1.50

The V

The C

Ca

Also by this author

As Caprice Langden
The Virgin Clause, the Calegaris, Book One[1]
The Virgin Temptation, the Calegaris, Book Two[2]
Princess of Pride, the Calegaris, Book Three[3]

AS DEBRA J. FALASCO
Contemporary Romance
Man with Money[4]
Man with the Mafia[5]
Historical Romance
Inevitable, the Tales of Chapel Hall, Book One[6]
Inhibition, the Tales of Chapel Hall, Book Two[7]
Indecorum, the Tales of Chapel Hall, Book Three[8]
Lord Ravenspur's Christmas Wish[9]

1.   https://www.amazon.com/Virgin-Clause-Calegaris-Book-ebook/dp/B085DCLWR8

2.   https://www.amazon.com/Virgin-Temptation-Calegaris-Book-ebook/dp/
B085RY2777

3.   https://www.amazon.com/Princess-Pride-Calegaris-Book-3-ebook/dp/B091NNY-
DX5

4.   https://www.amazon.com/Man-Money-Debra-J-Falasco-ebook/dp/B07R4NK5S1

5.   https://www.amazon.com/Man-Mafia-Debra-J-Falasco-ebook/dp/B07PS6R3YL

6.   https://www.amazon.com/gp/product/B07FYTW44S

7.   https://www.amazon.com/gp/product/B07VJJNXSP

8.   https://www.amazon.com/Indecorum-Tales-Chapel-Hall-Three-ebook/dp/B08KD-
FRWRC

9.   https://www.amazon.com/Lord-Ravenspurs-Christmas-Wish-Novella-ebook/dp/
B081DNWT23

Chapter One
-Noemi-

I remembered the taste of the restaurant's coffee — bitter because I didn't have my favorite creamer to sweeten it.

I remembered the clouds and the dismal gray morning that echoed my mood. The heartbreak of leaving behind everything, and everyone, I loved overshadowed my excitement about moving to England to work at my dream job.

I remembered how tired Lilly and I were because we sat up most of the night, reminiscing about our inseparable childhood years and wondering what the future would bring now that we went our separate ways. She promised to fly to England and visit me as soon as she could, a promise she had fulfilled.

I remembered that my brother Willis was busy with his senate campaign. I surprised him when I told him I was moving to England. He couldn't reschedule his campaign stops to drive me to the airport, so we spent some time together before he had to get back on the road. He wasn't the one who drove me to catch my flight, and he wasn't the one who sat with me before I had to get into the security line.

I remembered how **he** had taken one look at our tired eyes, red and puffy from crying, and insisted that he would drive us to the airport.

Dante was his usual quiet self on the road from Connecticut to New York City. While Lilly dozed in the front seat, I sat in the back, nervously clutching my carry-on, staring at the back of his neck and the rich, black hair I wanted to run my hands through.

I was going to miss him. Even though he rarely talked to me, Dante Calegari had been a fixture in my life for over a decade. His presence *meant security, safety. Whenever Dante was around, I felt an inexplicable sense of peace.*

In a modern world where anything could happen, I knew I would be okay because Dante was there. When he was traveling, I visited the Calegari home. No matter what Lilly and I were up to, especially in our teenage years and beyond, there was this sense that something was missing. The home was incomplete without him. Dante didn't know it, but once, his words helped me through the darkest time of my life, revealing a side of him that I had never met before; a side that had given me hope, bravery, and a sense of worth I hadn't experienced until then.

A side I had fallen in love with.

My mind had wandered to thoughts of what was never to be—a kiss, a night in his arms... in his bed. I wanted to know what it would be like to have those strong, muscular arms hold me again. To know what it would feel like to have his lips on mine, whether in a drawn-out kiss or feathering my cheek and forehead with tiny kisses that were meant to tempt me into giving him more. I wanted to give him more. To give him anything! All he had to do was ask.

But he never did. He was always cool; polite but distant. I was never anything more to him than his little sister's best friend. He didn't see me any other way.

When our eyes met in the rearview mirror that morning, I caught a glimpse of an expression I'd never seen on him. I blushed and turned away from the intensity in his eyes.

I couldn't hold his gaze. I never could.

Even once we arrived at the airport. Even when we sat at a table for three and I downed another round of bitter brew. Even as he shook his head at how many creamers I had to empty into my cup to make the coffee palatable.

Dante didn't speak to me, but our eyes kept meeting.

And I kept looking away.

I wanted to talk to him. To tell him that I'd miss him, just as I'd told his mother and brother the same thing that morning. Only with Dante, everything was different. I'll miss not being able to look at him when he didn't know I was watching. I'll miss the deep timbre of his voice when he said, "Hello, Noemi," as he walked away.

I'll miss the way he looked in the dark suits he wore like a second skin, and I'd miss the woodsy, citrusy scent of his cologne. It was the scent of my youth, of my dreams and fantasies, of an unfulfilled longing that left me with an empty feeling in my heart; a feeling that threatened to spill over if I didn't keep avoiding his eyes.

We lingered over our coffee and Lilly and I made idle chit-chat because we'd already poured our hearts out and just couldn't do it anymore. Our bravery wouldn't last.

"My flight boards in two hours," I said as I looked at my watch one more time. We could see the terminal from where we sat. The security line was long, but it moved steadily.

The smile fell from Lilly's face as she stood up. "Then I'm going to say goodbye now. I can't..." Her eyes filled with tears again and mine immediately did the same. "Call me when you get there, Noe. I... Dammit... I wasn't going to cry anymore."

We hugged, and then Lilly shocked me when she pushed away from me and grabbed her purse.

"I gotta go, Noe. I... call me."

I watched her walk away, her designer heels clicking on the tile, knowing that she was as much of a wreck as I was. I sucked in a deep breath, getting my emotions under control. My hand shook as I gathered my carry-on. I dropped the strap three times before a hand reached down and took it from me.

That time, I didn't look away when our eyes met. Dante held the bag out to me.

"Do you have everything you need?" he asked, his voice oddly husky.

I nodded; the words stuck in my throat.

"*Noemi?*" *he prompted, a look of irritation flashing over his face.* "*It's a long flight. Do you have everything... books, food?*"

"*Yes,*" *I answered quickly, his ire prompting me to respond.* "*I'm good. I packed some snacks. I'll eat a meal on the flight. I... I'm good. Thank you,*" *I added hastily.*

Dante nodded, but he didn't take his eyes off me. I thought he wanted to say more, but he didn't. He just ... stood there.

"*Thank you,*" *I said again.* "*For driving. Lilly is tired. And upset. I'm glad she doesn't have to drive back.*"

"*It's my pleasure,*" *he replied, but he said it as if it were anything but.*

My eyes shifted to the ground.

"*Have a safe flight,*" *I heard him say just as his feet started to move out of my line of sight.*

"*Wait!*" *I cried, looking up at him as he started to walk away. He had his back to me already but froze when I reached out for him.*

He turned to me with that unfamiliar look in his eyes. If he had any idea how much I needed him at that moment, how much I regretted the years of conversations we never had. I wish I had been a stronger woman, that I was the type of person who went after what they wanted and accepted nothing less than what I deserved. He told me once to not be afraid to take what I needed, to ask for what I wanted, but the words stuck in my throat, leaving me to swallow hard as I felt my cheeks start to burn.

"*You wanted something, Noemi?*"

How could he just stand there? In the last ten years, was that all I was to him? Just someone he gave a ride to the airport? Was there really going to be no hugs, no parting words, no bittersweet goodbyes?

The tears pricked my eyes again, but I pushed them away.

"*I just thought... Well, I wanted to say goodbye.*"

He blinked a few times. "*Goodbye.*"

What the... He turned and walked away?

My heart pounded as my body screamed, No! That wasn't the way it was supposed to be! I couldn't let him go. Maybe he had no need for more, but I did.

"Dante!" I called out, my bag hitting my leg as I ran to get to him.

"What?" he snapped, spinning around.

The anger in his eyes made me stop in my tracks just inches away from him.

"What do you want, baby girl?" he asked smoothly as he shoved his hands into his pockets. "I said goodbye. What more do you want?"

"What do I want?" I repeated incredulously.

"Yes," he barked then enunciated more slowly. "What do you want? You have a plane to catch and you're wasting my time."

"Wasting your... I... I wanted..."

I had no idea at that point what I wanted. Certainly nothing I could tell him. I wanted his arms around me. I wanted his mouth on mine. I wanted some show of emotion that said I meant something to him, even if it was just friendship. That if my freaking plane crashed on takeoff, he'd feel more than just annoyance because I wasted his precious time by trying to prolong our separation.

"I want a proper goodbye," I said quickly.

"A proper goodbye?" His eyebrows rose. "I thought 'goodbye' was a proper 'goodbye.'"

He angled his head and studied me. "But you want more, don't you?"

That husky note returned to his voice as his eyes swept over my face.

"Yes," I whispered.

"What?" he asked as he closed the remaining distance between us. "What more do you want, Noemi? Something to keep you from being disappointed? Something to make the agony of parting even greater as you fly across the ocean? Something dramatic and heartfelt, perhaps?"

I shook my head at his nonsense. "No. Nothing like that. I don't even know what you're talking about. I thought we were friends. I thought... is a hug too much to ask for?"

His jaw tensed as he studied me. "A hug? That's all? I must have disappointed you with mere words. But if you have your heart set on a hug..."

His arms stretched out and I moved into them. It was awkward and weird and the most bizarre hug I'd ever had. It felt forced. Unnatural.

As Dante's arms closed around me, he whispered in my ear. "No expectations, baby girl. This would have been so much easier if you'd had no expectations. Don't set yourself up for pain."

His arms stayed around me as I leaned back and looked up at him.

"I did what you said," I reminded him. "You said I could ask you for anything. I just want a real hug and to say... goodbye."

My voice broke and Dante closed his eyes at the reminder of the words he'd said to me four years ago. I stretched my arms around his neck and pulled him closer to me. I felt his body tremble just before his arms tightened around me. Movements stilled around us as I blocked out everything except the steel of his body against mine and the heat that radiated from him. Dante shifted on his feet and fitted me closer to him. A sigh or a moan, I don't know which it was, but for the first time in four years, I felt like I was where I belonged.

How could he not feel it, too?

Regret washed over me like a tidal wave. I waited too long, and his arms felt too right. I wasted years, and he couldn't begrudge me just a few minutes in the heaven of his arms.

After what seemed like an appropriate amount of time, but not nearly long enough, I dropped my arms from his neck, letting them fall to his chest.

Dante ran his cheek, rough and masculine, over my forehead, and I shivered. Another moan escaped from my lips and he made the movement again. I clutched the lapels of his suit.

Electricity pulsed between us as our eyes met. I licked my lips, prepared to say goodbye one more time. Dante's eyes followed my tongue before he leaned his head down to my ear.

"Get the fuck on that plane," he growled.

I BLINKED AWAY THE memories as I stared into the dark water that surrounded the *Mary Theresa* as she sat anchored off the coast of Barbados. I thought airport Dante was distant and confusing, but the man I know now, the man I bargained with over my virginity, that man was an enigma. Hard and implacable one minute, comforting and soothing the next. Was it crazy that I liked both Dantes?

Hard and implacable Dante made me feel secure. Nothing could alter his plans; not intruders or pirates or blown out windows. He handled each situation with deadly confidence. I didn't know anyone else who could have remained so calm and in control under those circumstances. I could rely on Dante. He was brutally honest and unapologetic. I knew I never had to worry about what was true or what was real. He'd be honest with me no matter what. I didn't doubt anything he said.

Comforting Dante made me feel valued, which was something I never expected to feel from him. He could have just arranged a dinner or a hotel room and coldly taken what I offered, but he didn't. Private planes. Yachts. Designer clothing. He went out of his way for me.

And the way he protected me... the way he stormed into the cabin and covered my body with his when the explosion shattered the cabin windows. I suppose he would have done that for anyone, but there hadn't been "anyone" else. Not like me, according to Cecile who said he brought women to the Grand Tropican, but he had never gone through such lengths to take care of them the way he had me.

What did it all mean? Did it mean anything at all? Dante spoiled me in the last forty-eight hours and he certainly didn't have to. Not to get what he wanted.

Butterflies rose in my stomach as I allowed myself to hope, even briefly, that he wanted me, that this was more than just a means to an end. I certainly didn't need the Cinderella treatment from Dante to get me to sleep with him. I didn't need to be bought.

"You're frowning."

Dante's deep voice took me out of my musings and back onto the deck where we had just finished eating dinner.

I turned my head to face him as he approached.

"We're anchored for the night. Captain Burrowes will take care of the window in the morning. You have nothing to worry about," he explained, misreading my expression.

I looked at him sideways. "I want to believe you—"

"But you don't." He stated flatly as he put his hands in his pockets and leaned on the railing next to me.

I took a deep breath, knowing that my lack of faith irritated him.

"When we were there," I nodded toward the island, "someone got into our hotel room and tried to murder us." My voice trailed off as I nodded toward the open ocean. "When we went to sea, someone tried to blow a hole in your boat. I'm not sure how I feel right now, being sandwiched between the two."

Dante didn't say anything. His brow furrowed as he turned to look out over the water. I was getting better at looking at him and not turning away. I studied his dimly lit profile, watched his jaw tighten and brow furrow.

The ocean water lapped against the side of the *Mary Theresa*. The air smelled of that salty, brininess one would expect. Under different circumstances, I would have melted at the ambience. But it had been a freaking unbelievably long day, and I hadn't relaxed enough to allow myself to enjoy anything since the explosion.

By his own admission, Dante had killed three people: the two pirates, and the man who had been in our bungalow. If I added in the two that he wasn't aware I knew about, he had killed five people in one day. Who could do that and then stand so casually on a yacht as if he had no cares in the world?

I suppose it wasn't a fair assumption. He had done all of it to protect me, to protect his yacht, his crew, and himself. The pirates had killed one of his men. Dante did what he had to do. A part of me understood that, b ecause I wanted to. I *had* to understand him. All Dante's actions were in self-defense or the defense of others.

But if I believed that, why were my thoughts so unsettled? Why couldn't I put all my faith in him? I missed the secure feeling that came with Dante's presence. It was there, but it felt just out of my reach, left somewhere on a beautiful island I never got to explore.

Chapter Two
-Dante-

I didn't have a clue what to say to her. I think I understood how she felt, but empathy wasn't one of my strong points. I wanted Noemi to feel secure. *Fuck!* I killed five people to make sure she was safe. If she knew that, she wouldn't point out to me how scared she was. She'd know that I had her best interests at heart. She'd know that every decision I made in the last six hours was based around her safety.

I needed some way to reassure her. We had eight days at sea; I didn't want her to spend that time feeling anxious, but I'd be damned if I knew what to do. Spoken words were my bond, but no matter how important words were to me, Noemi was different. My verbal reassurances didn't seem to help her. She needed more and for the first time ever with a woman, I felt compelled to deliver her expectations.

I should have been able to say, "you're safe, don't worry about it" and have her trust in that. But she'd been with me on our adventure for less than forty-eight hours. She watched me kill a man and had almost been cut to ribbons in an explosion. I considered the possibility that she needed more than words to convince her to put her faith in me and believe that I *would* control the situation.

"This isn't what you imagined it would be." I stated, trying to open a dialogue I loathed to have. I couldn't look at her but kept my gaze on the water below us as it lapped against the side of the yacht.

"Considering that I didn't know you were flying me to a tropical paradise then taking me aboard a luxury yacht suitable for a billionaire? This was all a surprise. No, I didn't expect to watch a man get killed in our bungalow, and I didn't expect to have a boat almost blow a hole in your yacht. Nope. Didn't expect any of that."

She tried to make light of it, but I could feel the razor edge of her tension in the night air. "But you expected something, Noemi. It's natural. You had some thoughts as to how you wanted our contract fulfilled, didn't you?"

"Of course I did. Your mantra, 'No expectations?' Sorry, I've failed. If I said no, you'd know I was lying. You're just going to have to be disappointed in me because I'm not a robot that doesn't have dreams."

"Tell me, *bambina*," I urged. She needed to fucking *help* me help *her*. "Tell me what you wanted. What you fantasized about."

I ran my fingertip over her lower lip, trying to pull the words from her with my touch. I saw the hesitation in her eyes. She wanted to answer me, but she held back. This wasn't the same as meeting a physical need. I lacked the intuition to be able to instinctively know what more she wanted.

"Tell me," I demanded hoarsely, my lips hovering above hers. I could give her anything, *anything* she needed, she just had to tell me what the fuck that was. I could give her the world if she asked me for it.

Her continued reluctance to share reminded me who I was talking to. Noemi's shyness, and her ability to come out of her shell, was always there, hiding behind her soft walls. She revealed herself when she needed to be strong, but she wasn't brave enough to show her deepest desires. If I needed her to speak to me, I had to give her the confidence to do so. My hand wandered to her hip and smoothed the fabric of her sundress over her curves. When she didn't answer me, I applied pressure.

"Noemi," I growled as I ran my lips from her jawline to her ear. "If you could have anything, have me anyway you wanted me, what would you want?"

My heart rate sped up.

Control. It was an illusion. I gave her a glimpse of it. She held all the power now. I'd do whatever she said. It would be my interpretation of her words, but she had the power to make me into any man she wanted because I was that lost, that desperate to make this easier on her. Yet, she remained silent, shaking her head as I pressed her.

"No words, Noemi?"

I gripped her thigh as my hand circled her ponytail. Fine. She wouldn't talk to that man when he tried to be nice to her, then she'd have to talk to the other one.

I gripped her hair, angling her head to the side as my lips roamed her neck.

"You need to tell me what you want, baby girl." I nipped her earlobe and she jumped, her hands reaching for my shoulders. "Or you get nothing."

Her mouth parted as the protest leaped into her eyes. Her tongue darted out to moisten her lower lip. Temptation filled her eyes along with indignation. I kneaded the curve of her hip, pushing her lower body against mine, grinding her against me, teasing both of us.

"I won't fuck you," I grated against her mouth, "unless you tell me how you want to be fucked."

She swallowed, her body slackening in my grasp. The harsher I was with her, the more she needed me, relied on me. And used her power to slay me. I lifted my head to look at her as she finally started to speak.

"But I don't want you to fuck me," she whispered as our eyes met.

"Liar," I accused as I started pulling the length of her dress up to her waist.

"Dante—"

My hand dipped past the edge of her panties. I could tell from the feel of the lace that her denial was a lie.

One corner of my mouth ticked upward with satisfaction. She squirmed as I drew one finger over the fabric covering her pussy, already damp and moist for me. I stroked her, watching her eyes close and her mouth part.

"You're not supposed to lie to me, Noemi. I'm disappointed." And pissed off that she would boldly try to deny herself what she very clearly wanted.

"You don't understand," she panted as I continued to lightly stroke her, slowly moving from one delicious end of her pussy to the other. Fuck, I wanted to taste her again. If she'd just say the word, I'd go down on her right there on the railing of the aft deck.

"I don't want you to fuck me," she moaned as I increased pressure and speed. "Oh... God, Dante..." She struggled to speak, and I was too much of a bastard to let her relax. Her hips pushed forward against my hand.

"I want... I want you to make love to me. That's what I dream of. That's what my fantasies are about."

My hand stilled as I listened to words that wrapped around my gut and squeezed, forcing the agony to surface.

She heaved a deep breath. "I want romance, gestures, the atmosphere." She waved her hand in the air. "This is all so perfect, but my ideal fantasy is to have you make love to me. I... didn't know the difference between fucking and making love until..." Her voice trailed off.

I couldn't control it. My body stiffened. I set myself up for this. I should have known what she'd say. If I had an empathic bone in my body, I would have known.

"I know you're angry because that's not what you want, and I'm okay with that," she added hastily. "But you asked, and you wanted your answer. So now, you have it."

Letting her dress fall, I took a step away from her. Her eyes immediately fell to the planks of the deck flooring.

My jaw tensed. *What the fuck had I done?* I told her I'd give her anything she wanted if she'd just tell me what it was. If she had groaned anything else, I would have scooped her up in my arms and carried her to the nearest cabin.

But this? What the fuck was I supposed to do with this?

I put even more distance between us as I took another step away from her. I needed a drink. Badly.

Noemi stood in the moonlight, her body hunched and frightened. Why could I read her when she was scared and nervous, but I couldn't tell when she needed more? If I had any fucking clue what she was going to say, I wouldn't have asked her. She knew what she told me wouldn't make me happy, not that I was ever happy.

I had two choices: comply with what she wanted as I told her I would or walk the hell away from her. Now.

That's what she thought I'd do. She thought I'd leave. She knew she'd angered me again and that I would leave her alone as I had on the plane. Noemi shifted nervously on her feet but kept her eyes downcast.

A demure fucking goddess. *My* goddess. Waiting for me to disappoint her.

Again.

Fuck, my dick was already hard but now it was engorged. *What the hell*? All she had to do was show signs of submission, let me control her, and he was at attention.

Five minutes and he could have what he wanted, but I needed five minutes to figure out how I was going to meet her demands. She wanted romance and ambience, and I didn't know how to do that shit.

"Stay here," I bit out.

Her shoulders sagged, and she nodded. Noemi gave up. She told me what she wanted and now, the power was all mine again.

I just didn't know what the fuck to do with it.

I ran a hand through my hair as I stalked to the wheelhouse where Captain Burrowes sat studying his instruments. He straightened up when I walked in unannounced.

"It will cost you, but they'll be here first thing to fix the windows. We'll have to dock for the morning," he said as I barged in.

"Aren't you married?" I blurted out.

His eyebrows rose at my uncharacteristic outburst. Captain Burrowes had been with me for five years, for the duration of time that I owned the *Mary Theresa*. He came with the yacht. We forged a strong relationship over the years. He was discreet and trustworthy. Like everyone else, he didn't have details about my life, but considering the man he'd worked for before me, his new assignment was a walk in the park. I kept him on after I killed his boss. The man who hired me was the yacht owner's brother. When he inherited his brother's wealth, he found out the man didn't have half the amount of money he'd bragged about. My client paid me with his brother's yacht, complete with the captain and crew. They'd seen a hell of a lot worse than me over the years and didn't blink at any of it.

But at my unexpected personal question, Burrowes crossed his arms over his chest. "Why are you asking?"

Why did talking to people have to be so fucking difficult? "Just answer the damn question."

His eyes narrowed. "Why?"

He was protecting his wife. I got it. I also knew he was married, and he knew I knew that, so what was the big fucking deal? I wasn't going to just come right out and ask for his help.

My eyes drifted past the board of instruments to the woman on the deck below. Noemi leaned against the railing, looking lost and forlorn. I wanted to build her back up, give her the strength she needed. I didn't have an idea of how to begin just like I had no idea how to ask Burrowes for his help. I never fucking needed anybody's *help*. A favor, maybe. A debt. I'd owe him if he could just give me a fucking clue what a woman wanted when she wanted romance.

What the fuck had she done to me?

My fists clenched at my side as I watched the light breeze blow her hair around her face. She tipped her head up and let it coast over her skin, the fabric of her dress blowing out behind her.

Why the hell was I trying to be someone I wasn't? I didn't do romance. She'd just have to live with it. If she didn't like who I was, to hell with her.

"Fuck it," I growled, yanking open the wheelhouse door.

"Fifteen minutes," Burrowes said behind me.

"What?"

"Give me fifteen minutes, then take her to the black cabin."

My head wanted to explode at the idea that he knew my weakness.

"Ten," I grumbled. I didn't even know what the hell I could do to keep her busy for ten minutes, but I still needed that drink.

I GAVE CAPTAIN BURROWES his time, then when Noemi finished nervously drinking her champagne, I took her hand and practically dragged her away. Noemi gasped as she looked around the black cabin, named so because everything in the room was made of black lacquer or covered in black fabric.

I didn't know what Burrowes had planned, but Noemi's face lit up when she saw the dozens of candles that illuminated the dark interior. The curtains had been pulled back to let the moonlight shine in. Someone had the same thought I did; a bottle of champagne sat chilling in an ice bucket. I didn't understand the point of the rose petals that were scattered on the bed.

I closed the door behind us.

"Did you do this?" Noemi asked with a shy smile and a hopeful expression.

"No," I admitted as I reached for her waist. "I'm not a magician, *bambina*. I was with you." It wasn't the answer she wanted, but it was the truth. She told me not to lie to her. This hardly seemed like a scenario that required going back on my word.

Her smile started to fall. "Did you ask someone to do it?"

"Does it matter?" Fuck. Why would that possibly matter?

"I guess not," she sighed. "It's beautiful. Thank you."

She said it as if I'd just gifted her a damn sweater for Christmas.

I should have felt something. Stung by her disappointment? Confused by her indifference? I wanted to please her, but the part of me that didn't give a damn, none of this mattered.

She told me what she wanted, and I promised I'd give it to her. Did the execution really matter? I didn't know how to do all the sentimental stuff, but I knew how to be honest.

"I don't know how to do this, baby girl."

She tilted her head and looked up at me. I couldn't help it. I reached for her ponytail again, wrapping the conveniently bundled locks around my fist.

"Do what?"

"Romance." I tugged and she moved forward. "Flowers. Chocolates. Candles. Sweet words. That's not me, baby girl. Never has been. Never will be."

"You could try... a little?" she suggested as she leaned into my arms.

"I did." I nodded towards the array of candles on the bureau. "I didn't do this, but I set it in motion, and you're still disappointed, aren't you?"

"No," she denied.

I put a finger over her lips. "Don't lie, *bambina*. I can't trust you if you lie."

"I'm not lying, not really."

Her hands landed on my chest, sliding up to rest on my shoulders. My body roared to life at the smallest of touches.

I covered her hand with mine, pushing it down to the vee of my shirt.

"Explain that to me, Noemi," I demanded. "While you unbutton my shirt."

Her mouth parted as she met my eyes, but she didn't hesitate. Her fingers moved to the first button.

"I'm not disappointed in the room," she said, licking her lip as the first button came undone.

Her hands moved to the second, released it, then moved down to the third, then the fourth. The edges of her fingers skimmed my bare skin as the fabric fell away. The heat rose between us. The closer her fingers came to the waistband of my pants, the slower her hands moved, the shallower her breaths became, and the less eye contact she made with me.

"You said you wanted romance. I can't give that to you."

Her hand hesitated over the last button.

"I know," she whispered hoarsely. "But you asked me what my fantasy was, and I told you. I never once *expected* all of that. All of *this*."

She waved her hand around the room. Capturing it in the air, I moved it to the button of my trousers.

Noemi's eyes drifted shut as she sucked in a nervous breath.

I leaned forward, rubbing my cheek over the top of her head, feeling her silky hair cling to my evening stubble. I kept my hand over hers, urging her toward what I wanted, what I believed we *both* wanted.

Lightly biting her lower lip, Noemi hesitated.

"Go ahead, *bambina*," I urged, not recognizing the husky tone of my voice. "Touch me. Please."

I didn't know the man who begged a woman to touch him, but when Noemi's hand lightly skimmed my abdomen, causing my muscles to tighten for her, I sucked in a shallow breath of relief.

No. I didn't know how to do romance, but my ignorance didn't take away from the heat that existed between us. I couldn't deny it and was quickly losing any desire to try. I burned for her, and all the flowers and candles in the world couldn't increase how much I wanted her. I didn't need any additional trappings when all I had to do was look at her.

And when she touched me... *fuck*. I felt more alive than I ever had. I led a life of depravity; of sadism, of pleasure taken from extinguishing the life of others. None of it compared to how I felt when I was deep inside Noemi.

I blew out a breath as Noemi dragged two fingers down my breastbone, skimmed my abdomen, and stopped just above my waistline. Her palms flattened against me, and she ran both hands up my chest to rest on my shoulders under my shirt.

"Off," I growled. The weight of the fabric felt like a blanket of stone that I needed to be freed from, but it was a freedom only she could give me.

With a flick of both wrists, Noemi released the shirt from my shoulders. Her hands roamed my chest at will. I did nothing to stop her delicate touches. Every sweep of her hand sent a shudder through my body, her touch a drug I was quickly becoming addicted to. I wanted her to stop so I could get inside her as fast as she'd let me, but I didn't want to end the pleasure. When I tipped my head back and groaned at sensations that were becoming unbearable, her movements slowed. Her hands traveled back to the waistband of my pants.

I opened my eyes to look down into hers. Hesitation met desperation. I needed her touch. I needed to be in her hands. I needed that softness sliding over my cock. I *needed* her.

Chapter Three

-Noemi-

"Yes," Dante hissed between his teeth, telling me what he needed as my fingers hovered over the button of his pants.

His stomach tightened; his entire body clenched as I slipped a finger inside his waistband. I didn't know the right way to do it. I'd never unbuttoned, or unzipped, a man's pants before, but judging from Dante's reaction, it didn't matter. I knew he'd help me if my inexperience was about to ruin the moment, but from the growl that escaped his throat when I popped the button through the hole, my inexperience didn't disappoint.

God, I wanted this. I've felt him inside me, hard and deep, but I haven't touched him. Not as intimately as he'd touched me.

I hesitated, my hand poised over his zipper. I looked up at him through my lashes. Dante's half-closed eyes were on me, so intense I couldn't look away. I pulled on the zipper, tugging it down one tooth at a time. His breathing picked up and I found... I liked it. My heart was already beating beyond control, lurching when I saw Dante's reaction to my touch. I wasn't sure I had the nerve to go through with touching him... there... but from his sucked in breath, taut stomach, and the size of him as I struggled to undo his zipper, he would take over when I needed him to. All I'd have to do was ask.

His zipper fell open into a sharp vee, and I swallowed, unsure what to do next. He must have read the uncertainty on my face.

His hand fisted my ponytail.

"On your knees, baby girl," he whispered hoarsely.

I didn't even hesitate. I dropped to my knees, my hands resting on his thighs. He didn't say anything but placed my hands on the waist of his pants and tugged. His hands fell away when I began to pull his khakis down his thighs. When they fell to his ankles, Dante stepped out of them.

I couldn't help myself. I leaned forward, nuzzling against his thigh. His answering groan ignited a fire within me. I turned my head and kissed the hot skin. His muscles twitched and a growl escaped him. He didn't wait for my help. Dante's cock sprung free, jutting up strongly in front of me as he pulled off his underwear.

I wanted to touch him. I felt like I *had* to touch him. I knew I'd embarrass myself if I did the wrong thing. I had no idea how to touch a man. I had no idea what Dante would like. I hesitated to go any further.

I looked up at him through pleading eyes.

Dante took a step back and extended his hand to pull me up.

He was completely naked in front of me as I stood there, awkward and unsure of myself.

"At this point," he purred as he walked me backward to the bed, "there isn't a damn thing you could do that I wouldn't like."

He leaned down for a quick, hard kiss on my mouth just before the back of my knees hit the mattress. His eyes searched mine.

"Have you had enough independence, or do you want to continue?" he asked as his hands slid under my caftan.

I didn't answer him right away because I didn't know!

"Does it have to be that way?" I asked, my words muffled as he pulled the dress over my head.

"What way?"

I tilted my head as his lips sought the curve of my neck.

"One or the other of us in control? Can't we just... both?"

I didn't even know what I was saying or whether it made any sense to him. Dante started to undo my ponytail. Gently. I was surprised at how gently he touched me considering how tense his body was.

"We can try," he muttered. "Although, I admit that doesn't usually work for me. But we can try... if that's what you want."

He ran his hands through my hair, fanning my dark tresses out behind me. His soft touches didn't prepare me for his strong grip around my thighs, pulling my legs up before roughly tossing me onto the bed. He lowered himself to his knees between my thighs while I fought to catch my breath. If this was both of us sharing control, it sure didn't feel that way. Dante sat back on his haunches, staring at me with an unreadable expression on his face. He was... waiting. Maybe it was my turn. I followed his eyes to my cleavage. *I could do this. I wanted to do this.* Reaching behind me, I unclasped the hooks of my bra, letting the straps fall and then removing it fully. His satisfied groan assured me I'd made the right decision. I thought it was his turn to regain control, but... apparently not. I followed his gaze lower to my panties.

I took a deep breath, wanting to do something sexy, like they do in books or on television. Move slow. Be deliberate. Put my hand... no, not there. Oh, God, how was it supposed to work? The candles were too bright. I couldn't hide my uneasiness.

I squeezed my eyes shut, ready to make my move and pull my underwear down in front of Dante. I just couldn't look at him when I did it. I started to tug when Dante's lips skated over mine before he kissed me long and deep, making me forget all about the last stage of my awkward striptease.

I moaned both from relief and need when I felt his firm touch sliding my panties down right before he cupped my sex. That gentle touch had returned. I eagerly opened for him, rewarded once again by his approving groan. I was wet and ready for him already, but he played and teased, giving not a care in the world to my growing sense of urgency.

"*Dante,*" I whimpered when his fingers continued to fondle me until I reached a fever pitch. I needed him, needed to feel him inside me so much I wanted to cry from the emptiness I felt while he denied me.

"*Dante,*" I pleaded again, grabbing his hand. Desperation created bravery. I couldn't let him continue. I wanted what I wanted, and I wanted *him*!

"Tell me what you want, *bambina.*"

Two fingers sunk deep inside me, and I stretched to meet them. I wanted fast and hard. I wanted him to make me cum , but Dante continued with long, slow, almost gentle movements.

Heavy breaths and strangled moans filled the room. I ran my hands up his forearms, over his shoulders, and anywhere I could reach so I could feel his lean muscles ripple as he moved.

When his lips returned to mine, I bucked beneath his mastery. He owned me, yet, still, he didn't take me over the edge.

"If you tell me what you want, I'll give it to you," Dante promised, his voice thick with lust.

"Tease," I murmured in his ear.

Dante's chuckle-growl vibrated against my cheek. "Now you know why I don't like it."

Emboldened by desire to make him understand how I felt, I ran my hand from his shoulder, down his side, and rested it on his abdomen. Inhaling sharply, Dante rested his head against my forehead.

"I dare you," he said breathlessly, throwing down the gauntlet of my desire for him.

Slowly, my hand crept closer to him. Dante's breathing became more erratic. I wanted to know what he'd feel like in my hand. Would he be as hard as he felt when he was deep inside me? I hesitated... again... We'd only been together a few times. I didn't have the confidence to grab the bull by the horns, so to speak.

When I lingered too long, Dante ground his hips against my leg, pushing his erection closer to my hand.

I needed him to tell me what to do. I needed domineering Dante to take over. I'd never touched a man there before. He knew that. He knew I was a virgin, or rather, had been a virgin, so he must have known I'd never touched a man.

I swallowed, wondering how long he'd let me suffer before he intervened, wondering when I would open my mouth and let him know what I needed.

Dante raised up on his elbow and stared down at me with curious eyes. "You've never touched a man before."

I started to shake my head but remembered his other mantra. "No. Never," I answered him timidly.

"The fuck," he muttered harshly under his breath. I felt his erection twitch against the side of my leg.

"If you don't touch me now, you're going to miss your chance," he growled. "I'm so hard for you I'm going to fucking explode."

My hand started inexplicably shaking. "Help me," I pleaded in a whisper.

Two hushed words ended any control I had, and I was giddy with relief. With a sexual gallantry that I had only dreamed about, Dante placed his hand over mine and spent the next several minutes guiding me, showing me how to please him and myself. After a few shy touches and several apprehensive strokes, I found my spirit. I loved touching him, hard as steel and soft as silk. I loved the way his lips parted, his eyes closed, and his hips thrust forward in my hand. I couldn't get enough of the way he shuddered and groaned. The balance shifted again. I couldn't get enough of how powerful it felt to watch a commanding man like Dante writhe beneath my touch.

The vulnerability Dante allowed wouldn't last long. I knew he had a limit, and I knew the second he had reached it when he grated,

"Enough." Within seconds, he was sheathed to the hilt within me, filling me, making me feel whole again.

"I'm going to make you cum so hard, every fucking crew member on this yacht is going to hear your screams."

I didn't know how I'd look any of them in the eye in the morning, especially after I screamed not once, but three times before Dante pulled out of me and pushed his erection into my shaking hands.

"That's it, *bambina*. *Fuck yes*," he groaned when I stroked him to his orgasm. I smiled against his mouth as he kissed me, shudders and spasms still rocking through his body. Getting control of his breathing, he wrapped me in his arms.

Words matter, as Dante always said. But mattering and meaning were two different things. I thought about the meaning behind the words Dante whispered into my forehead.

"A lifetime of firsts," he muttered, his chest rising and falling as he carefully avoided putting all his weight on me.

"What do you mean?" I whispered. Temptation made me bold as I kissed the throbbing vein on his neck.

"I've never let anyone touch me like that."

I blinked at his confession. How could that be? I know he liked to be in control, but how could he have denied himself that, especially when he seemed to like it so much. Why was I the first woman he allowed such boldness?

I couldn't read anything into it. I couldn't let myself think that there was a reason why he let me touch him, why he lowered his guard so much that he nearly came in my hand before he took me so fiercely. *No expectations*. If I allowed myself to believe I was something special to Dante, I would be sorely disappointed, and I was so tired of being disappointed.

But when I thought about the sex we'd just had, I realized it was more than that. Dante gave me options he hadn't before. He gave me a gift that night. He gave me control. Up until the last few minutes, I set the pace; I made the decisions. Yes, maybe he hadn't made love to me like I'd asked. But maybe he had in his own way. He was always honest with me. He said he didn't know how to be romantic but giving up a sliver of his hard-won control was enough of a gesture for me. And that admission that he'd never let another woman touch him the way I had? That alone was the sexiest, most romantic thing he could have told me.

Dante recovered enough to turn onto his back. I expected him to make his exit soon. No, not expected: I knew that he would. It's how he did things and I braced myself for it.

I curled against him, ready to take advantage of the time with him while I had it. I sighed with contentment when his hand dropped to my waist and the other smoothed comforting circles over my back. I relaxed against him, basking in his warmth as I anticipated the inevitable cold of being pushed away.

We laid that way for several minutes. Dante was quiet, but he wasn't in a hurry to leave.

"Thank you," I whispered to his cheek as I dropped a kiss along his jawline.

He grunted. "For what?"

"All of this." I waved my hand around the room again, indicating the melting candles and the chilled champagne. "I know you didn't do it yourself, but as you said, you set it in motion, and it's the thought that counts." I blushed in the darkness. "And what came after..."

A rumble vibrated through Dante's chest. "As long as you're happy."

Chapter Four
-Dante-

Noemi shook her head in the darkness, her hair sweeping across my chest. "I am. Romance doesn't have to have all the bells and whistles some people expect. I don't need all that."

She stopped and grabbed my arm. "Not that I don't appreciate what you've done for me. I'd be wearing yoga pants and t-shirts every day if you hadn't bought me all these beautiful clothes. I'm not ungrateful. It was very thoughtful and kind of you. That's what I like. Small gestures that show someone was thinking about me, not undying attention. I don't want someone to fawn all over me, jumping to do my bidding.

"It's too much and it's insincere. Sweet gestures are one thing, but I'd rather have honesty, sincerity, and thoughtfulness. Right now, you're the most romantic person I know."

"How the hell did you come up with that?" I wanted to laugh but it came out as a bark.

The smile dropped from her dimly lit face. Her hazel eyes held mine. She rarely looked me in the eye, but she'd done so more often over the last two days. Her confidence was growing. Her transformation bewitched me. Bewitched and terrified me. Tonight, she looked right into me, like she knew me, really knew me. The prospect sent chills down my spine that shocked each nerve ending in my body.

It was a lie. She couldn't really know me, because if she knew me like her eyes claimed they did, she'd run. She'd get as far away from me as she could.

"Well," she tilted her head to the side and peered up at me. "For one, you made sure I had my favorite coffee creamer on the plane, and you ordered my favorite breakfast."

I snorted, and she continued. That was a no-brainer. I'd watched how she made her coffee for almost a decade. The eggs benedict was by default: it was my favorite as well.

"And you rescued me—twice! If that's not romantic, I don't know what is."

"You think I would let you die?" I said. If she were anyone else, I just might have. I only stuck my neck out for the three people I was bound to by birth.

"No. I know you wouldn't let me die. And by itself, it doesn't mean anything significant. Lots of people would have gone above and beyond to save another's life."

For fuck's sake. My heroics were just what everyone would do? "Make up your mind," I growled.

"The coffee, the life-saving. The clothes, jewelry, massage. The wine!"

"The wine?"

"Yes. It hasn't escaped my notice that since we've been on the yacht, the Pinot Grigio has been flowing freely. I rarely drink anything else unless I'm not given a choice."

I smirked at her reference to the red wine the night before.

"And I know it's not all coincidence. I said I wanted romance and gestures, but you don't need to put pressure on yourself to come up with them."

She leaned down and ran her mouth over mine. "You're doing just fine."

"I don't need a pep talk," I said, and she laughed.

"Ah, I woke the beast. It's not a pep talk, Dante. I'm just letting you know that I don't need you to try too hard. I don't like all that fuss anyway. I just want you, as you are." Her voice fell as her confidence shifted. "It's all I've ever wanted."

"I'm okay with being in the shadows," she continued. Her eyes never left mine, but a small quiver broke her words. "The dark suits me just fine."

The dark? What was she trying to tell me? Noemi didn't know a fucking thing about living in the dark. What she experienced in the last forty-eight hours was nothing compared to what she could have seen. She stayed on the edge; one foot stretched into the dark like a toe dipping into a cold pool of water. She's still close to the light. One step was all she'd ever need to bring her right back into its rays.

But she's not lying. She's comfortable on the edge of the shadows. She's comfortable with me. If she weren't, she wouldn't be there. She questioned me, but she gave in to my demands. She wore my blindfold. She ate dinner two feet away from someone else's pet fantasy to please me, because I wanted to see how she'd react. She protested, yes, but she should have told me to go to hell when I locked her in the bathroom of bungalow six at the Grand Tropican. There was something about Noemi that made her comfortable in the little bit of the shadows I'd exposed her to, but she had no idea how dark it was on the other side of that line.

The idea of pushing her comfort zone, of bringing her fully into my world, clawed at me. Tonight was different. I caved into her. I gave way to what she wanted, let her take some of my hard-earned control. The exchange was temporary and we both knew it. I chose to give her that gift because I couldn't give her anything else.

She'd understand how meaningful that was if she knew what it cost me. She owed me now, and I planned to collect before the week was over. How deep into the dark would she be willing to go for me? I fucking loved that she liked playing in the shadows, but the shadows weren't the dark. Shadows move. They change. Sometimes, shadows don't even exist. Noemi's too good to know that the two aren't the same, but was I going to be the bastard who would teach her the difference?

I could show her. I could bring her into my wicked world. I could make her my queen of the night. But what I couldn't do was pretend.

"You don't know anything about the dark," I whispered against her neck. "There's nothing there for a girl like you."

"You're wrong, Dante." She arched her back as I sucked on the tendon of her neck. "There is something in the dark for me. Something I want very badly."

She pulled her head back to look into my eyes.

"Don't," I whispered, my throat tightening.

She had me by the balls already, and if she fucking said the words, I would never want to let her go. I would, because I had to, but for the first time in my life, I'd know the bitter sting of regret.

"There's you. You're there, Dante. And if going into the dark is the only way I can have you, then I'll go. I'd follow you. I don't want to be out here by myself anymore."

I didn't answer Noemi. It was all nonsense anyway, and there was no point in discussing it. She wasn't going into the dark with me. We had a temporary contract, the terms of which had been fulfilled.

The yacht windows would be fixed in the morning, then we were setting out to sea.

With no stops, Florida was seven days away. After the explosion, I informed Captain Burrowes of my change in plans. I collected a debt from another friend who owned a private island. We would anchor there for a night or two, spend a few days in Michael Bianchin's island paradise. Beyond that, we wouldn't see another person who wasn't captain or crew of the *Mary Theresa*.

My mind was made up. Noemi wasn't going into the dark or anywhere else with me, not if she wanted to stay alive. After Florida, Noemi was going home, and I was going after the bastard who tried to kill us. Twice.

"Go to sleep, Noemi. *Vai a dormire, angelo.*" I pushed her head down onto my shoulder, hoping she'd take the hint and stop talking. I wanted to be nice to her but if she pushed me, I wouldn't have a choice.

Fuck. I should have left the room already, but I liked the way she felt against me. I liked the way she curled against my side, the way her breasts pushed against my chest and her hair tickled my chin as I rested my head against hers. I should have been the ass I am and left her to her dreams. Instead, I took what I wanted, but not without a warning. My arm tightened around her waist.

"Okay," she said quietly. "Good night."

Her lips feathered over mine before she nestled against my chest.

My heart thudded loud enough to keep us both awake.

I'd never had a lover's goodnight kiss before.

A lifetime of firsts.

Chapter Five

-Noemi-

I've felt that warmth before, that beautiful pressure that claimed me, stoking my desire to a fever pitch. I wasn't alarmed when his firm hand stroked my body from neck to ankle, taking me from slumber to a carnal fantasy. I moaned when his mouth followed the same path before he wrapped my hair in his hand and pulled my head back. Dante's mouth traveled the length of my throat, pausing above my ear.

"*Fuuuuck.* I can't get enough of you," he groaned right before he angled my hips and sank into me from behind. I loved the feel of his weight pushing me into the mattress as I met each of his demanding thrusts.

"Take me, baby girl. All of me."

Again and again. His hips pistoned faster and faster as I took his length deeper.

The sun began to light the cabin with blues and pinks splashed outside the window. The view was stunning, but the feel of him claiming my body... I could have awoken to Dante's sexual demands any and every day of the week and forgotten that the sun even existed.

"WATCH YOUR STEP," DANTE warned as we walked down the gangway to the dock.

"Are you sure this is a good idea?" I asked, taking his hand as I reached the bottom.

"We'll be fine."

I looked behind me to the two crew members who were joining us on our excursion. Dante suggested a shopping trip to the village while we waited for the windows to be repaired. Nerves got the better of me, but I felt safer when Dante was with me than I did alone.

"Is that why we need bodyguards? Because everything is fine?" I smiled at the two men behind us but was met with stoic professionalism.

"Just a precaution," Dante answered as he helped me into the front seat of the same car we had driven yesterday. "You can shop to pass the time until the windows are repaired. They'll stay far enough away to give us privacy."

I frowned at him as I buckled my seat belt. "Why do I get the feeling you're not telling me everything?"

The two crew members got into another car that sat in the marina parking lot next to ours.

"Because you're amazingly and frustratingly perceptive."

He walked around the car and took the driver's seat.

He cupped my chin and looked down at me. "I thought their presence would make you feel better. No, I don't expect there to be any more intruders or pirates, and we'll be out in the open, but considering the luck we've had since we arrived in Barbados, I'm hoping they'll deter any pickpockets, muggers, or any other lowlife that has nothing better to do with his time than bother us. Okay?"

"I'd be with you." I covered his hand with mine.

Abruptly, he let go of my chin and started the car. "I may have to step away for a few minutes while you shop. Not for long, but I have some calls to make."

I tried to hide my disappointment by shrugging. "I guess I should do the same. I never got a hold of Willis, and I still need to call Lilly."

He nodded. Silent, brooding Dante had returned. He had been attentive all morning, just short of charming.

We didn't shower together, and I didn't ask to once the realization hit me that we had slept together—all night. Dante didn't get up and leave; no early morning sneaking out of the cabin. That was enough. We showered at the same time, but in different rooms. When we met again on the aft deck, he pushed the pads of my fingers against his lips and pulled out a chair for me. We ate breakfast overlooking the sharp blue water. Our conversation was minimal, and I was okay with that.

The marina wasn't far from a small village that offered everything a tourist would want: shops, restaurants, bars, and more shops. I worked hard on my psyche as we walked the open-air market. No expectations, but expectations weren't the same as desires.

We started out awkwardly, with Dante stiff and tense beside me as we strolled through the village. My nerves fed off his. I knew it was difficult for him. He didn't seem to be enjoying our outing which only served to increase my anxiety. To deal with it, I chatted. Nonstop. "Oohing" and "ahhing" over everything that caught my eye. To ease his anxiety, Dante offered to buy me anything and everything I picked up.

When I tried on the tenth bracelet, he offered one more time to buy it for me.

"If I let you buy me everything I've admired so far, my arm would be weighted down," I laughed as I put the bracelet back.

"You haven't let me buy you anything yet," he groused.

His arm slipped around my waist as he pointed to the jewelry in the case. "I'm serious, Noemi. If there's something you'd like, money's no object."

"It's not about the money. These things aren't expensive—"

"Then let me buy you what you want."

What I wanted couldn't be bought, but with his insistence, I began to understand him a little bit better. Dante was emotionally stunted. I'd known that for years. His need to buy me things, clothing or touristy knick-knacks, was his way of reaching out, of providing, of caring. He didn't know any other way to express himself, so he used his money. Years of information collided. The way he dressed, the way he provided for his family. Lilly! Suddenly, how he spoiled Lilly... It all started to make sense. What he couldn't express emotionally, he said with material things.

I leaned up and kissed him on the cheek. He grunted. His arm tightened around my waist.

"I promise. I will let you buy me something. Just one thing before we leave. But I haven't found it yet."

He frowned down at me. "If you haven't chosen something by the time the windows are done, I'm buying the whole damn shop."

"Deal," I laughed, knowing it wouldn't be a problem. I could easily pick out one item from the entire village but choosing that item would have to wait. A familiar pang started low in my stomach.

I ran my hand up his shirt to rest on his shoulder. "There is something you could buy me now. If you're so inclined."

His eyes narrowed. "I told you I don't like to be teased, but fine, I'll bite. What do you want, Noemi?"

Oh, God. He used that voice, the deep, sultry tone that weakened my knees when he said my name.

I licked my bottom lip, wanting to push myself. I wasn't a good flirt, but I couldn't resist. I stood on tiptoe and placed my lips just under his ear.

"I'm hungry," I purred in a voice I hoped was seductive. Dante's hands tightened as he transferred his grip to my hips.

"What do you want?" he asked bluntly as his fingers bit into the skin, barely covered by my minidress.

I angled my body into his but tilted my head back to look into his eye. Desire flared between us. His dark eyes couldn't hide what he wanted.

And the growl from my stomach couldn't hide what I wanted.

"A sandwich... or something? I'm really hungry."

Dante's chuckle-growl tickled the side of my throat. "I'll buy you lunch."

I jumped when he swatted my behind with a quick slap.

"And later, I'm going to make you pay for that."

My stomach flip-flopped at the lust that dripped from his voice. The shy girl from the past would have ducked and ran. I wasn't convinced that I had changed so much. A small smile escaped as I ducked my head into his chest instead.

TOURISTS PASSED BY while the sun continued to pour its rays down upon us. We chatted as we ate lunch at an outdoor café overlooking the beach. At least, I chatted. Dante was quiet, but not with the same awkward silence we started our day with. He listened to what I said, made a few comments here and there, and sat back in his chair, relaxed as the sunlight bathed his powerful frame.

He was at ease, even if he wasn't conversational. He was a Dante I didn't know anything about, and I wanted to rectify that. I wanted to know more than the obvious. I wanted to know why he was so reserved that a quiet girl like me seemed like a chatterbox compared to him. I wanted to know how he spent his time. Why did a stockbroker have to travel around the world so extensively? I wanted to know why he favored dark suits and what about me made him start calling me "baby girl" all those years ago?

I settled for what I thought were less personal subjects. I tried to talk to him about the Grand Tropican. I didn't reveal what Cecile told me about his visits, but I skirted around the issue, asking him how he'd found such an exclusive location, how often did he go, had he taken other women there—impersonal things like that. The question about the women popped out of my mouth before I could stop it.

He answered each question with a few brief words. "A friend," "Whenever I feel like it," and my favorite, "None of your business."

That particular response stung, but Dante soothed the irritation by running the pad of his thumb over my mouth. "Don't ask questions you really don't want the answers to, *bambina.* Finish eating your lunch so you can pick out your one thing before we return to the yacht."

I took another bite of my conch fritter and another swallow from my mauby drink, savoring the delicious freshness as it slid down my throat.

"Speaking of the yacht, how long have you had it?"

"About five years."

"And the crew? How long have you known Captain Burrowes?"

"The same."

I palmed my head and looked at him across the table. "And the name. *Mary Theresa.* Did you name it after your mother?"

"Yes."

I went back to my fritter. "Why?"

I couldn't read the expression behind his mirrored glasses.

"Because I couldn't think of anything else."

"What was it called before you bought it?"

"The Sea Princess, or some shit like that. I don't remember."

"Did you have to do much work on it? Redecorate? Anything like that?" I was desperate for a real conversation.

"No. It was fine the way it was. Now, I have a question for you."

I sat forward, anxious to share just about anything with him. "Okay. Shoot."

Dante lowered his glasses. "What happened to the shy, quiet girl who never used to talk?"

I laughed. "She got tired of the world passing her by, of people making decisions without consulting her when she knew she had something to say." I tried to make light of why I'd forced myself to change, why I moved to England and started a new life.

But Dante wasn't smiling as he listened to me. He studied me with unrelenting eyes.

I put down my fork. "I got tired of going unnoticed. I found my voice."

If my words hit home with him, then so be it. *He* was part of the reason I changed. I was tired of missing out on the things I wanted most because I was too afraid to chase them. I was always afraid of disappointment, so it was easier not to put myself out there. The whole "you can't miss what you never had" conundrum.

But it's a myth. You can miss what you never had and never even realize it until you were face-to-face with him again.

I toyed with the tines of my fork while Dante continued studying me with an odd expression on his face.

"Why?" I asked bravely, ignoring his advice to not answer questions I didn't want to know the answers to. I *had* found my voice, and while the heart of that girl still existed, she learned to go after what she wanted. "You should be glad I changed. We wouldn't be here if I hadn't."

That girl would never have had the nerve to approach Dante in his office and bargain over her virginity just so she could have one night with him.

"Yes, we would have."

I blinked with confusion at how aggressively Dante answered me. He reached across the table and took my chin between his thumb and forefinger.

"That deal was made the day you came back from England, Noemi. I didn't know you were home until the damn car ride to the party that night, but when I saw you, when our eyes met across the room… this is why I was pissed off at you for coming home. This was always going to happen, Noemi."

"I don't understand," I gulped. The anger in his eyes made me look away.

"Understand this, then. I liked the shy, quiet girl because she didn't have the strength to match me. She was lovely, but she didn't have a hold on me. Not like this girl, not like the woman you've become. I don't like her. I fucking need her. And that makes me mad as hell."

My breath hitched as I avoided his gaze. That brave girl didn't have a clue how to handle this. He lied. She wasn't so strong.

"Look at me, Noemi."

I glanced quickly in his direction, but a blur caught my eye, and I followed the familiar figure from a table not far from us as he hurried from the café.

"Oh, my God." I looked harder at the man as he skirted around the fence that served as the wall of the café. I clutched Dante's forearm as recognition dawned.

"What? What is it?" His eyes followed mine, latching onto the man in the clichéd Panama hat.

"That man," I nodded in the direction of his quickly departing back. "The one who's leaving now. I know him."

Dante turned his head, casually looking over his shoulder. He nodded at one of the crew members who sat at a table a few feet away from us. They had been so nondescript all morning, I'd completely forgotten they were there.

Dante made a gesture with his finger, pointing to the departing figure, and the crew member immediately stood up and started following the man.

"What are you doing?" I clutched his arm tighter. "Do you know him? Where's he going?"

"Just a precaution." He placed his hand over mine. "How do you know him, Noemi? I didn't know you knew anyone in Barbados."

"I don't really know him. I mean, I've seen him before, that's all. But it wasn't very pleasant."

"Tell me." The cold of his voice robbed all the sunshine around us. Dread filled my stomach.

"I should have mentioned something before." I felt guilty that I hadn't, and I didn't know why. "But first there was dinner, and dancing, and then afterward—" How could I have even thought about that man when Dante and I were going to be together for the first time?

"Noemi—" Dante's harsh growl hurried my speech along.

"He ran into me after my massage, when I was on my way back to the bungalow. He... he knocked me over. I thought he was going to help me up, but then he leaned over and said something to me."

Dante's eyes narrowed dangerously. The vein in his temple began to noticeably pulse. "What did he say?"

"He said..." My voice dropped to a whisper as I folded to Dante's dominance. "He told me to stay away from you. That you aren't who I think you are."

Dante stood up quickly, knocking the chair over. The remaining crew member joined us at the table, alerted I was sure by Dante's extreme behavior.

"I'm sorry," I stammered. "I should have told you sooner, but—"

"Yes," he bit out between gritted teeth. "You should have."

He turned to the crewman. "Take her back to the yacht. I don't care what else happens. Get her on board."

"Yes, Mr. Calegari." The tall, buff man did as he was told, extending an arm to me to escort me back to the yacht.

"Wait!" I cried, trying to get Dante's attention again.

He pulled some bills from his wallet and tossed them on the table to pay our tab.

"Where are you going? Dante—"

"I have some work to do, *bambina*. Go back to the yacht." He nodded to the crewman who started to pull me along.

"If you'll come this way, ma'am."

I turned to Dante as I stumbled forward, but he had his back to me as he pulled his cell phone from his pocket. The last thing I heard as I was practically dragged out of the café was Dante barking at someone, "Tell me you found that bastard."

Chapter Six

-Dante-

His blood should have dripped from the end of my blade. My knuckles should have been sore from my fist smashing into his face repeatedly.

But they weren't.

The bastard gave us the slip, disappearing into the market crowd. We tried to find him for over two hours, looking in shops, darting down alleys, pushing over trash cans.

We returned to the yacht without having captured our prey. I leaned on the railing, clenching and unclenching my fists, corralling the rage that coursed through me after missing my chance to take my fury out on that motherfucker.

He dared to touch what was mine. He knocked her over then threatened her—with *me*. Warned her to stay away from *me*. Who the fuck did he think he was?

The son-of-a-bitch would pay for that.

He wasn't fast enough when he made his escape from the café. He was stupid and sloppy. I thought he was better than that. He hadn't expected us to be there. He panicked when Noemi saw him, drawing attention to himself. Then he regrouped, pulling on his skills and training to give us the slip. I wasn't surprised by that. Pissed off, but not surprised.

When I visit his boss in New York next week, I'd let him know just how unhappy I was, both at his flunky's stupidity and at *his* interference in my life.

Noemi tossed her book onto the lounger when I approached her on the deck. "Did you find him?"

I shook my head, picking up the book so I could sit down. I flipped through the pages as I dealt with my uncharacteristic reluctance to start a conversation. I had to tread lightly. There were things afoot that I hadn't expected, and I couldn't reveal any of it. Not that I had any answers yet, but the search for those answers would bring things to light that needed to remain in the dark.

"Who was he?" Noemi asked.

I promised to be truthful with her, but there were things, so many things, that she could never know. The burden of years of secrets started to bubble, still containable but simmering below the surface as I chose my words carefully.

"I don't know." I tucked a stray strand of hair behind her ear. "Tell me what happened. Tell me exactly what he said when he ran into you."

She frowned but leaned into my touch. I squashed the urge to dominate, to conduct my interrogation with the same lack of mercy I would have usually employed.

She wasn't a lowlife piece of shit. This was Noemi. No matter how furious I was that she'd kept their encounter from me, I didn't need empathy to know that it was also not her fault. Later, I would have the opportunity to take my rage out on the person who was responsible. I'd let Noemi see my displeasure, let her know how disappointed I was. I'd find out if that mattered to her, and then, when I was alone in the black cabin tonight, I'd wonder why the fuck it mattered to me.

"I was on my way back from the massage. He was walking down the center of the path, heading right for me."

"Where did he come from?"

Dark tresses bounced as she shook her head. "I don't know. I didn't notice him at first. My mind was on other things."

A healthy blush filled her cheeks as she continued. "I was looking at the flowers and then... he was just there. I tried to move out of his way, but he adjusted and ended up walking right toward me and would have ran into me if I hadn't moved. When I stepped out of the way, I fell into the flower bed."

"Not hurt?"

"No. I would have said something then. I didn't fall hard. I landed on my knees. I thought he was going to help me up, but when he leaned over, he ..."

I raised a brow at her reluctance to speak. She'd already told me once, so I helped her out. "He told you to stay away from me. That I wasn't who you thought I was."

She swallowed and nodded as if those words couldn't be spoken again. "Why would he say that?"

It wasn't a lie when I answered her. "I have no idea."

I didn't know his motivation, nor did I know why he had been sent to sabotage our week together. I needed time to review the facts. Incidents were piling up. There had to be a connection between them, but I wouldn't figure out what it was by sitting on the aft deck with the most delectable woman I'd ever known.

I pinched the bridge of my nose. My carefully laid plans had been fucked with. No matter how much support I wanted to give Noemi right now, I had work to do. But I had to know one thing first.

"Have you been able to reach your brother yet?"

"No. He hasn't answered, and he hasn't returned my messages."

"Is that normal?"

I doubted that it was. Noemi and Willis weren't inseparable, but they were close. I couldn't imagine him not calling her back unless he had very specific reasons for not doing so.

"No, actually. It's not normal at all. I was going to try to call him again after lunch, but then..."

"I understand." I stood up to move away from her. I needed to concentrate, and I couldn't do that around her. "I have some calls of my own to make. The windows will be done soon then we can set sail. Try to call him one more time. I don't want him to worry about you. I'll be in the library. The door will be locked, but if you need anything, just knock."

I left a confused woman sitting on a lounge chair on the main deck of my yacht. I knew she deserved better from me. But I also knew that if I didn't start connecting some of these dots, she wouldn't be alive long enough to come to that realization herself.

Chapter Seven

-Dante-

Michael filled two shot glasses from the decanter on his desk. "I'll be leaving shortly. I wanted to be here when you arrived, make sure you were settled in. My island is your island for as long as you choose to stay."

"I appreciate your hospitality, but it will only be for a day or two. I need to get Noemi home, but I have to find some answers first."

"Like who had the nerve to put out a contract on Dante Calegari?"

"That's a starting place. You wouldn't happen to know anything about that?"

Michael frowned, threw back his shot, and poured another. "Nothing specific. Have you been online?"

I shook my head. I hadn't had the time, or quite frankly, the inclination, to view my death warrant. "But you have?"

Michael nodded slowly. "I was on the circuit, looking for a job."

"I suppose I should thank you for not taking that particular one."

It would have been humorous if Michael weren't a master of his game. If Michael Bianchin had wanted me dead, one: He would have carried out the job himself, not sent those bungling idiots; two: I'd be dead. Michael didn't miss. We were the best in our business. The minutiae that would determine which of us was better would be lost in a pool of blood. Yes, he'd probably succeed in killing me, but it would cost him his life as I took him down with me. Fortunately, we had enough mutual respect that it wasn't an issue.

He sat forward in his chair. "I think you'd be surprised at how many people didn't want that job or even approved of it being posted in the first place."

"Yet, someone took it. Who the fuck were they?"

"Hotshots trying to prove themselves. I take it 'they' are no longer a concern?"

"Amateurs. Someone let those men get slaughtered."

"Somebody out there has balls. Do you have any idea who wants you dead?"

I remembered what the first man said as I slid my knife across his throat. *"It's not about you."*

"I don't think anyone really does."

Michael's eyes narrowed as he leaned forward. He was a master of our game. Very few played it as well. He had as much interest in how the pieces moved as I did. He could very well end up a king on the run himself someday.

"How much am I worth?" As morbid as it was, I needed to know what price had been put on me. That number was another piece of a puzzle that hadn't revealed its picture yet.

"That's why this was a joke. A million. It was out there for hours before anyone snapped it up."

"Because they knew that anyone who had a chance of succeeding wouldn't take it for such a low price."

"And that's why it doesn't make any sense. Anyone who wanted you out of the way bad enough to actually make the move wouldn't have put out such a lowball contract."

"Unless it was never about me to begin with."

Everything that didn't make sense made perfect sense. Michael didn't know the things I knew about Noemi. He didn't know our past.

"Tell me," he urged.

"It was meant to be a distraction. The contract. The men sent to kill me. It was to keep me on guard. If I was trying to save my own life—"

"Then you wouldn't be paying as much attention to her." Michael was fast and there was no reason to elaborate. "Why the hell does someone want her dead?"

That was where our alliance ended. I had a lifetime of secrets to take to the grave. So, I just didn't answer him.

"This violence against innocent women seems to be going around," he muttered as he finished his last shot after several minutes of silence.

"What do you mean?"

"I'm not sure yet, but I'm going to a very small town in Colorado to find out."

That caught my interest. The contract I wouldn't touch. "The librarian?"

"Who the fuck wants to kill a librarian?" Michael ground out.

"Maybe she saw something she wasn't meant to see."

He shook his head. "No. Not this. There's too much money involved. And if it's mob related, they could have hired anyone. They don't usually use the circuit."

"True. But I don't see you taking this." If he did, he wasn't the man I thought he was.

"No, I won't, but my curiosity is piqued. I'm going to Leadville to find out what the big mystery is. Something about it... intrigues me."

"You're going to settle your curiosity? That's not like you, either."

"Let's just say I've had enough of watching innocent women pay the price for something some other fucker did."

I raised my glass to him. "On that we agree."

He looked out the window with an expression I was beginning to recognize—reluctance. Something had happened and Michael

Bianchin was beginning to doubt everything he believed in. *Fuck*. He wasn't the only one.

"Did you end up taking the Romano contract?" I needed to change the subject as much for my benefit as for his.

"No. Too close to home. Were you interested?"

"Not at all. While I don't condone what he did, there's worse people in the world."

Michael nodded. "I agree with you on that, also. They found his body in a burned-out car, you know."

I shrugged. The fate of a mafia Don who'd ratted on the entire New York underworld was a conversational distraction, but I didn't care about his fate. Not when Noemi's hung in the balance. Not when...*Fuck*!

Wide eyes stared at me from the doorway. It was my fault. I was sloppy... again.

Michael and I sat in his office with the door wide open like we were shooting the breeze after a cold beer. I let my guard down and talked to Michael as naturally as if we were discussing the weather. I thought I told her I'd come to get her. I thought she'd stay in her room. I thought... It didn't fucking matter what I thought.

My blood pounded through my veins as a torrent of emotions washed through me. Emotions I didn't know what to do with. My chest tightened. I don't know how much she heard, but if she heard anything it was more than enough. Put together with what she'd already seen...

Michael stood up to leave.

"No, we'll go." I intercepted him in the doorway.

Frowning, he turned to Noemi.

"Stay here. I'm leaving the island shortly anyway, and I still need to pack. It was nice to meet you, Noemi."

He took her hand, raised it to his lips, then smirked at me when I couldn't control the rumble that reverberated through my chest.

"If you need anything during your stay," he added more seriously, "please don't hesitate to ask Phillipe. He'll take care of you."

He said the last words while looking straight at me. "Dante."

He nodded at me then left the room.

That son of a bitch. He thought I would hurt her? Fuck, I didn't know. Was I going to hurt her? If anyone else had eavesdropped on our conversation, they wouldn't have lived to tell the tale, but how many times in the last few days had I faced the realization that no matter what happened, Noemi would make it through this alive. She wouldn't die by my hand or anyone else's...

But that was before she heard a conversation that was never meant for her ears.

Chapter Eight
-Noemi-

A stupid impulse lured me from my room, but thirst wasn't really stupid. I wanted something to drink so I went in search of tea, a bottle of water, anything! The maze of bungalows and gazebos connected by more flowered walkways was confusing, especially when you hadn't been given a tour.

As soon as the tender arrived at the island's shore, introductions were minimal. Dante and Michael rushed me to my room, and then closed the door on me like I was a child who couldn't listen to the big boys talk. It took about ten minutes to take the items out of my suitcase and put them away. After that, I wanted a cold drink, something to wash away the heat and the uneasy feeling I'd experienced since meeting Michael.

Michael Bianchin, I assumed, was a business associate of Dante's. He was nearly as tall as Dante, but much more... rugged. He was handsome, with copper streaks in his dark brown hair that complemented the green of his eyes. He was polite, but there was something about him that made me uncomfortable. Maybe it was the way he looked at me, like he could see right through me. Or maybe it was witnessing the immediate bond he shared with Dante? One that I struggled to build. I've never seen Dante act so familiar with anyone who wasn't part of his family. As soon as the two shook hands when Dante and I stepped off the tender, I was practically forgotten. Whatever the two needed to discuss so urgently, it trumped being social.

"Stay, unpack," Dante had murmured as he kissed my cheek. "I'll come back to get you."

But Dante wasn't serious, was he? I just wanted a glass of tea or lemonade. It really wasn't the same as saying, "Stay in this room. Don't leave until I come back to get you." But his exact words were lost. My mind was in a million other places. Maybe I heard what I wanted to hear. Maybe I blocked out yet another of Dante's unreasonable demands.

Unreasonable? No. If I thought that when I left my room, I'd have changed my mind. His demand was perfectly reasonable if he wanted to make sure I didn't hear their conversation.

A chill snaked down my spine, wrapping every nerve in my body in its icy grip. My heartbeat hammered; my blood pounded; the hair raised on my skin. Everything happened all at one time. I was in flight or fight mode, but I didn't want to do either one. What I wanted was to understand what I just heard.

Dante killed five men in two days. Possibly six. I wasn't sure about the man from the café. Maybe Dante had lied about finding him. Maybe that man was dead too.

"Dante—" I started to confront him, but he put a finger over his lips. He strode toward me, pulled me further into the room, and closed the door.

"There's been enough eavesdropping for one day, *bambina*," he said, his voice deceptively soft as he closed the door.

Bambina.... This was the Dante who had given me a ride home from his mother's birthday party.

This was the cold, distant man who said goodbye to me at the airport.

While the man I had spent the last few days with was certainly not warm and friendly, he was not the same man who stood before me. And the man I had been intimate with, the man who had touched me and shown me what physical pleasure was? That man was nowhere to be found in Dante's narrowed eyes and cold demeanor.

"We need to talk," I insisted when he remained quiet.

He crossed his arms over his chest and leaned back against the door. Was he blocking me in? He was angry, yes. I got it. He was furious about what I overheard, but he wasn't going to hurt me. Was he? He said he wouldn't. He promised me several times that he'd never hurt me. I tried to give him some time. Maybe he needed to gather his thoughts. But he was crazy if he thought I was just going to shrug this off and then go eat dinner with him later as if nothing had happened.

Finally, he spoke. The tone in his voice matched the void in his eyes. I couldn't take his detachment. I preferred his angry hostility over the black hole where his emotions should have been.

"You have questions. I understand that."

I started to talk, but he silenced me with one finger. "You shouldn't have listened at the door, Noemi. But you know that don't you?"

"Can I answer that or are you going to shush me again?"

His brow rose. "It was meant to be rhetorical, but if you have something to say..."

"Something to say?" I lost it. My voice rose, trying to pull something out of him, something he'd buried deep. I wasn't going to stand there and be made to feel like I was the one in the wrong. Not when it had been revealed that he was a... what exactly was he?

"Of course I have something to say, but are you actually going to let me ask questions?"

He shrugged. "You can ask."

"You said you wouldn't lie to me."

I was stalling. I had questions, plenty of them. I just had to decide which ones I really needed to know. Which answers could I hear and not get scared? Despite his aloofness, I didn't fear Dante. Something told me that could change with a few ill-thought-out questions. *Ill-thought-out questions?* The man just admitted to being a hired killer! My emotions went into hyperdrive, making me dizzy from confusion.

"And I won't," Dante replied. "I was part of the conversation you should never have heard, so I am aware of what you now know. I won't insult you by trying to lie about anything, but neither will I tell you things that you don't need to know." Dante responded as if he was talking to a stranger. "Go ahead. Where would you like to start?"

Where would I like to start? Where *would* I like to start?

"That's what you do? Who you are? You're not a stockbroker like Lilly said. You're a hitman?"

Dante shook his head as if I'd gotten it all wrong. But I hadn't. Things I couldn't imagine were true. I knew what I heard! It all seemed to fit. I should have been in complete shock, but I wasn't, and I was confused as to why.

"No. That's not entirely accurate. I am heavily invested in the stock market, but I'm not a broker. I never was. And I'm not a hitman. I'm an assassin."

"Assassin?" My tongue tripped over the word. "Aren't they the same thing?"

Dante answered me with a sigh and a look of disdain. "No, they're not the same. A hitman is low class. Unevolved."

I couldn't help but snicker at his tone. Being a hitman was beneath him. The absurdity hit me. His arms had wrapped around me with a demanding passion that I never knew existed, but also with a surprising tenderness I didn't know he was capable of. Those same hands took the life of others in exchange for money. The man I loved was a ruthless, cold-hearted murderer.

"Why?" I blurted out, my mind working fast to reason through it. How could I have fallen for a killer? Dante was intelligent, the smartest man I knew. He could do anything. *Be* anybody. And this was what he chose? "Why do you... do *this*?"

Dante tilted his head to one side. At first, I thought he wasn't going to answer me.

"Because, baby girl. Evil men lurk in the dark. Someone must hold them accountable. That someone, sometimes, is me."

"So, it's some kind of noble cause? Vigilante justice?"

"That's not it at all."

His voice lowered and his eyes darkened. This was the Dante I barely knew. This man scared me.

"When a bad man has to die, you need a worseman to kill him."

Anti-social. Confused. Emotionally stunted. Dante was many things, but bad? No. I didn't believe that. Even knowing that he was a hired killer, my heart could never think of Dante as a bad man.

"Is that what you are? A bad man?" I asked softly.

He cupped my cheek, a shadow passed through his eyes, then he turned away. I watched his body change. His shoulders straightened, his fists clenched at his side.

"The worst."

"I don't believe that."

He turned back to face me. "I don't care. Who and what I am isn't defined by your beliefs. No man is just one thing. I know that better than anyone. You've only known the man that I've shown you."

"I watched you kill someone, Dante. You never intended to show me that."

"An unavoidable occurrence."

What did that mean? "Unavoidable occurrence?"

"You were supposed to be asleep."

"You knew, didn't you? You knew those men were coming for us and you didn't tell me?"

"Yes. I made that decision, just like you made the decision not to reveal to me, until now, that you knew about the other two men."

"Those pills weren't ibuprofen, were they?" I asked.

"No."

"What were they?"

"Sleeping pills."

What the—? "You drugged me?"

"Are you fucking serious? Sleeping pills aren't the same as drugs. These were all natural, over-the-counter sleep aids. With the wine, they should have helped you stay asleep until our visitors were dealt with," he snapped at me. "Now, I have a question."

I eyed him warily. "I'm still feeling resentful that you basically tried to knock me out without my permission, but okay, shoot."

"How did you find out about the other men?" He eyed me suspiciously.

I swallowed hard. "I... there was a vent in the bathroom wall. I overheard you talking to the resort manager, or whoever that was."

His jaw clenched. "I see that hearing things not meant for your ears is going to be a habit with you."

"It wasn't like I locked myself in the bathroom. You're the one who put me there," I reminded him.

"That's true." A muscle ticked in his jaw. "Another in what's turning out to be a long line of mistakes."

From a heart beating too rapidly to one that skipped a beat. "What does that mean?"

A clenched jaw and narrowed eyes loomed over me. "It means I've made too many mistakes where you're concerned, Noemi. I've let you distract me."

"Distract you?" I interrupted. "It was your idea to take me on this island-hopping cruise of yours. There are countless different ways we could have fulfilled our contract."

"Exactly," he growled. "But I was too caught up in you to think straight."

Dante leaned over me, forcing my body back against the desk. He braced himself on his arms as he hovered over my bent body. His voice dropped to a near whisper.

"I wanted to show you what it would be like. I had one chance to make you mine, knowing it would only last a short while. I wanted to make you feel what you'd never felt before. I know you didn't need all of it—the resort, the yacht, the designer clothes—but I needed to give it all to you, and I'll be damned if I understand why. Just like I don't understand why you've gotten under my skin. You make me careless, sloppy. You make me *weak*. You don't understand how dangerous that is."

"Then explain it to me."

"I've told you not to ask things you don't really want to know."

"By your own admission, I know that you're an assassin. You kill people for money."

I thought the words spoken aloud would get a reaction out of him, but that was my own naïve expectation. He continued to watch me with a blank expression; I studied him in return. His clenched fists and squared shoulders gave him away. He wasn't as removed as he wanted me to believe. His secret was out. He never wanted me to know this much about him. Who would?

"How many people know this about you?" My stomach started to churn.

"Almost none. Michael is a rare exception. Of course, now you know his secret as well. I really wish you hadn't come looking for me, *bambina*."

I was an idiot. I sucked in a breath as the enormity of the situation took hold. A bad dream. This all had to be a bad dream. My mind bounced from one frenzied thought to another as my heart pumped furiously. He was a murderer, a friend. He was the hottest man I knew; and he was my... lover?

The air around me grew heavy. I don't know if it was from the heat, dehydration, or my body's reaction to my newfound insight into who Dante Calegari really was. When the room started to spin, harshly whispered words came back to me. *"He's not who you think he is. Stay away from Calegari."*

Was I going to faint? People didn't really faint, did they? I've never fainted before in my life but Dante's harshly muttered, "*Shit*," brought back another phrase of his. "A lifetime of firsts."

Strong arms surrounded me. Darkness took hold as I fainted for the first time in my life.

Chapter Nine

-Noemi-

I opened my eyes to blue fabric wafting in the breeze and the soft chirping of birds outside. A light breeze cooled my skin. My throat was parched.

I turned my head to the side. I was in my room, rather, the room I was assigned to on Michael's mystery island. The white walls and white rattan furniture weren't welcoming. While it looked feminine and fragile, it felt stifling and confusing. Or maybe that was just me, dealing with finding out the man I've wanted for years was an assassin.

A figure sat next to the bed. Winter hours created shadows around the room, but I knew who he was. Chair back against the wall.; hands steepled together as his elbows rested on his knees and he stared at the floor. That perfectly combed hair was messed up as though hands had run through it repeatedly.

"Dante?" My voice cracked as I tried to sit up.

His head shot up. "You're awake."

The relief in his voice almost made me smile through my discomfort and irritation, but it wasn't enough to make me feel any better.

"Yes." I looked around the room. "Is there something I can drink?"

"Outside on the patio. I'll be right back."

Dante left the room as I hauled myself up into a sitting position. I was embarrassed at having fainted, angry at his behavior, and confused about just about everything else.

Dante returned immediately with a glass of water. He handed it to me then returned to his chair by the bed.

I took a small sip, then a much larger one. The crisp, cold water slid down my throat, soothing the dry ache.

"You need to stay hydrated," Dante said sternly from his chair.

I wanted to act out like a spoiled child. *And you need to shut up!* But I held my waspishness in and went for sarcasm instead. "If that's your way of saying you were worried about me, I'm fine. Thanks for asking."

His eyes narrowed, but I didn't care if I made him angry. "How long was I out of it?"

"A few minutes," he answered with a pensive look on his face as he studied me. I stared back at him, completely at a loss as to what to say to this man I knew little about.

"Dinner is on the patio if you're hungry. You should eat. Get your energy back."

Food. That was his way of saying he cared about me. If I were expecting him to throw himself at my feet with warm words, I would have been heartbroken. But I was beginning to understand the man he was and the invitation to eat was as good as it would get. For now. I didn't know if I really wanted to eat, but I was hungry, and I knew I should put something in my stomach.

"Thank you."

I stood up and Dante jumped from his seat.

"Maybe... I should bring a plate to you?"

His hesitant tone stopped me as I took a step toward the door. While I had done a terrible job of connecting some dots, heck, almost *all* the dots, I didn't think I was mistaken this time. Dante was nervous and unsure of himself. He wanted to know that I was okay. He wanted to help me.

But he didn't know how.

I put my hand out, a momentary conciliatory gesture that I hoped he had enough social awareness to understand. His dark eyes stared down at my outstretched fingers before he took my hand in his.

His usually strong, firm grip was cold and clammy. He barely held my hand, but for that moment, I was glad that he tried.

The small patio table was set with a light meal of small tea sandwiches, fresh fruit, and macaroni and cheese. The odd assortment brought a smile to my face.

"It looks good," I said as Dante pulled out a chair for me.

"Michael sent it over. He was worried about you."

I took a cucumber sandwich from the tray followed by a large scoop of the macaroni. "Well, it looks delicious. I'll have to thank him. I'm sorry, by the way. I've never fainted before. And thank you, too."

Dante ignored the sandwiches and fruit and filled his plate with some of the mac and cheese. "For what? Making you ill?"

"I'm not ill. I'm sure... Listen, it was just the heat, and the dehydration, that got to me."

"Don't lie to me, Noemi. I'm sure our topic of conversation had a role in your passing out."

"I'm not sure you should flatter yourself so much."

He paused with his fork midway to his mouth.

"While that was not the most pleasant conversation we've had, and I still have a lot of questions by the way, I'm not usually done in by words alone. I didn't faint when I saw you take a man's life. I mean, if that were going to cause me to faint, it would have happened that morning. But yes, adding that to the heat and the dehydration didn't help, I'm sure. But I'm okay. I'll eat and drink and—"

"You're rambling."

"Yes, I'm rambling. I'm at a complete loss of what to say to you yet, I feel like I have to say *something*. I can't just sit here and have lunch like I'm not on a private island with a man who kills people for a living."

I put my fork down. "And yet, part of me feels like it doesn't matter. Like that man, whoever he is, has been around forever, but I don't know *that man*. I just know the man sitting in front of me. He's hard, and demanding, and arrogant and overwhelming, but he's also strong and giving. That man provides generously for his family. He's the man who comforted me when my parents died. The man I've wanted for so long..."

My voice trailed off in a pathetic sigh. "I'm a little confused right now."

I couldn't look at him anymore. I stabbed at my macaroni, trying to get enough to stay on my fork so I could take a bite.

Normally, the silence was awkward, but I think we both welcomed it. Dante didn't say anything after my tirade, and I didn't poke the bear. It was an illusion—some peace and quiet in a tropical murderer's paradise.

I was hungry and finished off most of the little cucumber finger sandwiches and almost all the sliced fruit. Dante stuck with the mac and cheese. We both drank the iced tea. We avoided conversation, explanations, and interrogations in favor of silence.

By the time we were done, I did feel better. The shaky feeling had passed, and my thirst was quenched. The nauseous feeling in the pit of my stomach had disappeared. Mostly.

"I should thank Michael for the food," I ventured to say.

I sat back in my chair, focusing on the picturesque setting around me. Lush green plants, simple rattan buildings, tropical flowers. I hadn't had time before to notice how beautiful Michael's island was.

"He's already gone," Dante said, standing up.

"Where'd he go?"

"Away. On business."

My mind went right to what it was I shouldn't have known. I swallowed another mouthful of tea along with the words that sprang into my head. *A business trip to kill someone?*

"I need to leave, Noemi."

"What? You're not leaving me here. You can't just drop me off an island."

"Calm down. I'm not leaving the island." He shook his head. "Why does this always have to be so difficult? I know I usually just disappear, but I wanted to let you know. I have some calls to make, some business to take care of. I'll be in Michael's office for a while."

"That's progress, I guess." I tried to be understanding. At least he had warned me this time and not just walked away, but it felt more like he expected me to sit back and enjoy a tropical vacation with a murderer. Surely he understood how bizarre this was?

Dante stood up to leave, thinking, I assumed, that he had done his good deed and told me of his plans. Loneliness crept over me quickly. I stared past him to the break in the landscape where I could see the beach through the overgrowth of trees.

My shoulders stiffened as his hands clasped them from behind. Dante nuzzled the top of my head with his chin. No words were necessary. I'd been comforted by that gesture before, briefly, at the airport five years ago. That night in the Calegari kitchen. When things were at their worst, this was Dante's way of reaching out.

"Patience, *bambina*. We'll talk more tonight," he whispered against the top of my head.

My voice stuck in my throat at his sudden gentleness. He could have been cold and demanding. There were times when his dominance was exactly what I needed. But he knew! He knew that what I needed right then was his humanity. I didn't need his take charge, wear my blindfold, autocratic behavior. I needed warmth and compassion. I don't know who was more surprised that he could give me that—me or him.

Chapter Ten

-Dante-

I found Noemi on the beach, toes tickled by the incoming tide while she reclined on a blanket, and the sun painted a horizon of blues, reds, and pinks for her viewing pleasure. The juxtaposition was clear but nearly absurd. I spent two hours immersed completely in my world—looking for answers, talking to associates and trying to piece together a macabre puzzle. Seeing her on the beach afterward brought forth the same sense of calm that coming home after a job did. Light. Familiar. Welcoming.

I hadn't expected that, given that she had discovered my secret, but I recognized it.

If nothing else in this world was real, she was. If I didn't know who I could trust, I knew I could trust her. I didn't know how I knew that. Was it because she didn't scream when she found out I made a living by taking other people's lives? Because she didn't insist that I put her on the yacht and immediately take her home?

Noemi wouldn't go back to Connecticut and tell my story to the world. To my core, I knew I could trust her, but I also knew I still had to make the point known. I couldn't risk anything. She had to understand the position we were in. Nothing could be left up to chance. Not that it would matter if she blabbed to the world. Even if they believed her, all she had was a conversation. No proof. No evidence.

If my crimes could be traced back to me, I'd be a dead man already.

If she ever spoke of it, I'd know it for what it was. Her betrayal.

I could never forgive her for that. I was prepared to live without her if I could continue to admire her from a distance. If she betrayed me, those feelings would change. The poison would spread through me, and I would no longer care whether she lived or died. Distance would be the only thing keeping her safe.

But there was more. I waited for her to bring it up. We hadn't gotten that far in the conversation before she fainted. That scared the hell out of me. I had yelled for Michael as soon as I caught her. Panicking, I wanted to call for a doctor to be sure she would be all right, but Michael pointed out that we were miles away from civilization. Phillipe, his estate manager, doubled as a medic when needed and took care of her by elevating her legs and checking her vitals. He said she'd be fine. I challenged him. Clearly, she wasn't fine, or she wouldn't have fainted, but Michael helped convince me that she needed to eat and drink something. I wanted to kick myself, knowing that she probably wouldn't have fainted at all if she hadn't overheard my conversation with Michael.

I wasn't convinced of anything until she woke up after just a minute or two. If she hadn't, I don't know what we would have done. I sat by her bedside, willing her to open her eyes and prove to me that she was fine. I should have stayed with her after we ate, but I needed that time alone. I needed to think about how the next few days would play out.

In the end, I went against everything I believed in and took the coward's way out, but I also hung my hopes on a frantically whispered prayer to the Virgin Mary that Noemi had forgotten half of what she'd heard and was so shocked by my revelation that the details of my conversation with Michael had been lost.

She turned her head when I lowered myself to sit beside her on the blanket. Ankles crossed, I clasped my hands around my knees and kept my eyes trained on the horizon.

I wasn't used to beating around the bush. I was tired of being confronted by my shortcomings with every conversation I had with her. The longer I stared at the waves, the more I pulled at the edges of a mask that refused to budge. The other man was in charge now. He wanted to ease her fears. He wanted to apologize for having ruined what was supposed to have been a once in a lifetime experience. He wanted more than I was willing to give and more than I ever deserved to receive.

Noemi bent her head so that her face was in front of mine, blocking the ocean view. "Hi," she whispered quietly, a shy smile on her face.

"Hello."

When our eyes met, I surrendered to what the other man wanted. None of this was her fault and it was my responsibility, not hers, to figure out how to make it all work. The burden of my sins caused the shadow in her eyes. It was unacceptable in every way that she had made it from the shadows to the edge of my darkness, but what happened after that rested entirely on my shoulders.

I grabbed her hand and pulled her up. "Walk with me."

I started to let go of her hand, but she grasped mine tighter. An unfamiliar panic set in, quickly squashed by the man who got his strength from giving her what she needed.

Noemi looked up at me with an expression that begged me not to disappoint her again. I squeezed her hand and gave a tug. One slow step at a time, we walked along the shore, reluctance heavy between us. She didn't want to let go of me and I didn't want to talk, but both were inevitable. She needed answers, but I didn't owe her anything... except her life.

The soft sand gave way to our steps as the waves created their music beside us. Just like the Grand Tropican, I'd been to Michael's island before, and just like the flowers surrounding bungalow six, I'd never noticed the pristine rhythm of the ocean or the gentle massage of the sand beneath my bare feet.

I cleared my throat.

"Ask," I invited her, the huskiness of my voice betraying me. "I can't promise to answer everything, or that you won't hate me when this is over, but you can ask."

She grasped my hand tighter. "I could never hate you. I may never fully understand you. But I don't think I could ever hate you."

I marveled at her naïveté as much as I envied it. I knew she had experienced pain in her life, yet she handled my sins with grace. A grace I hadn't earned. Soon, she'd know how much I didn't deserve her charity.

A shell caught my eye. I took her hand with me as I bent to retrieve the coiled treasure whose spirals wrapped around itself in infinite layers one on top of the other. With my free hand, I dusted the sand off the ivory and purple nautilus then flipped it through my fingers, over and over again. The movement soothed me as I waited for her first question. She wouldn't pass up the chance. I didn't have to tell her that she'd never get the opportunity to question me again.

If I had the nerve to look at her, I think I would have seen her pensive brow and wise eyes. Naïve, yes, but Noemi had an inherent wisdom. She had a way of extracting my truths without a word.

"How long have you been in this line of work?"

Easy enough. "I took my first contract when I was sixteen."

"That's so young," she gasped. Concern made her tighten her grip on my hand. "How? Why?" She stumbled through her questions. "That's awful, Dante."

She didn't know how awful it really was. What should I have told her? Because it was who I was groomed to be? Because I had been raised with a vendetta, decades in the making, and my inheritance from my father was the privilege of carrying out a promise I made when I was just a boy?

"That's not something I share, baby girl. Not with anyone."

"You said few people know this about you? Lilly? Gabriel?"

"No. No one in my family knows. As you said, Lilly thinks I'm a stockbroker. Gabriel... He knows I play with the stock market. He suspects more than that, but we don't talk about it. You need to understand, Noemi. I don't talk about this. It's not dinner table conversation. If you hadn't overheard me talking to Michael, if you didn't see me kill that bastard at the resort, we would never have had this conversation. Ever."

"What happens now then? I can't pretend I don't know—"

"I don't expect you to. But once you return home, this will never be spoken of again."

I had to make sure that happened.

"You said that you were a bad man, that when bad men needed to die, someone even worse had to kill them." She hesitated, a tumultuous expression in her eyes. "The men that you've killed, did they deserve it?"

Her attempt at vindication touched me. She didn't believe I was a bad man. She was looking for a way to justify the monster.

"I thoroughly vet every contract I take."

"They were guilty? How can you be sure of that?"

"Because I spend a considerable amount of time investigating them. I go to bed with a clear conscience, Noemi. I've never taken a contract on an innocent person."

"Is that why you're gone so much? You're investigating these people?"

"Yes."

"You said 'person.' You've killed women, too?"

She was dangerous with her ability to see through my words. But it was also a relief. It meant this conversation wouldn't drag out unnecessarily as minute details were picked slowly apart. It needed to be quick, like the removal of a band-aid where slow exposure only prolonged the pain.

"Evil tendencies don't inherently belong to men. Women can be just as immoral."

"Immoral?" she whispered thoughtfully. "Exactly what type of people have you..." Her voice trailed off as if she couldn't bring herself to say "killed" one more time.

"People who deserved it."

"Says you," she challenged.

"Says me."

We stopped walking and I turned her to face me.

"I'm not talking about the average wife beater or street corner thug, baby girl. Every single one of them deserved everything they got. And more."

She tilted her head as she sought to understand a world she knew nothing about.

"So, you're their judge, jury, and executioner? What type of people deserve to die because Dante Calegari decreed it so?"

"The worst mankind has to offer. Pedophiles. Human traffickers. Men and women who sell other men and women as slaves."

"Sex slaves?" she asked tentatively.

"Yes. Among other things." Things so unspeakable even I couldn't say the words out loud. Especially not to her.

Her voice softened as she looked away from me. "Children?"

"Yes."

I was brutally honest with her, but she had no idea the wicked cruelty that existed in this world. I wanted to plant the idea but not taint her with the gory details.

"So then by killing these people, you're actually saving lives? Innocent people, including children, are spared because you got rid of the men–*people*–who victimize them?"

One corner of my mouth ticked upward. She was still trying to find the good in my actions. I couldn't fault her for that. On the surface, it was exactly the way she portrayed it.

But I knew better.

"Don't try to paint me as a hero, Noemi. It's not like that."

I couldn't tell her that I enjoyed my work. I couldn't admit that with the first contract I accepted at the age of sixteen, I was lucky that I'd found a way to take my twisted rage out on people no one would ever miss.

We started walking again. She was quiet. I could almost hear her mind working, grinding through everything I said. Thinking. Analyzing. Trying to find something redeeming. Connecting the dots.

But she wouldn't be able to. She didn't have all the pieces of the puzzle, the jigsaw of what my soul should have been.

The sun continued its descent, leaving the sky awash with the reds, golds, and yellows of a tropical sunset. We continued walking in silence until Noemi grabbed my arm.

"When you and Michael were talking, you said that you didn't think the events of the last few days were about you. Is that why you're telling me all this now? Someone's trying... me? This is about me? Who would want to kill me? I don't understand, Dante—"

Our conversation triggered her memory. Her bottom lip quivered as fear took over. I reached for her, knowing that my arms could give her the comfort that my words couldn't, because the fuck if I had any answers to give her.

Her arms wrapped around my waist as naturally as if we spent every evening in this position. Her head bowed against my chest and I rested my cheek on the top of her head.

"I'm working on it, baby girl. If I had the answer—"

"You wouldn't tell me," she finished for me in a huff.

"You're right. About saving your life, no, I won't tell you."

"But it's my life," she grumbled. "How am I supposed to live it knowing that someone else is trying to end it?"

"Listen to me," I grated in her ear, angered again, not by her fear, but by the audacity someone had to threaten her, to instill that fear in her to begin with. "I'm not certain yet that what I said to Michael is accurate. It was just a thought. Even if it's not true, I'm not going to let anything happen to you. I think I've proven that already. You're with me. You're perfectly safe, you understand?"

"But what about... after?"

We hadn't talked about after. I knew she wanted more than just one night, just one week, with me. I'd known that from the beginning, though she hadn't mentioned it. If I made the offer, she'd take it, but it wasn't going to happen, and she had enough self-preservation and self-respect not to bring it up. I couldn't say anything that would get her hopes up; couldn't lead her to believe this week was anything more than a means to an end, even though I knew that was a damn lie.

This week was *everything. She* was everything. My beginning and my end. Once the week was over, I'd walk away from her, find the bastards who'd set this in motion, and make them pay for what they were putting her through. My guilt wouldn't let me walk away without knowing she would return to the life she deserved because there was no way in hell she was ready for the life she thought she wanted. A life with me.

Noemi trembled in my arms.

"I'm working on it, baby girl." My voice lowered. I wanted her confidence. I needed her to believe in me. "You're going to be just fine, but you're going to have to trust me."

There was no hesitation in her voice as she simply replied, "I do."

Chapter Eleven
-Noemi-

I thought our first kiss on the veranda was the kiss to end all kisses, but that one...

Dante held my face in his hand while his index finger traced the shape of my lips with a feathery softness I didn't know he was capable of. He never stopped surprising me, but this gentleness, this Dante that I didn't know yet, was a much nicer surprise than finding out he was an assassin. Like everything about him, the notion was such a complete contradiction my head hurt from trying to understand it.

"I see you," he said throatily, dropping a whisper of a kiss onto my parted lips.

I closed my eyes and leaned forward, wanting more than such a chaste touch. My mind still reeled from everything I'd just learned, including that I was possibly someone's target, though I had no idea why anyone would want to kill me. The thought made me shiver as I reached out for Dante's strength. I wanted him to hold me. Wanted his touch to remind me that he was in charge and that I could surrender all of this to him. I believed he'd make it better.

"Overthinking. Trying to solve this. That's my job. You think too much, Noemi."

His mouth skated over my cheek before reaching my ear. I gasped when his hand touched my chest. He didn't fondle me as I anticipated but placed his palm flat against the opening of my coverup.

"I feel you. Your heartbeat has increased. Has anyone else ever made your heart beat this fast or is it just for me?"

"Just you." He had to already know that since there were no others before him.

"You think I already knew the answer to that question, don't you? The answer's yes, I did. But I needed to hear you say it, *bambina*. Remember? Words matter. What I can see, what I can feel, what I can hear. That's all that matters to me. Your body talks to me in ways you don't even understand."

I tilted my head to search his eyes. "What is it telling you now?" I asked breathlessly.

One corner of his mouth ticked upward. "That you want to dance with me again."

He stepped away from the surf, holding my hand and stretching my arm out.

"You haven't been paying attention," I teased him back. "I don't like to dance, remember?"

I knew what he was doing. The conversation had taken a sour turn and he was trying to distract me the same way he had on the plane when the fear of flying held me in its grip.

"Oh, I remember very well."

With a determined tug, he snapped his wrist, pulling my body up against his.

"I remember how good you felt in my arms, how your body pressed up against mine. I remember how the tension eased from you, and how your arms slid around my neck once you relaxed. Yes, *bambina*. I've paid attention. I will remember *everything* about you."

Will? I wanted to ask him what he meant but asking that question meant facing the answer. He had no intention of there being an "after" for us. We'd go back to Connecticut. He'd go back to his secretive life and I'd go back to longing for someone I could never have. Only once I returned home, it'd be worse. I'd had a glimpse of what heaven could be like. Dante Calegari was a temptation, but he'd always be just out of my reach.

Dante's hands rested on my hips. He stood there waiting for me, letting me make the decision. And, yes, he knew what I wanted. Forget the dancing. Leaning against him while we swayed back and forth wasn't really dancing anyway, was it? It was just another excuse to be back in his arms. To wax poetic about the beauty of a starry night, a warm tropical breeze, and the roaring surf that drowned out everything except how much I needed him, how much I wanted him, and how very little time I had to keep living in this fantasy world he had created for me.

I closed the distance between us and wrapped my arms around his neck. "Dance with me, Dante. Before I wake up and find out that none of this is real."

He buried his hand in my hair, angling my head to that familiar position that let loose the butterflies in my stomach.

"Tomorrow, I'll ask you why you think this isn't real. Tonight, I don't give a damn."

The gentleness was gone. The Dante I knew I could count on had returned, demanding, forceful, taking as much as he gave as his mouth devoured mine. At some point during that kiss, we started our dance, creating a rhythm that belonged just to us, witnessed only by the sand, surf, and stars. Our mouths came together again and again as our bodies reached out for one another.

Dante picked me up and carried me down the moonlit path to my room. Kicking the door open, he didn't set me on my feet until we were inside. The room was completely covered in shadows with a strip of moonlight streaming through the window, highlighting the bed.

I didn't wait for his demands or hesitate in order to protect my own sensitivities. I knew what I wanted. I was the one who offered him my virginity. If I could do that, the power was mine.

When my feet touched the floor, I pushed away from him and smiled at his confused expression right before it morphed to one of surprise, then pleasure, as I started to untie my wrap. I'd never seen so many emotions cross his face in such a short span of time.

He tilted his head, studying me with a wicked gleam in his eye. He crossed his arms and leaned against the door with a cocky "I dare you" stance.

"Challenge accepted," I said as the lace coverup fell to the floor.

I wielded the power I finally recognized I possessed. Of course, he would fight it. Dante Calegari gave up control to no one. I was okay with that, too. I'd fight him for it and enjoy every second of the battle because that night, I planned to win.

Chapter Twelve
-Noemi-

The beach chair was in a reclined position. To be discreet, I had to raise up on my elbows and lower my sunglasses to admire the view.

When I awoke on the third morning of our extended stay on Michael's island, which I had since learned was called Smuggler's Island and had a rich past all its own, I turned over and hugged the pillow, breathing in deeply Dante's scent, the only part of him I had that early in the morning.

As expected, Dante was absent. During the three mornings we'd spent on the island, I found out he was an early riser and slept hardly at all. Most mornings, I was awoken before dawn by his wandering hands and demanding lips. We'd make love until the sunrise interrupted the darkness of the room, then, exhausted, I'd fall back to sleep while Dante went to do... whatever it is that Dante does in the early morning hours.

That morning, that "something" was taking a swim in the surf before breakfast. Normally, I wouldn't have cared what he was doing. It was too early to be up, but after he'd told me that dolphins had joined him in his swim yesterday, I eagerly made myself get up, put my hair in a ponytail, put on a bathing suit and one of my coverups (this attire being almost all I've worn for three days), and walked the path to the beach, stopping once, of course, to get a cup of coffee from the main house.

Dante didn't notice me at first. I relaxed in one of the beach chairs while the sun came up and the tide continued to recede. The sunrise was on the other side of the island, but the sky was still beautiful with its shades of grays and blues. The early morning gulls screeched, and the sanderlings kept me company as they hunted their breakfast along the shoreline.

Out past the breaking waves, Dante swam the length of the shoreline, back and forth, using something along the shore as a marker. I kept my eyes trained on him, anxiously waiting to see if a dolphin would join him again that morning. He was a good swimmer. He was much further out than I would be comfortable going, and he had more endurance than I could have dreamed of possessing. Back and forth he swam, pausing a few times to dive under the surface or to catch his breath before he was off again. During one of his breaks, he must have scanned the shore and found his audience. He paused then gave me a quick wave before diving beneath the water once more.

After watching intently for the dolphins that never appeared, I switched to drinking my coffee and watching the sanderlings scamper as they picked their meal from the wet sand.

When Dante's imposing figure emerged from the surf, I gave up my zoological interests and focused on the dominant species. I should have balked at my sexist attitude, but I was just a girl, and he was just the man of my dreams, with broad shoulders, sculpted muscles, and washboard abs.

As he got closer, I followed the dripping path of ocean water as it trickled down his chest, glistening on the bronze of his skin, highlighting every hard angle along the way.

"Still shy after the last four days?" His towel fell to the ground as he lowered himself into the chair.

I chose to ignore his attempt to bait me. I kept my eyes trained on the horizon. "No dolphins today?"

"No, no dolphins today."

"That's too bad. I got up early just so I could see them."

"You're not a good flirt, Noemi," he chuckled softly.

"What?" I turned to him, confused by his statement and even more by his uncharacteristic laughter. "I wasn't trying to flirt with you."

"Oh, I am well aware of that." He laughed again as he pushed his wet hair back to reveal the warmth in his gaze.

Island life was good for Dante. Each day, I saw more and more of his humanity. With each meal we've eaten together, each moonlit walk, each night spent under the stars, Dante's softer side revealed itself.

"You could have stroked my ego by letting me think you were up early so you could catch me in the water."

"And that makes you laugh?" I teased. "You never laugh, but you get a kick out of my inept banter?"

"It's not inept if it holds my interest."

I tilted my head as I studied him. "I'm glad I'm here then. I get to save you from striking up a one-sided friendship with a sea turtle."

"I'm sure a sea-turtle is an amiable companion. Quiet. Reserved."

"The two of you would have a lot in common, but you'd never find out because neither one of you would ever talk."

Dark, dominant Dante was heart-stopping sexy. Smiling Dante was adorable.

"I've never seen this side of you before. I like it."

The smile fell but didn't completely collapse. "Must be the sea air. Or the sun."

"Yes, the environment. I'm sure that's what it is."

His hand cupped the back of my head, dragging me toward him. "What else could it possibly be?"

"The stimulating, interesting banter?"

The last thing I saw before his lips met mine was the return of that smile.

He kissed me deeply, but not urgently—giving, not taking, slowly drawing from my lips again and again.

Too soon, he pulled back from me, tracing the pad of his thumb over my lips. "I'm going to go shower, then we'll have breakfast. I have some work to do afterwards."

I flinched at the words. I couldn't help it. Whenever I thought about Dante's work, morbid thoughts took over.

He frowned at me. "Just some phone calls, Noemi. Everyone on this island is safe."

"Sorry. I think it will take a while to get used to—"

He stopped touching me and stood up abruptly. "I'm not very hungry. I think I'll skip breakfast. I'll be in Michael's office after my shower if you need anything."

The naïve girl in me wanted to sit there and wonder what had happened to change his mood so quickly; but I knew. It was another reminder that the island and all the magic it held was temporary. Sighing, I gathered the towels and started walking back to my room. If I hurried, I could have caught up with Dante, but it was clear he wanted to be alone. Oddly, I was okay with that.

If anything had come from our time together, my confidence had grown, at least where he was concerned. There were issues to face, but he'd given me what I needed. He said it. I held his interest. I used the ploy of my virginity to get his notice, but it was me, my words, interests, my conversation, that kept his attention. And he had been attentive. It wasn't a figment of my imagination. The abrupt change this morning was the first incident like it in three days.

This was more than lust and a man taking advantage of a woman's offer. This was more than just "fucking." We talked. We listened. And today, we actually laughed and smiled. Maybe facing the changes he had to have felt was more than he was ready for, but Dante couldn't deny they were there. Island Dante was a different man. I hated that one day, he'd be gone. He hadn't told me when yet, but sooner rather than later, we were going to get back on board the *Mary Theresa* and wave goodbye to Smuggler's Island and the memories that would remain there.

The only problem I had was that I wasn't sure which man would be aboard that yacht with me.

After a quick shower and a solitary breakfast, I needed a distraction from the loneliness that took over in Dante's absence. I'm not sure how he managed it, but Michael's island came with a cell phone tower. I hadn't wanted to try during the last few days while I had Dante's full attention, but now seemed like the right time to call Willis again.

And like the last two times I tried to reach him, my call went straight to voicemail.

"Hey! It's me... again. Everything's still good. I hope you got my messages. We're about halfway done with our cruise. Should be back in a few days. At this rate, I'll be home before you call me. Okay. Well, if you do get this, call me back. I'm kind of starting to worry now. Love you."

It wasn't like Willis to be so unreachable. Not for me, at least. He had a team of people around him, assistants and interns and people whose jobs I didn't understand, pulling at him and making sure his time was well choreographed. But he always made time for me. Even if he couldn't speak right away, he always called me back. We had stayed close over the years. Even after our parents' deaths, when his career was just starting to climb, he was always there when I needed him. I missed him like crazy when I moved to England, but he came to visit a few times and we video-called weekly.

His political career had taken off like wildfire when I was still in high school and now, he was the incumbent senator from New York, sitting on the Armed Services and Foreign Affairs committees. Due to his position, he was also on the Intelligence Committee. When I couldn't reach him the first time I called, I wasn't surprised. But after a few days, when the return call never came , I started to worry and tried again.

This was my third attempt with no results. He always called me back. Late at night after an event; early in the morning on the train to his office. He found a time and a place, but he *always* called. I'd been so caught up in my rapture over Dante that I hadn't been worried until now.

It was funny that with all the craziness I'd dealt with that week, not being able to speak to my brother was the thing that made me the most nervous. I'd try one more time before we left the island. If I hadn't heard from him by the time I got home, I'd bypass the house in Connecticut and head straight for New York. Someone in his office would know where he was.

I scrolled through my phone until I found a number I never had to use before.

"Senator Petrafuso's office. How may I help you?"

"Jenny? This is Noemi. How are you?"

"Oh, hi! I'm well, thank you. How are you? It's great to hear your voice. Willis said you were home now?"

Jenny's words were the reassurance I needed. At least, he knew I was home, and he wasn't missing in action somewhere. She was his assistant and knew his schedule better than he did.

"I am, yes. Well, I'm on vacation now, which is why I've been trying to get a hold of him. He hasn't returned my calls, so I was wondering if everything was okay?"

"Hmmmm. That's strange. I know he always makes a point of calling you. But there's nothing to worry about. He's fine. He'll be back from Washington this afternoon. I'll grab his cell phone when he gets here and see if it's working properly. Maybe he never got your message."

"I don't know. I've called three times now. It rings and goes to voicemail. Are you sure he's okay? Is he super busy right now or anything?"

"No more than usual. Don't stress about it, Noemi. I bet it's a problem with his phone, that's all. Listen. I'll take a good old-fashioned paper message and shove it into his hands as soon as he walks in this afternoon. Okay?"

I breathed a sigh of relief. "That would be wonderful. Thank you so much Jenny." I didn't want to leave her the whole spiel, so I kept it brief. "Just tell him I've been out of town, but I'll be back in a few days. I'll call him again when I get home, but he can call and leave me a message on my cell. I'll check it as soon as I can. Or he can call me tonight if he's able to."

"Got it. I'll push the last option. There's no reason why he can't call you this evening. His calendar's wide open after six tonight. No, wait. That's tomorrow. He has a fundraising dinner tonight at The Met. But don't worry. I'll make sure he finds the time to call."

I hung up, breathing a little easier, but still worried. There are some things in life that are steadfast and reliable. Some things could be counted on irrefutably and their presence meant all was right in the world: Willis Petrafuso's brotherly support was the most consistent thing in my life and I had called him and left three messages with no response.

To borrow a phrase from Dante: *what the fuck was going on?*

Chapter Thirteen
-Noemi-

Tr ue to his word, Dante did his disappearing act before breakfast. I didn't see him all day. I gave him the space he needed,
and it hurt. After attempting to call Willis, I had another one-way
conversation, this time with Lilly's cell phone. Loneliness set in. I felt
the loss, abandoned by my temporary lover, my brother, *and* my best
friend. I ended up being the one trying to make friends with sea tur-
tles, lizards, and some inquisitive tree frogs while Dante holed up in
Michael's office doing who knows what.

I spent most of the morning on the beach, lathering on the sun-
screen before it got too hot for me, which usually occurred before
10:00 am. A quick dip in the ocean, a shower, a change into another
sundress, and I was set for a cozy afternoon with the hammock, a
mocktail, and the thriller I'd stolen from Dante's yacht.

I read for hours, stopped for the light lunch Michael's staff prepared for me, then forged on again, determined to get to the end of
my book. My ambition was undone by the heat, my heavy eyes, and
my earlier than usual wake up time. Sometime after the third body
was found, my eyes closed.

I dreamed of vibrant colors. Of talking sea-turtles. Of Dante,
smiling as we walked through the surf together, splashing each other
like we were in some cheesy laundry commercial. At least, I thought
it was Dante. I never really saw his face clearly. We ran through the
waves, laughing as he caught me around the middle. When I turned
to face him, I couldn't see his face. I got scared. It wasn't him. I didn't
know who he'd become, but I knew he wasn't Dante anymore, just a

faceless man. I broke into a run, dragging my feet through the waves as I tried to get away from him, but he caught me, pulling me down beneath the waves. The salt water poured into my mouth, burning my nostrils and lungs, stealing the air from me. When I bobbed to the surface, I tried to scream for Dante, but the man pulled me down again. This time I couldn't get up. He pinned me with his hands, forcing my head below the water. I gulped mouthful after mouthful of water. My lungs burned as I resigned myself to drowning. Arms came around me and I used what last bit of strength I had to try to fight them off. But this man didn't try to drown me. He pulled me from the water. I wrapped my arms around him and held on. I still couldn't see his face, but when his lips covered mine, I knew who he was.

"Dante," I murmured, surrendering to his lips as they coasted over mine again and again.

"Right here, baby girl. It's time to get up."

I shook my head. I didn't want to get up. I hadn't drowned, and now I was in the safety of his arms. I wanted to stay there, with him, in the surf on the island. I found a side of Dante that I cherished. If I woke up, that Dante would be lost to me forever.

His firm lips kissed and coaxed, landing then flitting away again, teasing me, drawing me further out of my sleep with each touch. Instinctually, my arms wound around his neck.

"Hmmmm, this is a nice way to wake up."

One corner of his mouth ticked upward. "I didn't want you to sleep through dinner."

I scooted over as he settled on the hammock beside me. It was one of those woven rope models that twisted ominously when he lowered his powerful frame into it. I giggled and clutched at him as it teetered precariously, threatening to spill us over, tossing us into the sand and crushed shells below it.

Dante stretched out, pulling me onto his stomach to cover the length of his body. With his weight and mine aligned, the hammock eased into a gentle swaying motion that brought forth a familiar feeling of contentment. We weren't dancing in a ballroom or swaying in the sand and surf, but the gentle rocking motion had the same soothing effect, pushing aside my usual defenses and lowering my guard.

"I missed you today."

The words were out, and I didn't regret it. I kissed the edge of his jaw, loving the rumble that tickled my ear as it lay against his chest.

He expelled a deep breath. "I know. I wanted to find you earlier, but some things came up that I had to deal with."

"Do you want to talk about it?"

"No," he responded firmly. "That's the last thing I want to do."

"Okay." The silence hung between us.

"I needed to get through all these calls today. We're leaving tomorrow. It will be a few days before we can make calls again."

"I know we have to leave soon, but I'm going to miss Michael's little island."

Dante pulled my fingers to his lips, pressing them firmly against his mouth. "Believe it or not, I will, too."

My heart fluttered, making me bold, his confession giving me strength.

"Take what you need."

"Ask for what you want."

"Words mattered."

"No expectations."

All of Dante's mantras flashed through my mind as I ran my hand through his thick hair. It was now or never. His surliness had passed. The Dante I was in love with was with me tonight. I had to take a chance. Even if he broke my heart, which was nearly a guarantee, I had to try.

"I know we'll have a few days left on the yacht, but when we get home... Maybe I can cook for you sometime? You could come over for dinner."

He stiffened beneath me, but his voice remained soft as he whispered, "Like a real date, Noemi? Like a couple?"

"We could—"

"That's not ever going to happen, *bambina*. I tried to make this experience everything you ever wanted, every dream you ever had for your first time. Despite the obstacles in our path, I wanted to give you the world in exchange for the gift you gave me."

He moved us to where we were laying on our sides facing one another.

"That's why you didn't share the experience with anyone else. Why you chose me. No one else was worthy. No location, no scenario, could match your dreams. Only I could give you everything you wanted.

"I gave you everything I thought would make this special for you. If you wanted to be wined and dined, I took you to the most elite restaurant money could buy. We danced on the sand with only the moon to light our way. I gave you the sunset in my arms every night as the ocean breeze caressed your naked skin. We laid beneath the stars while the smooth rocking motion of the yacht lulled you to sleep after I fucked you into exhaustion."

Dante's voice drifted off and with one shake of his head, became a whisper. "But when this is over, *bambina*, it's over. When we go home, it all ends. I'm done."

I couldn't believe he was so heartless, that everything we shared, everything we'd done, was just a means to an end. I refused to believe it, but he seemed to. Was I a fool? A dreamer? I didn't believe for one moment that this was all just some Machiavellian plot to have my virginity then discard me like a used suit. But he believed it, and I didn't have a way to convince him otherwise. So, I'd bide my time.

There was a way to get through to him, I just had to find it. After all, I found a way to get him here. I'd find a way to keep him.

"I understand." I said, hoping I hid my disappointment.

"No, you don't," he whispered harshly as he fisted his hand in my hair and twisted my head. "There's no fucking way you can understand what you've done to me."

"Then why does it have to end? Why can't we—"

"Because there's no place in my world for you, Noemi."

"Why am I even here then? Why the yacht, the island? Why did you even bother—"

"I told you. I wanted to give you everything—"

"But this wasn't the everything I wanted. I want you."

"And fuck, baby girl, you have me. More of me than anyone else has ever had."

Tears pricked my eyes as I bit back the only argument my heart could put together. I wanted to tell him how I really felt. Not just how much I wanted him, how much I needed him physically. He created a stirring within me that no one else would ever be able to soothe. I wanted to give him everything he'd given me and more. I wanted to give him my heart.

"But that's not enough." My voice broke and I lowered my eyes to hide the anguish.

"I don't have anything else to give, *bambina*. Trust me. You're not going to want the man I'm about to become. You definitely won't want what's left of me afterward."

"But I have you now." I whispered bravely.

I put everything I had into that kiss. I kissed Dante with all the longing that had been bottled up inside me. I kissed him the way he'd shown me to kiss, not with the hesitation of a shy woman, but with the mastery of a lover. With passion, and determination, and pride as I leaned into him, wanting to get as close to him as possible. There were enough things between us: our pasts, his present, my regrets.

There was no room for extra space and wasted air. I needed to be so close to him you couldn't tell where one of us began and the other ended, to become a part of him, just for one more night.

Something about the way he held me, about the way he picked me up like a bride, growled "fuck dinner," and carried me to my room. Something about the way he laid me gently on the bed and expertly removed what little bit of clothes I wore. Something about the way he kissed every inch of me, from the tip of my toes to the hair on my head. Something about the way he closed his eyes as he sank slowly, inch by slow, delicious inch into me, told me what I was afraid to hear. He made love to me that night—taking me slow and deep, again and again, continuing to give more than he took. I understood it for what it was. His goodbye.

Chapter Fourteen

-Dante-

I found her on deck, in her usual spot overlooking the water. I watched her from the shadows after having not spoken to her all day.

Our night together still haunted me. I couldn't escape how completely and utterly perfect she had been. I now knew why it was called making love. Every move was deliberate, not born of need or some primal urge. She was like no one I'd ever experienced before—not just physically or sexually. We connected that night in a way we hadn't before. I knew what she meant when she said she hadn't known the difference between making love and fucking.

I was a fool who didn't know the difference either. Until she showed me. It unmanned me to know that would be the last time we were together. We'd be back on U.S. soil in two days. Two days during which I'd interact with her as little as possible. I moved my things out of the master cabin and moved into the black room.

That was a fucking disaster. For a man who needed little sleep, a completely sleepless night is a recipe for disaster. Everything in the black room reminded me of her and the first night I'd tried to "romance" her. Everything reminded me of the way she'd gripped the black satin sheets as I rutted into her. The way the light shown in through the window brought back the memory of her body bathed in moonbeams like she was now, leaning into the darkness while the light fed off her.

I couldn't do it. I wanted to keep her, make her mine forever, but I knew I didn't have that right. There would be no more blindfolds, no more carrying her to the bedroom, no more feeling her pulse as she orgasmed around my dick, coming hard for me when I pushed her past her limits.

She was perfect for me, and she was never going to know it. I knew when we made our contract that I was going to break her heart. But I had no idea she'd break mine. Fuck. I didn't even know I had one until she shattered it with her shy eyes and beguiling smile.

It was painfully clear how wrong I was. Every breath I took as I watched her solitary stance hurt like hell as I tried to get more oxygen into my system.

I needed air. I needed *her*.

But I wasn't going to have her. When we arrived in Florida, I was going to put her on a plane to New York where she'd be met by one of my brother's goons who would drive her home to Connecticut.

I hadn't forgotten about the men who'd tried to kill us, but since this plan was known only to me, she'd be safe. I made her reservations before we left the island. She'd be back in New York before anyone knew where she was. By the time anyone got wind of it, she'd be back home in Connecticut under Gabriel's protection.

I called him before I left the island. He was pissed off about something, but I brushed it aside and told him what I needed for Noemi. I heard Lilly squawking in the background, but I ignored her as well. Whatever shit drama was going on at home, I didn't have time for it.

I had questions and I had a list. People owed me answers and quite possibly, their lives.

MY BAD HUMOR RETURNED, either in anticipation of the work I had to do or from anxiety over Noemi's distance. She shut me out. I did what I had to do and stayed away from her for two days,

strengthening my decision to walk away from her. It was what needed to happen. Other than dinner the last two nights, during which I
barely spoke, I spent no time with her.

I went to her room to help her carry her luggage so we could
disembark, but as soon as I knocked, she opened the cabin door,
grabbed her suitcases and sailed past me as if I were a ghost unseen. I
bit my tongue, knowing I deserved her disregard.

When I started to pull the cabin door shut, I noticed the master
closet doors were still open. All the clothing I'd bought her, including the gowns from Barbados, were still there, left behind as a sign of
their owner's independence.

With determined strides, I caught up to her, barely holding my
tongue until I unleashed my anger on her when we reached the main
salon.

"What the hell are you trying to pull?"

"Me? I'm not pulling anything," she answered.

"So, you pick now to start lying to me? Why the fuck are the
clothes I bought you still hanging in the fucking closet?"

"Because I don't want them. There. How's that honesty for you?"
She spun around to face me, jabbing her finger in my chest.

"You just spent the last two days ignoring me. How did you
think this morning was going to go? Thank you for treating me
like dirt the last few days, now please, may I keep the expensive
wardrobe? I don't want to see those dresses ever again."

"I told you how this would end." I felt like a fool even as I said
the words that didn't mean shit considering how selfish I'd been the
last few days.

"You told me that when we got back home, we were done. Well,
we aren't home yet, and we certainly weren't home two days ago
when you started giving me the cold shoulder. We had two more
days." Her voice softened as she lost her bravado. "And you wasted
them."

Holy shit. She didn't understand. How could she? I hadn't given any thought to how it would make her feel. I had to steel myself against it. Despite her fury, it was the right thing to do. I wouldn't back down.

"You wouldn't understand, so I won't bother to explain. What do you want me to do with your things?"

"Try me. And they're not mine. They're yours. Save them for the next woman you cart off to paradise. Or burn them. I don't care."

I ran a harried hand through my hair. This was why I didn't do this shit. But it was better this way than the alternatives. And it would get worse before it got better.

"Fine. Have it your way."

I stepped back, gesturing for her to go before me so we could get the hell off my yacht.

Noemi remained quiet on the drive to the airport. She didn't even ask me where we were. A car met us at the pier, and she sat in stony silence until we got to the airport. She was pissed at me, and I deserved it. But she didn't know just how cruel I could get.

The car I'd ordered dropped us off at her airline. I walked her to check-in where I used my credit card to get her boarding pass. She was all messed up. I could feel her anger and anxiety. I wanted to take her in my arms and tell her that everything would be okay, but I couldn't guarantee her that. Not yet. Someday soon, I'd be able to. Maybe she'd forgive me. Maybe it wouldn't be until after she'd moved on and put the memories of our week together into a forgotten vault. Maybe it'd be after she gave her body to some other fucker who could take better care of her than I could. Someone who hadn't laid out a calculated plan to break her.

I masked my emotions and turned to face her with the single boarding pass in my hand.

Confused, she looked at it, then at me. I just stood there without a fucking clue what to say.

"What's going on?" she asked, her voice trembling.

"Your flight leaves at one-fifteen. Do you have everything? Your passport, that book you've been reading?"

Like fucking deja-vu. I was putting her on another plane, flying her as far away from me as I could get her. Sending her away before I could really hurt her. But it was too late for that.

Tears welled up in her eyes as she looked up at me.

I couldn't fucking help myself. I swiped her lower eyelid with my thumb as the moisture started to spill over.

"Don't cry, *bambina*."

"Then tell me what's going on," she insisted, her voice strong through the tears. "Where's your boarding pass?"

"I'll get it, but it's for a different airline."

"You're not going back with me? You're deserting me?"

"No, I'm not going back with you, but I'm not deserting you. You'll get on the plane and fly back to New York. One of Gabriel's men will meet you at the airport and drive you back to Connecticut."

Her eyes widened in disbelief. "But what about... what happened? The man in the bungalow? The pirates? You're sending me out there alone? What kind of bastard are you?"

I sucked in an angry breath. I wasn't angry with her, but at the circumstances that put us here. That my plans had to change. In the end, it didn't matter. The result was her anger and heartbreak.

"It's better to get it over with, Noemi. There isn't going to be an us, so there's no reason to go on pretending. You'll be safe on the return flight. No one knows your travel plans but me."

"And the man who's supposed to pick me up from the airport."

"That hasn't been arranged yet. Gabriel will not send someone until you arrive and, on his life, he will send somebody he can trust."

She blinked at me. "So, you are deserting me? Just like that. We're through."

"Yes, Noemi. What we had is done."

"And you're going to go raise your hell now, or whatever you want to call it?"

I pulled her to me quickly. Anyone passing by would think it was a lover's embrace, but she had to know what a precarious situation she was in.

"I'm putting my trust in you, Noemi. What we had, the things we discussed, are private. Do you understand me?" I whispered harshly in her ear.

She tilted her head up. "Are you threatening me?"

For fuck's sake. I was. I wasn't. The fuck if I knew what I was doing.

"Yes," I answered casually because that's the man who was in charge right then. "But I believe I can trust you, can't I?"

She started to nod.

"Words, Noemi," I growled in her ear.

"Yes, you can trust me."

I fisted her hair, my lips hovering over hers. "Don't disappoint me, *bambina*. I'll know."

She stiffened in my arms, peering up at me with a mixture of fear and resentment. "I haven't lied to you. Your secret is safe with me."

My secret wasn't safe with anyone, but I would play the hand I was dealt until I was the one holding all the cards again. When all the pieces came together, I'd make it up to her.

"Good. Now, get the fuck on that plane."

My arms fell away from her as I took a step back. I couldn't look at her.

I turned away, leaving the carnage in my wake. I took the most beautiful woman in the world, gave her everything that was mine to give, then broke her. I deserved every bit of the hell coming my way.

Chapter Fifteen
-Dante -

I crossed my leg and waited patiently as the key turned in the lock and the door swung open. He left the light off as he walked into the room, crossing to a side table near the entryway where he laid down his laptop bag. He loosened his tie as he approached the bar.

The pop of a stopper being removed.

The clink of glass.

The gurgle of liquid being poured.

He needed a drink at the end of the day.

"You might need to make it a double."

One corner of my mouth ticked upward when he didn't jump at my warning.

"I was wondering how long you were going to sit in the dark before you said something."

He knew I was there. He was more perceptive than I'd given him credit for.

"How the hell did you get in here?" he bit out as he leaned against the bar and snapped on a small light.

The room was barely lit. My corner remained dark, but I could see him as he leaned against the sleek black lacquer.

"No reason to be alarmed. It wasn't easy, actually."

"It should have been impossible."

"You're right," I agreed. "If you'd like, when we're done with our discussion, I'll let you know how I was able to break your system."

"Wonderful," he drawled, tossing back the last of his drink.

He filled a shot glass with the amber liquid in the decanter and extended it to me. I never drink while I'm working so I shook my head. He set it on the counter and turned determined eyes back to me.

I ignored the expectant look on his face. "That was a dick thing to do."

"You broke into my home to call me names? What you think might matter if I knew what the hell you were talking about."

"Where do you want to start? I have a list of dick things you've done the last two weeks."

"A list? I can think of one thing that probably didn't make you happy and I don't give a shit. I did what I had to do, and I'd do it again. But I'm assuming it's too late."

"Why do you say that?" I liked that he was at least taking responsibility for his actions.

"You're standing here, aren't you? And she's back home? Mission accomplished."

"She's home. Safe and sound."

"I doubt that."

If he'd been anyone else, he'd already be in pain for what he'd done. "I don't like people interfering in my life."

"Are we back to the dick things you think I've done? I did it because I wanted you to stay away from her."

"I appreciate your honesty." And I meant that. It was a relief to know I wasn't going to have to threaten him to get the answers I needed.

He got more relaxed as we started to talk, pulling out a barstool and studying me across the room.

"You didn't break into my house to ask me questions you already know the answers to. Why are you here?"

He was right. I knew what he'd done and why. At least, as far as Noemi was concerned. But if my suspicions were correct, and they usually were, he knew more information, information that I need-ed to understand—like who put a contract out on me and who tried to kill her. He may not understand the full implications of what he knew, but he knew something.

"How did you know where we were?" I started to build my case with information that really didn't matter but would get him talking.

"How do you know half the shit you do? I have my methods just as you have yours."

I wasn't surprised. His connections were what moved our re-lationship forward from acquaintances to something more primal. Neither of us had expected to see each other at the negotiating table, but that's where we'd found ourselves years ago.

"Ours has been a lucrative relationship over the years. I'd hate to see it end because you made poor choices."

"It wasn't *my* choices that put us in this situation, Dante, and you know that."

"Noemi is a grown woman. She can make her own decisions." And as it turned out, her own demands.

"You're not the kind of man she needs in her life. You're not right for her. We both know that."

"You can sleep easier knowing that's not going to be an issue."

His eyes narrowed. "You fucking bastard," he hissed as the mean-ing of my words sunk in.

I ignored his insult and continued with questions. "Is that why you had your associate follow us? He wasn't particularly good at hid-ing."

He signed. "He wasn't supposed to hide. He was just supposed to make her nervous. Make her question what she was doing, in Bar-bados, with *you*."

I nodded in understanding, but I felt my first pang of discomfort at his words. No matter how long we'd known each other, knowing that he thought I wasn't good enough for her sent a current of anger through me. He knew me, my character, my career, but he didn't know the man Noemi knew. No one did.

"He wasn't supposed to get caught," he grated. "I chewed his ass for what happened at the restaurant. He didn't scare her too badly, did he?"

"Wasn't that your intent?"

"No. Yes. Hell, I don't know. I couldn't just call her and tell her not to go with you. I had to do something more drastic."

"Tell me, then, just how desperate were you to keep me from her?"

"What do you mean? Wasn't that enough?"

I watched his movements, looking for a tell that said he was lying. I'd never known him to be a liar. He was one of the best men I knew—until he pulled that cryptic warning stunt.

I suppose I couldn't blame him. If Noemi were my sister, I'd do everything I could to protect her from an ass like me, including putting out a contract on the bastard if that was the only thing that would get his attention.

I crossed my leg and leaned back in my chair. I wanted to see if Willis would slip and reveal something I needed to know. Too many pieces of the puzzle were missing. Desperation wasn't a feeling that sat well with me.

"I hear my life is worth a paltry million. You and I know from our previous negotiations that there's only one customer who pays such a small price to have someone else do their dirty work."

Willis tilted his head and pictures of Noemi looking at me the same way flashed through my mind. Six or more years had passed since I'd seen brother and sister together, side by side, but there was no mistaking the family resemblance.

"We didn't take that contract out on you, if that's what you're asking. I may not want you involved with my sister, but I have no reason to want you dead."

"Maybe you don't. But someone does."

"It's not us," he denied, then spoke to me in his senatorial tone. "The federal government has no reason to want to kill someone who performs such beneficial transactions on our behalf. You need to look somewhere else for your answers."

I barked out the laugh. "The federal government wouldn't give a rat's ass if I lived or died. I don't exist as far as Uncle Sam is concerned."

It was a sordid affair that brought my neighbor and I together. The good Senator from New York was part of a closet group of politicians who worked behind-closed-door deals to help rid the world of some very nasty individuals. I don't know who was more shocked, me or Willis, when I showed up to negotiate the first contract I took for the United States government. All under the table, of course. The deals were never official and there was nothing but a verbal agreement and an exchange of funds once the job was done. They didn't pay as much as the other contracts I took, but the government was a lucrative, reliable customer and if it had been anyone besides Willis pulling the strings, I would have done one job and moved on. Our negotiations involved no one but me and him. I never had any contact with anyone else. I knew I could trust him. We'd worked together off and on for six years. If he were going to fuck me over, he would have done so by now.

Or maybe he just had. "You know about the contract on me?"

I didn't ask him how he knew because I knew he wouldn't tell me. Willis Petrafuso had another persona. The less the two of us knew about each other's dark sides, the better off we'd be. Secrets were meant to be kept and history told me Willis was as good at that as I was.

"I just found out."

"It's only a few days old, so that's not saying much."

"What did you want me to do? Call you while you were seducing my sister, which I am very pissed about by the way."

"She's been trying to reach you. That's another one of those dick things I was referring to."

At least with that he had the decency to look contrite. "I know. I fucked that up. I didn't know what to say to her. I was afraid I'd give myself away, so I thought I'd just keep my mouth shut."

That wasn't like him, usually. There was more on his mind than his sister's virginity. While he said he was pissed about the two of us together, there was more he was worried about. And I'd be damned if I discussed details with him. Noemi was a grown woman. Her life was her own to share or not share as she chose. I didn't owe him a goddamn thing, and the fact that he hadn't punched me yet told me he was well aware of that.

"So, you have no idea who set up the contract and you had that asshat follow us just to scare her away from me? It didn't occur to you that she'd want to know why someone would go to such lengths?"

"It did, but I didn't care. Besides, the fool wasn't supposed to get caught. *You* were never supposed to see him. She's my sister, Dante. What would you have done if you were me?"

"I'd have stayed out of it."

"No, you wouldn't have," he said softly, studying me carefully. "There's no fucking way you would let your sister date a man like you."

If he had taken out a knife and shoved it into my heart, it would have felt better than the way his words sliced through me. He was right. Of course, he was. That's why I had left Noemi trembling with tear-filled eyes at the airport. That's why I made her care for me, buying her silence with her heart, just so I could ruin her and walk away with no regrets.

Because she was an angel.

And I was the devil.

And the universe knew we didn't belong together.

"Do you have any other questions? If not, you can see yourself out since you let yourself in."

Willis' nonchalance shocked me. He and Noemi were close. I expected more from him, which made me the biggest hypocrite on the East Coast. Despite telling me to see myself out, Willis followed me to the door.

"If I hear anything about the contract against you, I'll pass it on."

I turned back to him as I opened the door. "I'd apprecia... ugh, *what the fuck?*"

My jaw took the brunt of Willis' fist as it slammed into my face. The words were rhetorical. I didn't need an answer to my question, not when I could supply it myself.

Rubbing my jaw, I straightened up and shook off the pain reverberating through my head. "If I didn't understand why you did that, this would end quite differently, my friend."

He shrugged. "You earned it. I'm just wondering if you understand why?"

"I assume it's because I slept with your sister."

"No."

I winced with anticipation, steeling myself for the next blow which stung every bit as the first one. I didn't know Willis packed such a punch. My fucking jaw was going to kill me in the morning, but I knew I deserved it.

"That one was for sleeping with my sister. The first one was for breaking her heart."

I stopped rubbing my jaw. "She's a grown woman."

He crossed his arms and leaned against the doorjamb. "She's my sister. Grown or not. We've been friends for years, Dante. But one of the things that forged that friendship was Noemi's relationship with your family. Don't take that for granted. In fact, considering the position you're in, don't take any friendships for granted."

When he started to close the door, I put my body in its path.

"Don't get mysterious with me. I'll bypass the cryptic crap and let you know that someone, several someones actually, tried to kill me this weekend. I took them out before they got into the room your sister slept in. Someone else tried to blow a hole in the side of my yacht. Outside the cabin your sister was changing in. I know I'm a cold-hearted bastard, but if you know anything about why someone wants to end my life, you might want to consider your sister."

"Why? You walked away from her, or did you forget that?"

Words echoed in my mind. *It's not about you.* Then it was about her. It had to be about her.

"I haven't forgotten a damn thing." But someone was going to wish that I had.

Chapter Sixteen
-Dante-

I needed to be alert and aware. Instead, I was pissed-off, and my fucking jaw hurt like hell. The only thing I looked forward to was taking my frustration out on the next person on my list. I told Noemi hell hadn't broken loose yet and after my conversation with Willis and letting him beat my face in because I'm a dick, I was ready to start delivering on that promise.

I suffered being Willis' punching bag because I deserved it. I knew what I was doing when I took Noemi to Barbados. I knew what would happen. Her emotions were involved. There was no way to avoid hurting her. I could have said "no" to her proposition, but the temptation was too great. I had to have her, and I regretted nothing.

But I also couldn't get her off my mind. Willis' well-placed jabs weren't what made me angry. It was that I agreed with why he hit me that pissed me off. During the flight to New Orleans, Noemi was all I could think about when I should have been focused on reviewing my hastily arranged plans.

For a wealthy man, he had a pathetically useless alarm system, but in the end, I decided not to break in during the middle of the night but to use the front door in the middle of the afternoon.

I pulled up in my rental and rolled down the window, allowing the stuffy, humid air into the cool air-conditioned SUV. I leaned on the intercom and wondered what the fuck Christian Delacroix was thinking to leave himself so vulnerable.

"Can I help you?" the faceless voice crackled through the aging system. Delacroix was about ten years behind the times.

"Dante Calegari for Mr. Delacroix."

I took my sunglasses off and stared at the massive wrought iron gates in front of Delacroix's estate.

"Is he expecting you?"

"If he's the sneaky bastard I expect he is, then yes, he's expecting me."

"I don't understand. Mr. Calegari, do you have an appointment?"

"Tell Mr. Delacroix I'm outside his gate. I'm getting hot and irritable. He'll make an appointment for me."

"I don't... wait there. I'll check with his assistant."

I turned the music up on the radio. "I'll be right here."

Two minutes was all it took before the heavy gates creaked and slowly started to part. Once the opening was wide enough, I followed the tree lined pavement to the end of the drive. I parked the rental right outside his fucking front door which opened before I reached it.

A butler. The son-of-a-bitch had a butler.

"If you will follow me, Mr. Calegari."

Delacroix was living in a different era. He either thought he was untouchable, or he was adept at hiding the extent of his security measures. I didn't think he was that cocky, but he was the king of the New Orleans underground, so maybe I underestimated how much fear that placed in others.

I followed the silver-haired gentleman down a long hallway lined on either side by tacky velvet wallpaper and badly painted portraits of people Christian didn't know. Those stodgy plantation owners and uppity women were not related to him. He was an orphan from the south of France with not one drop of American blood in him. Like me and the *Mary Theresa*, he inherited his estate as a reward for a job well-done. It seemed every time I saw him, he had a new piece of property or a shiny new toy to show off. He owned several dummy corporations that made it appear as if he were the quintessential New Orleans businessman, but I knew some of his truths.

I was shown into a billiard room where Christian stretched over a table, attempting to make a corner shot. He looked up when I entered and waved the butler away. As soon as the massive double oak doors closed, Christian took his shot and sank the striped ball he was aiming for.

"Do you play?" he asked as he circled the table, looking for his next opportunity.

"No," I answered. "I don't have time for games."

He nodded, then chalked the end of his stick. "I understand. Billiards is something I acquired a taste for later in life."

"How fascinating," I drawled. I said I didn't play games, but I was playing his... for now.

"I was surprised to see you outside my gates," he said as he lined up behind the six ball.

"No, you weren't."

My matter-of-act statement caught him off guard. His grip slipped causing him to miss the shot.

"You knew I'd come here. Not only did you expect it, you wanted me to make an impromptu appearance. You get to keep up pretenses that way."

He put the stick back in the wrack before turning to face me. "You're more intuitive than I anticipated. Yes, I knew you'd come... eventually. I did think it would take longer though. After all, it's what I'd do."

"You'd visit the man you thought ordered your death?"

"Yes. If he let me in to see him, it would prove his innocence."

"Or he's just really good at playing the game."

"My friend, if I were that good, you wouldn't be here. What is it that I can do for you?"

"How did you find out about the contract?"

"From the boards. The same way anyone else would."

"But you said you didn't have details. Couldn't confirm any-thing." I walked around to the side of the table. "You said you'd heard a rumor. Didn't have all the facts. Why are you lying to me?"

Christian threw his hands up in the air. "Yes, you have me there. I lied when I said the contract was a rumor. I saw the information myself. I also saw the value of the contract. It didn't make sense. I thought I'd buy some time to do some research."

"Or to sell me out. You're the only person who knew I took your fucking plane to Barbados."

"Well, me and my crew."

"It's all the same to me. They're your people. Not one of them would try to kill me without your blessing."

His demeanor changed. "I have a traitor in my midst, Dante. I didn't take that contract out on you nor did I tell anyone of your travel arrangements."

"And you can't tell me how the men who were sent to kill me arrived less than twenty-four hours after I did?"

"I wish I could. I only let you in here so that you could watch me with your own eyes when I tell you that I have no idea how those men found you."

He should have had me searched when I arrived. I pulled my handgun out of the holster concealed by my suit jacket. I leveled it at him. At least, he had the bravado not to show fear.

"Then how do you even know about them? Who told you?"

He blinked, realizing his mistake.

"Put the gun away, Dante."

"No," I declined, coolly. "I don't know what the fuck game you're playing, and I don't think I want to bother to find out."

"You can't kill me."

My eyes narrowed at him. "You and I both know that's not true."

"And you and I both know that if you really wanted me dead, we wouldn't be standing here talking about it."

His confidence wavered as the sweat beads formed on his forehead.

"I'm not going to kill you," I drawled as I put my gun back in my holster. "Not today."

He knew something about what was going on, but I couldn't beat it out of him. Not yet. I needed him alive.

Already, my favorite hacker was working on his system. Delacroix had gotten lazy, thinking he was above everyone else. He should have been spending his money on more than luxury jets and high-end hookers. Judging by the antiquated alarm system and the outdated com, Marco would have access in just a few hours.

All of that was beyond me so I paid a college kid three quarters of a million dollars to do my hacking for me. Untraceable. All done through dummy accounts. Maintaining the fake accounts was more of the "work" that kept me busy. Marco didn't know who hired him, but he'd copy everything he could get his virtual hands on and send me what he found. I would have to wait a few more days before I received his encrypted files, but my travels had been productive.

Willis' reaction told me that he had nothing to do with the contract on my life. The fact that he didn't call me and tell me about the contract when he discovered it only reassured me that he wasn't involved. He didn't bait me. Didn't draw me into something. Didn't lure me out into the open. The U.S. government didn't have any reason to take my life. In the five years that Willis had been the unofficial government representative who hired me to extinguish the life of some undesirables, Willis never once mentioned his sister. Our personal lives were separate from our professional co-existence. He wouldn't use her to get to me.

I was less certain about Delacroix. Did I think he was orchestrating my death? No. But did I think he knew a hell of a lot more than he revealed? Damn right I did. The sweat on his brow gave him away. I never killed an innocent man, but I wasn't sure Delacroix was innocent.

But he was safe for now. They all were. Until I figured out what the hell it had to do with Noemi. I can protect myself but protecting her was paramount to my ability to live. If anything happened to her... If I couldn't stop whatever the fuck was going on...

I LAID MY HEAD ON THE cool hotel pillow. My fucking head hurt.

I had feelers out in my network. I had bribes placed with the right people. I didn't have anyone I could fully trust, but I had to give myself a time-out. Word could eventually get around. Even in the dark, people talk. I didn't want to come across as desperate. Everyone would expect me to want to know who had made two unsuccessful attempts on my life, but I had to make sure the power remained mine. I couldn't be viewed as weak.

The ache in my gut returned as I reached for a swig of the cheap scotch I got at the liquor store on the corner. No. I couldn't be seen as more than a man seeking revenge for a plot to kill him.

The truth was, for the time being, I was fucked. I had to protect Noemi, but in order to do that, I had to walk away from her. That was my intention all along, but now, it wasn't my choice which made me feel manipulated.

Restless, I stood up and walked to the open window. I pushed aside the hotel room curtain and stared out into the New Orleans night, so brightly lit I wondered how anyone could fall asleep with the multi-colored lights shining through their windows.

I frowned into the night, my body tense and my mind wired. I liked my easy, cut-throat world. I chose my victims carefully and my clients even more carefully. I didn't like being manipulated, and I didn't like complications.

And that's what Noemi was; a wide-eyed, red-lipped, soft-spoken complication.

And I missed her.

I threw back another swallow, a heftier one that time. I wanted to feel the burn scorch the back of my throat. I wanted the physical discomfort to match the emotional one. From somewhere deep inside me where the heart of a young man lay dormant, Noemi claimed a piece of me. I missed our conversations and the way she tilted her head right before she argued with me. I missed her soft voice and the way I felt whenever she was near me. I didn't even have to be touching her and her warmth bonded me to her.

I even missed the way her eyes teared up when she saw the bastard I really was.

Fuck airports. I couldn't walk into one now without the memory of breaking her.

Or maybe I was delusional. She had cried, but maybe she was fine. She had been back home for four days. She and Lilly were probably having lunch and shopping. She had mentioned she wanted to start job hunting. She would spend her time writing her résumé and searching for suitable positions.

With a growl, I sat in the corner chair, steepling my fingers and bracing my elbows on my knees. I stared at the ugly, Mardi-Gras inspired carpet with its fireworks of green and purple fibers, but all I could see was Noemi on the beach; Noemi walking in the surf on Smuggler's Island; Noemi bathed in moonlight on the deck of the *Mary Theresa*.

Noemi—strong and bold when she needed to be, but sweet and submissive when that was what I needed from her. Others may have thought her weak, but she met me at every turn, laughing at my whims, drawing me out of myself all while she was becoming a part of me.

I couldn't walk away without fighting for her. I had work to do. Delacroix. Her brother. One of them was the puppet master in all of this. I was leaving New Orleans in the morning. I did what I set out to do there: I poked the hornet's nest.

Then I waited for what was next. I checked the gun I had hidden under the pillow, then I made sure the knives I strapped to my calves were secure.

I was ready. I turned out the lights and returned to the chair in the corner.

It was just past midnight when the doorknob jiggled. I had chosen the older hotel for its squeaky floors, outdated hardware, and seedy clientele. It helped that the man at the counter had a drug problem and the extra cash made his Friday night a lot brighter.

I stayed in my corner, waiting for whoever it was to make the mistake of breaking in. How was this as fucking easy as the last time? If it were me, the fact that the chain door guard wasn't in place would be the clue that my unwanted appearance was, nonetheless, expected.

Whoever this amateur was, he continued to jimmy the decrepit deadbolt giving himself away with a "yeah, baby," when he finally succeeded.

I shook my head, feeling a small amount of reluctance for what I was about to do to the person on the other side of the door.

A young male, scrawny and carrying a small handgun, make and model undeterminable in the dark, pushed the door open, stopping as he walked inside. He shut the door quickly, but the brief stream of light from the hallway illuminated him well enough.

I shook my head. This was no assassin, and I was damned insulted that these were the people continually being sent to kill me.

"I hope you have the calvary coming soon," I said from my corner as I stood up.

"Oh, fuckin' shit!" the kid cried out.

"Let me guess," I leaned over and switched on the desk lamp. "You're just here to rob the place?"

He blinked, unsteadily waving his gun at me.

"You scared the crap out of me."

"You weren't expecting me?"

"Fuck no. They said the room would be empty. They said to just come up here, get into the room and help myself to whatever I found. I just had to trash the place while I was doing it."

"Sounds fucking stupid to me. What are you supposed to be looking for?"

"They didn't say."

"Who are 'they'?"

"Uh, I'm not sure. A couple guys pulled up in a dark car. Asked if I wanted to make some money. I said, 'hey, doesn't everybody?' I thought they just wanted me to suck their dicks, or something like that."

"Are you a prostitute?" I asked him point blank.

"What? No! I mean, not officially, but you know how it is. Occasionally, to make a little extra cash." He shrugged.

"Give me the gun before someone gets hurt," I ordered as he talked.

"Oh, uh, sure. They said it wasn't—"

I turned and aimed at the wall behind me. It'd wake the neighbors, but we were done talking anyway.

"What the fuck man!" he yelled as his body jerked in reaction to the pop of the gun. "There weren't supposed to be any bullets in that."

"What's your name?" I asked him as I emptied the bullets from the chamber.

"Donald," he answered quickly as he started backing up.

"No. Don't do that, Donald. You took a job, now you have to finish it." I indicated the room. "Go ahead. Trash it."

"What? Man, I don't understand what's going on here."

"That makes two of us. Now, trash the room." I walked over to the bed and pulled my gun out from under the pillow. "I promise you. This one is loaded."

"Okay, okay! Don't frickin' shoot me. I'll do it. Where should I start?"

I shrugged. "Do whatever you would do when you trash a room. And you have about a minute. Go on, get busy."

I snapped off the desk light.

"Wait! It's dark in here. How am I supposed to—"

"Clock's ticking, Donald. I'd start with the dresser drawers if I were you."

I heard him pull open drawers while he muttered under his breath. He opened them, then slammed them shut again.

"Dude, there's nothing in here."

"Dude, I'm not your dude. About thirty seconds left."

He moved over to the closet. "Man, you're not going to kill me, are you? I don't understand what's happening here."

"What's happening here, Donald, is that you're not a very good liar."

He stopped moving.

I reached under the bed and pulled out my suitcase while I kept my gun pinned on him.

I knew men and I particularly knew how dishonest men acted. The high-pitched voice, the breathlessness. He was antsy, but not antsy enough.

"I'm not lying," he insisted, more quietly this time, like I'd believe him if he just insisted it was true.

"Those men set you up. You're not getting out of this room alive. Now, go stand in front of the window."

"What the—? Dude, you're nuts."

But he did as I said. Poor dumb bastard. I took my suitcase and opened the door just a sliver.

"Wait? Are you leaving?"

"Yes, I am. One of two things will happen: Your friends will arrive and find you here alone and they'll kill you or they'll kill you where you stand without even bothering to find you."

"That doesn't make any sense. You're leaving, I could just walk right out the door after you."

"Oh. Yeah. Thanks for pointing that out."

I pointed my gun at him and shot at his shin. He screamed as the bullet shattered bone and he crumpled to the floor, clutching his bloody leg.

"Oh, man. What the hell man!" Strangled groans and cries mixed together. "You fucking shot me!"

"You'll live. Sorry, I take that back. You're going to die, but it won't be because I shot you."

The red laser dot appeared, first on the wall, then bouncing around the room while it looked for its target.

"Looks like your friends are here."

"Friends? Ha!" he cried out. "Fucking Delacroix isn't a friend of mine. He said this would be easy. That I'd be set for months with the money I earned, I just had to keep you busy. He didn't say I'd get shot!"

I closed the door behind me. Things always seem to take forever, when really, our conversation lasted less than five minutes. No one had called the police until the first gunshot. It would take them a few minutes to get to this part of town.

I quickly walked down the hall and took the back flight of stairs to the ground floor. I pushed open the back door just as I heard the sirens approaching. Calmly, I put my suitcase in the trunk of my car.

I wasted a throwaway gun and my newest fake ID on that kid who'd gotten mixed up in something that was over his head.

But he gave up the man who hired him.

As soon as I drove out of New Orleans, I switched vehicles, ditching the one I'd stolen the day before behind the grove of trees where I had parked the rental. I pulled out my phone. It was 3:00 am, but he'd answer.

"Dante?" he said clearly.

"Your friend is dead."

"I don't know what you're talking about."

"Someone shot him through the window as I was leaving."

"I don't understand."

"What did you think would happen? Never mind. It doesn't matter. Someone put a bullet in his head. I hope you weren't close to him. I don't think you'll recognize him after tonight."

Delacroix was silent as my words sunk in.

"I didn't hire him, Dante. I don't know who did."

"I don't know what the fuck I did to you, but you should know, you're at the top of my list now."

"I didn't take that contract out on you, and I did not send that kid to kill you. Is he really dead?" His voice was oddly quiet, laced with more compassion than I'd ever heard from Delacroix.

"I didn't stick around to check the body."

"You've made a grave mistake, my friend. I always thought you didn't take innocent lives."

"I'll simply repeat what you said. I didn't kill him. If I were you, I'd be more worried about who did. I take that back. I'd be more worried about me."

"Don't do this, Dante. I know about your girl, remember?"

My voice dropped. I let every bit of the ice in my veins manifest. "If you think threatening her will help you, you're wrong. She means nothing to me."

"Yes. I can believe that. Someone already tried to kill her twice and yet, you walked away from her and left her all alone."

"That's interesting. We discussed the contract on me, but I never said anything to you about someone trying to kill Noemi. I'm done chatting, Delacroix. The only hope you have to stay alive is to give me some proof, that you're not the one behind this fucked up mess. Until I get that information, until you convince me otherwise, you're my next contract."

I hung up on him.

Back in the car, I put the burner phone along with the fake id and credit cards that I used at the hotel into a baggie and put them into the suitcase for disposal.

I was buying time with Delacroix, time for him to decide if whoever was pulling his strings meant more to him than his own life did. He gave himself away when he mentioned Noemi. He was either sloppy or very clever.

If he didn't kill that kid, someone else did. But he's the one who hired Donald and put him in harm's way. As far as I was concerned, Delacroix might as well have pulled the trigger himself.

He was also wrong about Noemi. She may have been back in Connecticut, but she was never alone. Gabriel made sure of that.

Though my little brother would take care of her, my stomach still clenched at the thought of what was coming next. I sure as fuck couldn't trust Delacroix, and no matter how many men Gabriel had surrounding Noemi, there was always the chance one of them would slack off. Gabriel would be pissed if he ever heard me say that out loud, but if he had idiots like Jacko working for him, then I had reason to worry.

I pulled an alternate phone out of the glove box. It was 3:00 am in Louisiana and even later in Connecticut, but I knew he'd answer.. I just had to know that Noemi was all right.

He answered on the third ring.

"You'd better not be dead," Gabriel growled.

"I'm fine," I answered.

"Good. Then I can kill you myself."

I heaved a sigh and started the car. "Take a number."

He groaned into the phone. "Do you need anything? What can I do?"

"I'm fine. Just... busy with work." What I really wanted was on the tip of my tongue, but I couldn't push the words out.

"Hmmmm. And that's why you're calling me at 3:00 am. To tell me how busy you are."

"Yeah, something like that."

I heard the rustle of covers and Gabriel's voice became a little clearer.

"Noemi's fine," he said quietly. "I have people watching her house. I have a team following her. So far, there's been nothing suspicious. She's stayed to herself since she came home. We haven't seen much of her. She was here yesterday, chatting with Ma."

"How is she?"

"She's pissed at you, bro. Probably plotting your demise for being the heartless bastard you are."

I rolled my eyes while my heart sank. I knew she'd be angry and that our travels wouldn't remain a secret. Like she had told me, she and Lilly talked about everything, but Noemi wasn't the one I was referring to when I asked that question.

"I meant Ma," I clarified.

"She's fine. She has another round of testing next week. Nothing major happened this week. Some random things like forgetting where she put her purse or that she already poured a cup of coffee. Stuff like that.

"Are you really not going to ask about her? You're more fucked up than I thought," Gabriel growled when I didn't say anything else.

"I just asked about Ma," I snapped back.

"I was talking about Noemi!" he barked. I heard him take a deep breath. "Look, I don't know what happened between the two of you when you went wherever the hell it was you went, but the woman who came back is not the same woman who left. Big brother, I love you, but you have some serious explaining to do."

"I'll be home soon," was all I said right before I hung up.

If he thought I had some explanations to make now, wait until he saw what was going to happen next.

Chapter Seventeen
-Noemi-

I needed to be sleeping but I laid there with a heavy ache in my chest, weeping and crying one minute, then punching my pillow and pissed off the next.

I knew my relationship with Dante wasn't going to be permanent. He never led me on or pretended that our trip to Barbados was anything more than a means to fulfill our contract.

At least, not in the beginning.

But once we arrived at Smuggler's Island, I got to know a different side of him. I got to see the Dante of my dreams, still dark and demanding, but not as distant, not as remote as the man I'd known in Connecticut.

I got to know his gentle half and with that knowledge came hope. I wanted desperately to believe that what we had, what we experienced together, could be more than a one-week stand.

But the way he treated me with such disdain once we boarded the *Mary Theresa* to return home shattered all those hopes. I realized he didn't want anything to last beyond our trip, but to abandon me at the airport? To put me on a plane and walk away? He didn't even put me on the plane. He just handed me my boarding pass then left.

When I first came home, I thought I'd be okay, but as the hours and days passed, my anger grew along with the overwhelming ache that took up residence in my heart. When did I become such a crier? Yes, I was an introvert, but I had never been the overly emotional sort who cried at the drop of a hat. Not until Dante came back into my life. I was getting nauseous from bouncing back and forth between fits of tears and fits of fury.

As much as I wanted to hate Dante, I couldn't. My predicament, along with being my torture, was also completely my fault. I set myself up for the fall. Dante had warned me, long ago, about opening myself up to more pain than I could handle. It may have taken five years, but his prophecy came true.

I bargained with the devil and he won. He got my virginity, and I got a broken heart. He was off doing God knows what while I tried to put the memory of the best week of my life behind me.

I tried to move past it, but that wasn't easy when I found myself in his home as early as the next morning after I arrived back in Connecticut.

True to his word, one of Gabriel's employees had met me at the airport with one of those cheesy "Noemi Petrafuso" signs.

"That's me," I said to the tall, heavy set man who held the sign with as much enthusiasm as one would when sent to run an errand that was the equivalent of babysitting.

"Right this way."

No greetings, no conversation. He did, however, take my bags for me as he led me to a dark SUV. The drive from New York to Connecticut was longer than it should have been. I guess most things would be when you spend the time replaying one five-minute conversation over and over again.

When we were about ten minutes from home, I received a text from Lilly. We never managed to connect during my travels with Dante so this time, I answered her right away.

Lilly: Gabriel said you're on your way home. OMG! WTH is going on?

Me: Long story.

Lilly: Dinner tonight. I need to know everything!

Me: I'm tired. Rain check for tomorrow?

Lilly: OK. Breakfast?
Me: Sounds good.
Lilly: 9. See ya then.

I TIPPED MY HEAD BACK and turned to watch the scenery pass by in a blur of green and blue. I was not ready for Lilly's inquisition. She'd want to hear all the gory details, but this was her brother we would be talking about. This was Dante. His privacy meant a lot to him and no matter how irritated I was, I couldn't betray his trust. Lilly would understand. She'd have to.

But when I arrived for breakfast the next morning, Lilly was nowhere to be found.

I knocked on the door and was allowed in by another one of Gabriel's employees. It wasn't any of my business, but it seemed as though there were more of them hanging around the house than usual. Even a few sitting out in a car in front of the street. I didn't know Gabriel employed so many people, but I didn't recognize any of them except Jacko who was sitting in the kitchen with Gabriel when I walked in.

As soon as I walked into the room, Gabriel jerked his head toward the door. Jacko gave me a smile but immediately left the kitchen through the back door.

"The weary traveler returns." Gabriel said as he spread his arms wide.

I couldn't help but smile at him. A good morning hug from Gabriel Calegari was familiar and comforting, but it was a far cry from waking up in his brother's arms.

"Thank you for sending someone to pick me up," I said as I stepped into his arms. He was warm, and strong, and... not Dante.

Breakfast was going to be torture. I had barely slept the night before and there I was thinking that I could be in Dante's home while I tried desperately to forget him.

"My pleasure. Coffee?" Gabriel offered.

I pulled out a barstool and plopped myself down. "You might need more than one pot, but that's a start."

"That bad?" Gabriel laughed as he poured the coffee into a mug he set it in front of me before reaching into the refrigerator and getting a container of French Vanilla creamer. "Here. I know you can't live without this shit."

"Bad enough. I didn't sleep well last night."

Gabriel's dark eyes studied me across the granite countertop. He leaned on his elbows, all the laughter fading from his eyes.

"Are you okay, Noemi? I know he's my brother, but I'll punch him in the face if you want me to. Hell. I don't even care if you want me to, I may do it anyway."

I achieved the desired ratio of coffee to creamer and took a quick sip. "No, no physical violence on my behalf, please."

I'd had enough violence to last for quite some time. I just wanted peace, quiet and normal. Right then, having coffee with Gabriel and chatting about something other than his brother was the normal I needed.

"Alright for now, but if you change your mind, just say the word. It's been a long time since I've had a chance to try to drop him on his ass."

Gabriel took a drink from his own mug, a large gray monster of a cup with the word "Bossman" on one side in bold black letters.

"Bossman?" I laughed.

One side of his mouth rose in a smile that reminded me so much of the half-smiles Dante would occasionally let escape. Gabriel's smiles were more frequent and more easily given, but he looked so much like Dante then that I could have stared at him all morning.

"A gift from the guys," he chuckled softly. "They think they're funny. So, what brings you here this early in the morning after a restless night? Shouldn't you be sleeping in?"

"Lilly invited me for breakfast. Where is she?"

Gabriel immediately stiffened. "She was supposed to meet you here? Are you sure?"

"Yeah, I'm sure. She texted me on the way home last night. Look."

I pulled my phone from my coat pocket and showed it to him.

Gabriel's brow furrowed as he took the phone from me and read Lilly's text.

"Is everything okay?" I asked when he didn't say anything.

"As far as I know. Look at this."

Pushing his phone across the countertop, Gabriel pointed to the screen. "She sent me this text last night."

"*Too much wine. Crashing at a friend's house. See ya tomorrow night*," I read. "Tomorrow night? She must have forgotten about breakfast. That's odd. Who's the friend?"

"I don't have a clue," Gabriel muttered. "And she didn't call you to say she wasn't going to be here?"

"No. I've had my phone with me and there's no missed calls. You look worried, Gabriel. Should we be worried?"

"No," he answered quickly. "I'm sure she's fine. If she had too much to drink, she probably just forgot. I'll just send her a quick text," he mumbled as he walked away.

He lied to me. I could clearly tell he was worried. Lilly was a spoiled Italian princess, but she wasn't forgetful, and she didn't drink so much that she had to spend the night at people's houses.

I took a sip of coffee but didn't notice the taste as my worries settled in, especially when Gabriel furiously typed into his phone. It was like I wasn't even there when he paced the room, then exited through the swinging door.

I didn't know whether to wait or go home, so I sat there, drinking my coffee and worrying about my friend until a cheerful voice distracted me.

"*Buongiorno*, Noemi!"

I hopped down from my stool to greet Mrs. Calegari.

"No, no, stay there." She waved her hand at me. "I just came for more coffee." She reached for the pot. "And what are you doing here so early? Didn't you just get home?"

I knew better than to give her details that would make her worry. "I thought I'd try to catch Lilly by surprise, but she has other plans."

"That girl," Mrs. Calegari shook her head. "She's a wild one. I'm so glad you've come home. Maybe you can be a good influence on her again, like when you two were younger. She listens to you, you know."

"She's just spirited. I think she has some big things coming in her future." I remembered Lilly's comments about opening a boutique, but I didn't know whether she'd shared her dreams with her mother, so I kept quiet.

"Well," Mrs. Calegari leaned on the counter the same way Gabriel had and I smiled. "If that 'big thing' is in the form of a tall, handsome man, then I will pray that the 'big thing' arrives quickly! She needs someone who will make her settle down."

I shrugged. My experience from the last week with Dante made me appreciate Lilly's cavalier attitude toward romance. "I don't know. I think it's good that she's strong and independent."

"She can be strong and still fall in love. It happens all the time, *bambina*."

Bambina? I choked on my breath. She never called me that before. Why did she start now? I was doing well until that moment. It wasn't easy being in his home, with reminders everywhere, but hearing that term of... was it a term of endearment? It sounded so different coming from her.

"I don't understand what she's waiting for," Mrs. Calegari continued.

I shrugged as I struggled internally to regain my composure. "Maybe... she's just waiting for the right person to come along."

I shouldn't have looked at her, but our eyes met, and her compassion and understanding were more than my fragile psyche could handle.

In times like that, I missed my mother. I wanted to be able to sit down and talk to her about Dante, to get her advice, woman to woman. Mrs. Calegari was his mother. While she had been a substitute parental figure to me for years, she was the last person I could discuss Dante with.

"I suppose that's possible," she said softly. She reached out and covered my hand with hers. "I shouldn't rush her. The right man is always worth waiting for. Don't forget that, Noemi."

I blinked several times. "People... get lonely. Sometimes, the waiting feels so long."

"That's true. But he's worth waiting for. When he's the right one," she said softly.

She knew. I fought back the tears that threatened to spill over.

"Give him time, *carina*. He's a smart man, but even a smart man doesn't always see what's right in front of his face."

"How much more time does he need?" I whispered; my voice hoarse from holding back the emotions. "I don't think I have another decade in me."

She patted my hand. "I know him better than anyone. I don't think you'll be waiting much longer."

Mrs. Calegari believed a lifetime of lies if she thought she knew her son. Like me, she only knew the side of him that he presented to the world. She didn't really know him at all. But I couldn't tell her that. What could I say? *Your son kills people for money.* Did it matter that they deserved it?

Instead, I forced a smile to my lips and covered her hand with mine. "I hope you're right."

"Of course, I'm right. A mother knows her son and she knows what's right for him."

Did she know what he'd done to me? Where we had been and what we had experienced together? How much *did* she know about any of that? Did she have any idea what he'd done to me? While she may know that he and I would be good together, her predictions could be nothing more than wishful thinking. If she didn't know her oldest son was a killer-for-hire, then how reliable was her claim that I was the right woman for him?

THREE MORE DAYS PASSED. Three long, unending days that merged into the beginning of a miserable week. I tried to put Dante out of my mind, focusing on mundane tasks like updating my resume and searching for a job. I found several that I was interested in, but none that screamed at me. I had time. My savings would last a while. It wasn't like I had a house payment or anything.

In that aspect, I was spoiled. Our family home was paid off and Willis took care of the bills, something I would change if I ended up staying in Connecticut permanently. If I found a local job and remained in the house, I would insist on taking over the bills. It was another thing I needed to speak to my dear brother about, but we kept playing phone tag.

A storm the night before left a couple of inches of snow behind. I spent some time outside, shoveling the driveway and the sidewalk. I'm not sure why I did the driveway when I still wasn't driving my car, but it kept me busy for a while at least.

When I came in, I saw I had a missed call from Willis. I put the tea kettle on then listened to his message.

"Hey, Noe. Sorry I haven't called. Just been really crazy around here. Listen, we need to talk about Christmas. If I'm going there or if you want to come up to the city. Think about it. Let me know what you want to do. Yeah. Glad you had a great vacation. Call me back."

Great vacation? I had left him several messages and I don't think I referred to my vacation as "great" in any of them. He sounded hurried and preoccupied.

I had no idea what I wanted to do for Christmas. I hadn't thought that far in advance, but the holiday was less than two weeks away. If he came to Connecticut, I needed to get a tree and decorate. Our family decorations were stored in the attic. It wouldn't be too much of a hassle to bring them down. I could keep it simple—dig out just what I needed to trim a small tree and it would be cute to put the stockings we used as kids over the fireplace.

By the time I finished drinking my tea, I decided decorating for Christmas was exactly the distraction I needed to keep my thoughts away from Dante. Despite an ocean between us, Willis and I always spent Christmas together. He usually flew to England, but there was one year when his present to me was tickets to spend the holiday with him in New York. We did it all: the Rockefeller Center tree lighting, ice skating, and watching the Nutcracker Suite performed by the New York City Ballet. A homey Christmas wouldn't be the same, but it was what I needed. I'm sure Willis would understand if I decided to stay home. Traveling again didn't appeal to me at all.

Hours later, my mission was a success. I dug through mounds of boxes covered in years of dust. I found enough decorations to cover a small tree then realized it was a pointless exercise. When my parents were alive, we always got a real tree. Willis and I upheld the tradition when it was just the two of us.

"Well, I guess that's another welcome distraction. I need to go get a tree," I said to no one. "Which I cannot do since I don't have a car."

My newfound holiday spirit crashed and burned. "I can do this," I muttered. "I'll just borrow Lilly's car, or call Gabriel. They'll help me get a tree."

Lilly and I hadn't connected since she came home the night of our forgotten breakfast. She had apologized profusely and said she'd make it up to me even though she offered no explanation for why she had missed breakfast.

But her phone rang and rang then went to voicemail. Something was up with her. I had enough on my mind but worrying about Lilly wasn't going to be one of them. I could at least confront her.

I knocked on the Calegari front door and Jacko answered.

"Hey, Noemi. How are you?" he asked as he stepped aside.

"I'm fine. Thanks. You?"

"Sure. Great. Hey, since we have a second alone. I wanted to apologize to you for the way I acted at the party that night. You know, it was the alcohol and well, I just thought you were a pretty girl, you know? I didn't mean any harm."

His quick apology went straight to my heart. "It's okay really. No harm done."

"Well," he looked bashful and awkward as he asked, "maybe I can make it up to you sometime?"

It should have been a fun, flirty moment, but Dante's words came back to me. *You're not a good flirt.*

"Sure, I'd like that." Would I? Not really. I was just being polite, but his face lit up with a smile.

"Would you? Hey, that'd be great. Maybe we could—"

"Jacko, don't you have something you need to do?" Gabriel interrupted us as he walked into the entryway.

"Yes. I was on my way out when I found Noemi at the door." Immediately, he turned and started to leave, tugging his winter hat over his head. "We'll talk about it when I see you again, I guess. Bye."

"Bye," I answered as he hurried to leave. I turned to Gabriel. "Bossman angry?"

He laughed good naturedly, but I could tell he was irritated with Jacko. "Bossman has work that needs to be done and Jacko is already late. So, what's up Noemi?"

"I was looking for Lilly. She didn't answer her cell."

"Yeah." He shook his head. "I don't know what's up with her. She was up and out of here by eight this morning. Said she had something she needed to do."

"Really?" Maybe she was working on her boutique idea and still hadn't shared it with her brothers.

"Did you need something? I have no idea when she'll be back."

I smiled my best surrogate sister smile. "As a matter of fact, I do. Christmas is coming and I need a tree, but I have no car, sooo..."

Gabriel stroked his goateed jaw and nodded. "A Christmas tree, hmm? That can be arranged. Give me an hour or so and I'll take you to get a tree."

"Then I'll be back in an hour."

"No, I'll come get you when I'm done. This thing I have to do may take a little longer, but the tree lots are open late. Maybe we'll get a bite to eat afterward."

For the first time in days, I felt like smiling.

Chapter Eighteen
-Dante-

A fucking Christmas tree. First crossword puzzles and now a Christmas tree. I slammed the car door shut and watched from the driveway as Gabriel and Noemi tried to get the small tree untangled from the ropes that tied the Douglas fir to the top of Gabriel's Lexus.

It should have been me. While I was flying around the country trying to figure out who was playing puppet master with our lives, the woman I'd been losing sleep over was being protected by my brother. She was eating dinner with him, according to what Ma told me when I arrived home. The two were scouring the lots like a married couple looking for the perfect Christmas tree.

My gut had tightened when my mother told me where Gabriel was and who he was with as soon as I walked in the door and found no one home but her and some of Gabriel's henchmen.

I should have stayed in the fucking house. Instead, I went to my car to get the jewelry I'd brought home for Ma and Lilly. When I flipped open the lockbox in the trunk, two black velvet boxes looked up at me, but the small, generic, white cardboard box next to them had all my attention.

I picked up the nondescript square and steeled myself against the memories of sand and surf, of briny salt water and endless walks along the beaches of Smuggler's Island. Of dances in the moonlight and nights of unspent passion.

I never got my fill of her. No matter how many times I had loved her during that week, I was never satisfied.

I never would be.

I tossed the box back into my lockbox and shoved the two high-end velvet cases into my coat pocket. When I looked up, Gabriel's car had pulled up in front of Noemi's house. Noemi and Gabriel got out and proceeded to laugh with each other as they struggled to release the tree.

Slamming the trunk lid got their attention. They both turned my way. Gabriel waved at me with a goofy-ass grin that I wanted to punch off his face. Noemi's eyes widened and she gave me a weak smile before turning away.

I thought we were over that shit. I knew she wouldn't be excited to see me, but I thought she had at least learned to face me. In less than a week, we were back to square one? Her, finding comfort with my family, and me standing alone out in the cold.

Fuck that.

I ignored them and went back inside.

I went straight to my office and poured a shot of scotch.

Maybe I was wrong. Maybe the week we spent together didn't have as much significance as I thought it did. Maybe I was the only one questioning my very being, wondering who the fuck I really was and guessing about what would be left of the man I am when I moved on without her.

I took a chance. I played with fire and I was still burning. For her.

For the first time in my life, I wanted to be wrong. I wanted everything I did to keep her safe to be a mistake so I could throw open the door, march through the snow and sweep her up in my arms. I wanted to sit in front of the fireplace with her then help her decorate that damn tree.

I reached for the Dalmor and poured another shot. I downed it and moved on to a third as I sat down at my computer and pulled up video footage of Noemi's house. The tree was still laying against the side of the car. When I couldn't find Noemi or Gabriel, I switched cameras, checking every perimeter shot that gave me a glimpse of the Petrafuso home. Finally, I found them.

Noemi stomped through the snow with Gabriel beside her as she approached the walkway to our front door.

Fuck. What now? A cozy hot chocolate in front of the fire? I'd kill him. I didn't need to explain shit to him. He knew how I felt about her. He even *said so.* What the hell was up with him bringing her home to throw their friendship in my face?

All I saw was red. I fucking lost it. I slammed my laptop shut. My blood pounded so hard I barely heard the commotion in the kitchen as I approached. I slammed the swinging door with the palm of my hand and welcomed the pain that reminded me who I was.

"Watch out!" Gabriel yelled, pulling Noemi out of the way of the door as I stormed into the kitchen.

"What the fuck is going on?" I demanded.

Gabriel tried to push Noemi behind him. "Nothing. Stay there," he ordered her as she tried to get around him.

"No," she hissed back.

"Stop fucking telling her what to do," I seethed. Who the hell did he think he was to command her like that?

"I was trying to—You know what. Never mind." He jabbed his finger in my direction. "I was trying to keep her from barging into your office but now, I don't care. Have at it. Apparently, the two of you need to talk through some shit. Or maybe talking isn't what you need at all, but I'm too much of a gentleman to say what you really need."

"Get the fuck out of here," I growled at his suggestion.

Gabriel crossed his arms and leaned against the counter. It'd been a long time since I knocked my kid brother on his ass, but his smug expression begged for it.

"Stop it!" Noemi cried out. "He's right."

She faced me with her hands on her hips and a fire in her eyes. Damn, I missed that fire. Barely seen, but once it was lit, she was beautiful. My need for her nearly strangled me.

"I want to talk to you," she demanded. "How dare you—"

"Not here."

I grabbed Noemi's elbow and steered her toward my office, overly conscious of her scent and the feel of her next to me as we walked the hallway.

I closed the door to my office with a sharp snap and gave her a little nudge as we walked in. She stumbled forward slightly then glared at me.

That's it, baby girl, get angry. It would make it that much easier for me to slip into my role and be the bastard I really was.

"What are you doing? Why are you acting this way?" she asked warily.

"Because this is who I am. You knew that. I never made you any promises, Noemi."

Her eyes narrowed. I had to say those things. I had to push her away, but I wasn't prepared for the agony that ripped through me when I did.

It was one thing to ignore her, to pretend she didn't exist. It was another to look her in the eye and lie, then see the moisture pool in the wake of my tyranny.

Noemi stared at me and I turned away to face out the window to avoid her.

"You couldn't even bring yourself to smile at me?"

She challenged me, wanting an explanation for my behavior, but I had none. What could I say? *Because being near her was like having my heart ripped out?* Because I didn't want to leave the impression that I was still interested in continuing our relationship even though as she stood there looking sweetly furious, my dick made his interest known.

I wasn't over her, not by a long shot, and my body couldn't pretend that I was.

"If it mattered to you, why did you look away? And don't tell me it was because you're shy. We passed shy that night in bungalow six when you stripped in the bedroom just because I told you to."

She gasped, but I kept my back to her, not to be lured in by green eyes and red lips.

"This isn't you. I know you want us to be over, but this man... this isn't the real you. Not the real you," she repeated, trying to convince... who? Me, or herself?

"You're wrong," I snapped, turning to her. "That man? The one who took your virginity, who said sweet things to you on the beach?"

Pour it on. Make her hate me. Make *her* be the one to walk away because I couldn't. Now that I had her there, in my office, away from prying eyes, in a space that I owned, *that I commanded*, my fantasies of taking her on my desktop were minutes away from being realized.

"He's the fake," I continued harshly. "He wasn't real. That man never existed."

"You're wrong," she whispered. "I don't know why you're doing this. But I know you... I saw *you*. That man exists. Maybe he's another side of you, one you keep hidden and suppressed, but he *is* in there with that man you allow to be seen. I've tried to do this your way, Dante, and until I saw you in the driveway tonight, I thought I had succeeded. But as soon as I saw you standing there, everything I felt, everything I experienced with that man, came back. I know you and I know what I mean to you."

She took a few tentative steps toward me. "I know that no man is just one thing. I know about your life, and the man that you try to hide, and now I understand more about the man you allow to be seen. But you showed me another side of yourself. You showed me a man who had a heart, a man who could laugh, and tease, and ... a man who could make love to me and control my body with just a look and a touch. I know there are two different men inside you, Dante, and God help me, I want them both."

I shielded my black heart so the filth I spewed wouldn't affect me.

"Don't you get it, baby girl? They don't both want you."

The cold I'd pulled forth wasn't enough. Her cry cut through me. Stabbing pain shot through my heart.

I masked it like I always did because that's who I was. An expert.

Noemi wasn't sophisticated enough to pull off such a lie, to seduce with no regard. She wore her heart on her sleeve. Her speech was as much a declaration as a confession, even if she didn't say the specific words. But I knew. I knew her and she couldn't hide her feelings.

Unfortunately, the man she fell in love with was a figment of both our imaginations. He couldn't be allowed to exist. He was a weak fool.

To keep her alive, he had to die.

I allowed myself a moment of weakness, a moment to bask in what I'd discovered. The temptation was real. I couldn't live with her hating me. If I couldn't find a way to get us through this, it wouldn't matter that she loved me.

When this was over, I would take over hell to get her back. I'd be whatever kind of man she wanted me to be. Until then, she had to stay the fuck away from me.

She said she knew me. Knew who I was and what she meant to me. If that were the case, would she wait for me? It would be easier if she did, but in the end, it wouldn't matter. I'd steal her. Kill whoever I had to. Rip her away from whatever happiness she'd found just so I could keep her. Until then, she had to stay away.

I steeled myself. Channeled the baser instincts that made me the killer I was.

"It was fun, Noemi. We had a good time. And who knows, in another time, another place..."

I traced the edge of her cheek with my thumb, and she closed her eyes at my touch.

"But it's over. You made me an offer and I accepted. I took your virginity. I took you. But you're not a virgin anymore and the allure... well, it's just not there anymore either, you understand. I got what I wanted. Now, it's time to move on."

She looked at me through narrowed eyes. "I don't believe you."

My hand dropped to my side and I shrugged. "I don't care."

I steeled myself against the look in her eyes as the tears poured unhindered down her cheeks.

Her shoulders fell in defeat, but the feeling that I'd won, that I had gotten what I wanted, left a bitter, flat taste in my mouth.

I turned my back dismissively and walked around my desk, a move meant as much to block her out as it was to give me a few seconds to bolster my resolve. With my peripheral vision, I saw her walk to the door and pull it open.

I prepared myself for her exit, for the best thing that ever happened in my life to walk away and leave me.

I kept my eyes down until the sharp snap of the door and a hurried movement caught me by surprise. I tensed, not prepared for the fiery woman that stood in front of me.

I glanced up at her, feigning disinterest with one finger tapping on the desktop. Noemi was small but regal in her stance.

My fucking queen.

The trail of tears through her makeup marred her otherwise flawless beauty. The smudged mascara. Red, swollen, fuck-me lips.

Fuuuck.

Her siren's song called out to me like a meal to a starving man. I could have devoured her on the spot and not given a damn about consequences. If only I could have given myself that luxury.

The man I once was would have done it, would have taken what he wanted and not cared about another soul. But the man I'd become, he would die before he let anything happen to her. He was the one calling the shots tonight.

And she knew it.

With her next words, Noemi shattered my icy composure.

"*I. See. You.*"

One pink-tipped finger waved shakily in my direction. She had regrouped. Her back straightened and her eyes turned to steel.

"You don't fool me. I see you," she repeated. "And you're scared."

She turned, closing the door behind her with a deceptive softness.

I white-knuckled the edge of my desk. I let out every raw, burning emotion I had with a roar that could be heard through the soundproof walls. With a strength I didn't know I possessed, I gripped the edge of the mahogany executive desk and flipped it over, sending papers, pens, and the Madonna flying into the air. Mary crashed near my feet and shattered into tiny unrecognizable pieces.

Just like what was left of me.

Chapter Nineteen
-Noemi-

Despite my coat, my whole body shook as I walked back to my house. I knew Dante was emotionally distant, but I had no idea he was that cold-hearted.

He stood there with that remote expression on his face and wanted me to believe that he no longer wanted me. I understood that we were through. I got it. Dante very thoroughly made sure there was no trace left of the inexperienced woman I was. Our agreement had been fulfilled in every way, but for him to stand there and insist that the attraction had died along with his willingness to continue the relationship was cruel. We were over, but that didn't give him the right to treat me like I wasn't worth a speck of his time. That I wasn't worth the effort a fake smile would have cost him.

I stopped at the edge of the drive and pivoted to face the white colonial the Calegari's called home. Why did I not believe him? The words stung; they hurt like hell, but I didn't believe them. They weren't convincing. There had to be more. What was I supposed to do now? He returned home and poof, everything was supposed to return to where it was when we'd left?

I shook my head. No, I saw him. I could feel the turmoil in him, no matter what stupidity left his mouth.

I looked back at my Christmas tree, still leaning against the side of the car where I had left it when Dante coldly ignored me. Part of me wanted to drag the poor thing inside and start decorating while the other part wanted to march back into the Calegari home and have it out with Dante.

"I'd let it go for the night if I were you," Gabriel said as he approached from the side of the house where the kitchen door opened to the driveway.

"I don't know what to do," I muttered. Sad. Frightened. Angry. I didn't know what to feel, let alone what to do next. "Am I supposed to walk away? Pretend nothing happened?"

Gabriel put his arm around my shoulders and pulled me against his side. "I wish I had answers for you, Noemi, I really do. Dante is... well, he's Dante. He's my brother and I love him, but I don't know if I always understand him."

Slowly, we started walking back down the driveway to the sidewalk. Gabriel had been like a brother to me for years. I valued his opinion especially when it came to his enigmatic brother.

"I'm asking you for your best advice. What do you think I should do? Walk away? Let it end here?"

"I can't tell you what I think you should do because we're not the same kind of person. I can tell you what I'd do," he said as he let go of me and took hold of the Christmas tree.

"What would you do?"

"I'd fight like hell for the woman I wanted. This thing between the two of you... Noemi, you thought you were hiding your feelings, but we've known. We've all known for years how you felt about Dante. I know this is more than just a physical connection for you. He knows it, too. He just won't admit it."

"Why? If he knew how this would end up, why did he go through with it? What has he told you?"

I rapid-fired questions at him as my mind raced. I didn't know how much Gabriel knew about our week, but it was obvious that Dante had told him something when he asked Gabriel to send someone to the airport to pick me up. I had no idea what excuses he had given. I never asked.

Gabriel pulled the Christmas tree to his shoulder, and we walked to the back door of my house.

"He didn't have to tell me much. It was obvious that the two of you left together when you both disappeared that night. Dante left his usual message that gave us no information at all, but he did say he was with you and he told Lilly and Ma not to worry. Then, a week later, he called and told me that you were coming home. He gave me your flight number and said to have someone pick you up at the airport."

"Like unwanted baggage," I muttered as I put my key in the lock. Oddly, it turned with no resistance. I must have forgotten to lock it when Gabriel came to pick me up, but I was fairly sure that I had.

"No, not like that." Gabriel said firmly as he set the tree by the back door. He put his hand on my arm. "He cares about you, Noemi. It's just that he doesn't know how to show it."

"Why is that? I don't understand how he's so different from you and Lilly."

"He's just wired differently, that's all. It wasn't easy being my father's oldest son. Dante was raised with different expectations than Lilly and I were."

"Can I say that doesn't make much sense to me? You were the one who inherited your father's business."

"That's true, but Dante is the head of our family. There are certain expectations that come with that. Dante had a lot of responsibilities growing up and our father was hard on him. It was different for us younger kids."

My brow furrowed as I was torn between asking nosey questions and trying to put the pieces together on my own. I was afraid that if I started asking too much, I'd reveal too much. Dante said no one in his family knew what he did for a living. They believed his stock market story, but that didn't make any sense to me either. Lilly may have never given it a second thought, but Gabriel was too smart to not suspect something. Maybe he had doubts and never acted on them. Maybe, since Dante was head of the family, no one questioned him about anything. And was it that upbringing, those responsibilities and expectations Gabriel mentioned, that not only cut Dante off from his emotions, but also turned him into a killer?

It wasn't likely that I'd get all my answers while standing in the doorway. "Come in out of the cold. Can you help me put the tree in the garage? I have a bucket of water we can put it in."

We got the tree set up in its temporary home, but I no longer felt like decorating.

"Thank you for your help tonight. And for listening to me whine about your brother," I said as I walked Gabriel back to the door.

"Anytime, Noemi. You know that. Can I add one thing?"

"What's that?" I said with resignation.

"If he means something to you," he said quietly, "and I mean, if he *really* means something to you, you're going to have to fight for him. Dante isn't going to make this easy on you because in his stupid, prideful way, he thinks he's doing the right thing. You have to prove him wrong."

He chucked me on the chin then turned to walk away, leaving me as confused as I was before we had talked. Had this family always been so mysterious and confusing or was it a recent development?

I closed the door and locked it. I leaned against it for moral support then decided to trade the wooden panels for a cup of tea and a hot bath, not necessarily in that order.

I walked through my dark bedroom and flipped on the light in the bathroom. Hot water, a liberal sprinkle of Epsom salt and a dash of rose oil. I let the water run while I turned on the light in my bedroom and walked to my dresser. I glanced in the mirror as I bent to open the drawer where I kept my pajamas then froze.

I looked around the room quickly and nothing else was out of order. The brown envelope on the bed wasn't mine. I hadn't put it there, and I did not recognize it, but it was addressed to me in big black letters: *Noemi.*

My heart skipped a beat as I slowly walked to the bathroom and shut off the water. I stood in the doorway, eyeing first the envelope, then the phone. Someone had been in my home and left that envelope for me to find. Calling the police was my first instinct, but the romantic in me thought... perhaps it was from Dante? A love letter? An apology?

I sat on the bed with a heady reluctance that quickly gave way to my erratic heartbeat. I picked up the envelope and pulled out its contents.

I blinked as I read the first page. Once. Twice I read it. Then again.

What the hell was this? Who would do *this*? I read the note for a fourth time. "*You know who he is. Now you know what he's done.*"

I looked from the printed note to the paper behind it. It was a copy of my parents' obituary and a picture. I cried—openly and hard. The picture was a car—the wrecked remains of an ocean blue, 2008 Audi. I remember the color because my mother wanted that particular car because she fell in love with the color.

"I've always wanted a blue car," she laughed the day she drove it home. "After nearly twenty years of brown cars, I finally have my blue one."

She loved that car and drove it everywhere, including to a party the night she and my father swerved off the road and hit a tree head on.

I never thought about the details. I never let myself think about the agony they may have endured, but there was no mistaking the car in that photo. I looked at it closely through the tears. No. There was no mistaking the vanity license plate my Mom had ordered, FINAL-LY 5, alluding to the four different shades of brown cars she had driven before she finally got her blue one.

I wiped away the tears, but it was useless as they kept falling. I still cried regularly for my parents. On their birthdays, their wedding anniversary, the anniversary of the day they passed. The pain of their loss never went away but the tears changed over the years from choking sobs to silent streams to simmering pools. Looking at pictures of mangled metal and broken, jagged glass brought back the gut wrenching cries.

The trauma returned two-fold as I struggled to both catch my breath and draw some kind of connection between the note, *"You know who he is. Now you know what he's done,"* and the tragic death of my parents.

My broken heart could only come up with one conclusion. Someone was trying to tell me that the man I loved had killed my parents.

Chapter Twenty

-Dante-

It had been a long time since I overindulged in alcohol. I was on my fifth shot of Dalmor and well on my way to getting the most drunk I'd been since I turned twenty-one and endured that rite of passage.

I spent a few minutes cleaning up the mess I'd made, the desk much heavier and more difficult to set upright than it had been to tip over. I used the papers to scoop up Mary's shattered pieces but couldn't bring myself to toss the broken porcelain into the trash. Maybe there was a way to save her. Superglue or some shit like that. I pulled open the top drawer of the desk and dropped the pieces inside.

I tossed my jacket over the back of my chair, unbuttoned my shirt and kicked my legs up to rest on the top of the desk, tipping back in my chair and wishing to hell that tonight had never happened. I braced my shot glass against my forehead and sucked in a deep breath.

I tried not to engage her, but Noemi was determined, and I was weak and going around in constant circles.

I wanted her.

I needed to stay away from her.

I needed to protect her.

I needed to avoid her.

She challenged me. She saw through me. If she saw my fear, and called me out on it, couldn't she also see what she'd done to me? Did she know how deep she'd gotten under my skin? She'd managed to reach parts of me I didn't know existed anymore, parts I had lost touch with in my youth. Parts that were torn from me by the reality of what I'd been born to do, of who I was destined to become. The more pieces of myself that I found, the more I needed Noemi. Those shards were useless without her. In the deep puzzle of my tormented psyche, she was the only one who knew where those pieces fit.

I had no fucking clue what I needed.

I just knew that I needed her.

Right then, I needed to know that she was all right.

Fortunately, my work laptop was still in my travel bag. I hadn't smashed it on the floor with Mary. I pulled it out, logged in, took a deep, guilt-ridden breath and accessed the camera system.

I needed to go backward. I wouldn't be able to see much, but I wanted to know how she'd been when she left the house. Was she crying? Did she march away with as much indignation as she'd expressed in my office? Was she as confused as I was?

I rewound through footage of Noemi leaving through the kitchen with angry and determined strides. I changed cameras and watched her walk slowly down the driveway where she stopped. Gabriel met her in the driveway, and it looked like he... I leaned forward and squinted at the screen. He put his arm around her. Pulled her into a hug. Touched her. He was my brother, and I knew his actions were platonic, but I didn't care. Was I jealous? Fuck yes I was, and it was another unfamiliar, uncharacteristic emotion that pissed me off.

In my unjustified anger, I smashed the rewind key, going back further than I intended. The screen blurred by and I stopped, but I leaned in again at something that didn't make sense. I fast forwarded, watched for a second, then rewound again. Noemi and Gabriel leaving. Rewind. Gabriel walking to Noemi's house. I watched the footage of Gabriel and Noemi leaving in Gabriel's Lexus. Fast forward five minutes and another car pulled up in front of her house.

What the fuck?

I watched a man get out. I couldn't see his face. He wore a long coat and a knit winter hat. He walked up her driveway to the side of her house outside of camera range. He didn't knock on the front door like a visitor would. He went to the side of the house. Why? To hide? To not be seen? Was he a friend?

I marked the time and took several screenshots of Noemi's mysterious visitor. Desperate for an explanation, I switched through all the outside cameras looking for another glimpse of him, but I couldn't find anything. The man in the knit cap wasn't the only thing I couldn't find. I know Noemi left with Gabriel and she'd be safe with him. Gabriel had his own group of shadows who followed him from a distance to ensure the boss' safety. I went through the footage and found one of Gabriel's SUVs on camera as it discreetly pulled away from the house and followed Gabriel and Noemi.

Which meant no one was watching Noemi's house when Knit Cap arrived. The hair on the back of my neck stood up, and my hand shook. I fast forwarded again. Five minutes. He was out of camera range for five minutes. What the fuck was he doing?

Years of instinct kicked in. This wasn't just a "bad feeling." My intuition was never wrong as the result of decades of evil honed into skills that no man should possess.

My nerves made me fumble through the combination on my hidden gun safe. I took a deep breath. *Focus, Dante, fucking focus!*

I grabbed my Glock 26 and headed out through the doors of my office to the back yard. From there, I ran to Noemi's house. Shivering in the cold, I rang the doorbell then banged on the front door. She didn't answer soon enough for me, so I banged some more and yelled her name louder. "Noemi! Open the door! Noemi!"

If anything happened to her it was my fault. I let down my guard. I should have made sure someone was watching her house 24/7 whether she was in it or not.

My heart plummeted when she still didn't answer.

"Godammit, Noemi! Open this fucking door!" I yelled, not recognizing the desperate, scared man I'd become.

She should never have been in this position. She should never have been alone. I should have been with her; guarding her, protecting her, picking out fucking Christmas trees with her.

I leaned on the doorbell and banged again, only stopping when the door was jerked open.

She was a mess. Ratty hair, tear-soaked face, blood-red eyes, and smudged makeup.

"My God, are you all right?" I pushed past her to get in the door.

She closed the door but didn't step away from it. Her shoulders shook with her sobs. I'd seen her cry before, but I hadn't seen tears like that since the night I held her before her parents' funeral.

"What the fuck happened to you?" I asked, my voice hoarse with worry and the nagging fear that something had gone horribly wrong.

She wrapped her arms around her middle and jumped out of the way when I reached for her.

"Noemi? *Bambina*, come to me. Tell me what's wrong."

Every part of me protested at the distance between us. *Don't let her keep you away. Hold her. She fucking needs you right now.*

She shook her head and backed away from me. I dropped my arms. "Noemi? It's going to be okay. Just talk to me. Are you hurt? Did something happen? Did someone hurt you?"

I was going crazy watching her fall apart in front of me. My eyes raked over her. I didn't see any physical injuries, but no one cried like that for no reason.

"Let me help you, baby girl," I pleaded in a whisper.

"Help me?" she choked out. She blinked rapidly and wiped her eyes with the back of her hand. "You can't help me."

"I can. I promise. Tell me why you're crying, and I'll do everything I can to help you. Just tell me what's wrong."

"No!" she screamed at me. "You. Tell. Me." She jabbed her finger in my direction again. "You tell me the truth, Dante." She started sobbing again. "Please. Just tell me the truth."

"I will," I whispered, my voice echoing her pain. "Just tell me what you want to know. I don't know what you're talking about, Noemi. What truth do you want me to tell you?"

If she asked me if I cared about her, I'd tell her I did.

If she asked me if I needed her, I'd throw myself at her feet and beg her to let me show her how much.

If she asked me if I loved her, I'd vow to spend the rest of my life proving to her that I did.

My body shook with the realization that I would mean every word I would say.

I loved her.

"What do you want to know, *bambina*?" I asked again, preparing to bare what was left of my black soul to her.

She swallowed loudly but raised her head to meet my eyes.

"Did you do it?" she said as she sucked in a breath. "Did you kill my parents?"

My heart stopped beating. I wasn't black-hearted enough to not feel her pain. I wasn't cold enough to walk away and leave her where she was, wondering if the man she'd fallen in love with was capable of such a heinous act, even though I knew I was. My past caught up to me, but I had the truth on my side. If she'd believe me.

"No," I said firmly.

How the hell had we gotten to this point? And so damn quickly? I had secrets. The truth about her parents' death was one that I vowed years ago I would take to my grave.

"It wasn't me. I didn't kill your parents."

She believed me. And she saw through me again.

Noemi tilted her head. "But you know someone did? You know... it wasn't an accident?

I reached a hand out to her, willing her to come to me. I promised her I'd never lie to her. Somehow, something had come her way, some bit of information had been discovered that should have remained buried. The details of her parents' deaths were just the beginning. Opening this chapter of her life would plunge Noemi into more agony than one person could bear. I wanted to shield her from that, but I didn't know how much she had found out and I just promised, once again, to tell her the truth.

"Don't lie to me," she said through gritted teeth as I hesitated to answer her. "Don't you dare lie to me. Do you know who killed my parents?"

I squeezed my eyes shut and opened them to hold her tortured gaze. I nodded. "Yes, I do. I know what happened the night your parents were killed."

Chapter Twenty-One
-Noemi-

Not, "the night your parents died," or "the night you lost your parents." Dante's specific words echoed in my mind like a train in a tunnel.

"I know what happened the night your parents were killed."

They were very deliberate words chosen by a man who made his living taking the life of others. A man who, until now, had been someone I trusted, even if he was a ruthless bastard. But did I believe what he told me?

I searched Dante's face, looking for signs of the truth. There were many things that I didn't know about Dante Calegari, but I did know that his lack of emotion meant that showing feelings was nearly impossible for him to do.

I couldn't read the expression on his face or the look in his eyes because I wasn't used to seeing so many emotions there. I couldn't decipher them all. Pain. Fear. Warmth. Strength. Each one of those emotions warred with the other, and Dante did nothing to suppress them. I saw every piece of him, and I knew what I saw was the truth, not wishful thinking on my part. Not a fantasy or a dream. It was as real as the anguish that tore through me.

"It wasn't an accident. Someone killed my parents. It was deliberate?"

Dante shook his head again and stretched his hand out to me. "It was... and it wasn't. This is a long story, Noemi, that needs to be told from the beginning."

"Okay. Then start at the beginning," I sniffed, not sure I was ready to hear what he had to say. "But... could you say it again? Tell me that you didn't kill my parents."

This time, I reached out to take his hand and watched a wave of relief wash over him as he clasped my hand in his. Dark eyes rife with pain held my gaze steadily.

"I did not kill your parents."

I waited for him to make a comment, to say he was insulted that I could even think he could do such a horrible thing, but he let the clarity of his words speak for him. He was capable of murder, but was he capable of taking away the lives of two of the people I loved most in the world?

Those thoughts brought up a new wave of panic. I grew nauseous and the room got a little fuzzy. "Why?" I gasped. "Why would anyone want to kill my parents?"

He tugged me toward him, and I went easily, much too tired to try to do this on my own. I wanted his arms to hold me, wanted his body to give me the strength that had been depleted in my own.

"Sometimes," he answered huskily as he rested his chin on the top of my head and folded me in his arms, "as children, we don't know everything about our parents' lives. Remember, Noemi? No man is just one thing."

I sagged against him, letting his body take my weight. "I'm not in the mood for your riddles tonight, Dante." I tipped my head up to look at him. "If you know what happened that night, I want you to tell me. All of it."

He frowned and gave a barely perceptible nod. "If you're absolutely certain you want to hear it, I'll tell you everything I can."

"I want to know," I whispered, tucking my head against his chest again.

His arms tightened. "Then I'll tell you," he said in my ear, "but not here. Pack a bag for the night."

Oh, God. I wasn't in the mood for any more of Dante's mysterious travel plans. I started to shake my head, but he interrupted me.

"Please, Noemi," he asked softly. "It will be hard for you to hear this in your family home. I think it would be better if we leave."

"I don't want to go to your house either," I protested. "I don't want to see any one right now. Not Gabriel, not Lilly. Not any of those men Gabriel employs. I just..." I looked up at him. "I just want to be with you right now. No one else."

"I understand. I wasn't suggesting we go to my home. I have somewhere else we can go where we'll be alone. No one else. I think it will make it easier for you to hear what I have to say."

"Is it far?" I was so tired. I didn't want plane rides and blindfolds and cryptic words. I just wanted answers.

"No. Just across town."

He was quiet and comforting as he waited for my response. Deep down, I think he was right. And there was still the issue of someone having been in my house! I hadn't even mentioned that to him.

"Alright. Yes, I'll go. It's okay if I pack a few things?"

"Of course," he answered quickly as he pushed a lock of hair out of my eye. "If you don't mind, I'll come with you."

It was a relief to not have to ask him.

"I have something I want to show you," I said as I pushed open my bedroom door.

Everything was as I'd left it when I finally decided to go downstairs and find out who was banging on my door. I hadn't recognized Dante's frantic voice until I'd gone downstairs.

Dante followed me into my room, stopping respectfully just inside the doorway.

He looked at the papers scattered on the bed. "What happened when you came home, Noemi?"

I pulled my overnight bag out of the closet and tried to stay busy as I explained it to him. I had to. If I just stood there, if I looked at those pages one more time, I was going to lose it again.

"I was cold and honestly," I said as I set the bag on the bed and turned to face him as he leaned against the doorjamb, looking every bit like he belonged there, "I was still angry with you. I came upstairs to take a bath."

Dante ignored the papers strewn about the bed and let me tell my story. He glanced into the open door of the bathroom where the tub was still half full of water, but he didn't say anything.

I walked to my dresser and opened a few drawers to get some pajamas, a t-shirt and sweater, a pair of jeans and some underwear. I returned to the bed and started to fill the bag.

"I found that envelope with my name on it in the middle of the bed. I wasn't scared at first, not until I read it, and now, I realize that was entirely the right reaction to have."

That confession made Dante's eyebrows raise. "Someone had been in your home. *Uninvited*."

"I know," I sighed. "And I guess that makes me an idiot. I mean, for a second I got nervous, but then I saw the envelope and I thought... you know, the romantic in me thought..."

"That it was from me," Dante finished for me while my cheeks lit up with embarrassment.

"Yes."

"So, you decided to open it? Can I see what you found inside?"

I wasn't touching those damn papers again. I waved my hand toward the bed. "Sure. I'll just go get my toiletries."

I let Dante peruse the contents of the envelope while I gathered what I needed. I took my time, not in any hurry to discuss the note that implied that Dante was the person responsible for my parents' death.

When I was finally brave enough to come out of the bathroom, Dante looked up from the pages in his hand with a furious frown on his face, his demeanor lightening as he studied me.

He shoved the papers back into the manila envelope. "Do you have everything you need?"

I could only nod, preparing to get scolded for not using words and not caring one damn bit if I were.

But Dante didn't say anything either. He took my toiletry case from me, added it to the top of the bag, zipped the bag, tucked the envelope under his elbow and put his arm around me.

"Then let's get the hell out of here."

I followed my usual locking up procedures while Dante waited in the kitchen doorway. We stepped outside the door. While Dante waited on the stoop, I started to lock the door then paused, staring at my key, then at the pristine lock.

"What is it?" Dante asked.

I turned to look at him. "The door was locked when you came over."

"Yes. If it weren't, I'm not ashamed to say, I would have barged in. Why?"

"How did they get in?" I asked more to the universe than specifically to Dante. "There's no sign of a forced entry. The door wasn't locked when I got home, but I am ninety-nine percent certain that I locked it when I left. I always do. But if they didn't break in... did they have a key?"

Dante listened to me patiently. "You don't have an alarm system, do you?"

"No. Although, this day and age, we should have, I suppose. Especially with the house being empty for so long. I think Willis just never got around to setting it up."

The Dante I was more familiar with returned. "I'll take care of that as soon as we return," he said as I locked the door.

"It's okay. I'll get Willis—"

"Willis already had his chance and he didn't do it. I'll take care of it. At least then, I'll know it's done."

We started to walk down the driveway, and a memory of the last time we'd taken that walk together broke through the sadness and gave me a little something to smile about.

"It seems odd," I teased lightly.

"What's that?" Dante asked as he opened the trunk of his car and put my bag inside.

"No blindfold this time." I laughed lightly as he held open the car door for me.

When I bent to climb in, he whispered near my ear, "maybe later," and I shivered. The door snapped shut, and he entered on the driver's side.

I didn't pay much attention to the drive. It had been dark for hours. The streetlights flashed through the car as we drove down familiar streets and past recognizable landmarks. About a block past the Bridgeport Public Library, Dante turned down a street then pulled into the driveway of a townhome in a row of average looking townhomes.

"Where are we?" I asked.

"My home away from home. You'll see."

Dante took my bags out of the trunk. An average walkway led to a basic two-story townhouse. The front door was painted a lovely teal blue, but when Dante unlocked the door and ushered me inside, I found out that door was the last bit of color I'd see.

I looked around the open concept living area. The beige walls and black furniture suited him. Oddly, when Dante walked in and set my luggage down, taking off his coat, he looked like he belonged there more than he did the Calegari home.

"Can I get you anything?" he asked politely. He seemed nervous, and Dante Calegari was never nervous.

"Just some ice water, please," I answered.

He went to the kitchen and returned with a glass of water. He handed it to me then went to the bar across the room where he poured himself a drink. I walked around the room, stopping to study the black and white artwork that hung on one wall.

"How long have you had this place?" I asked. Lilly had never mentioned that Dante had a second home. Wasn't it also strange that his second home was in the same town he lived in?

"About twelve years now."

"Why? I thought you liked your house."

"I do, but it's home. This is where I do most of my..." he hesitated. "Most of my work."

I swallowed and nodded. I didn't ask for details, but I could imagine him sitting at the glass coffee table with his laptop, orchestrating the means of someone else's demise.

"Let me show you around and then we'll get started."

The townhouse was small, so the tour didn't take long. I should have dallied, prolonging the time it would take before I had to face the past, but I also wanted to get it over with as quickly as possible. Dante showed me the guest room and *ensuite*, his bedroom, and the room he used as his office.

"Make yourself comfortable while you're here," he said when our tour finished, and he ushered me into his office. "All I ask is that this room remains off limits unless I'm in here with you."

I sat on the big, overstuffed sofa that took up one wall. "I have no reason to be in here, Dante." I hugged one of the pillows to my chest. "You can trust me."

"I know I can," he nodded.

He pulled some keys out of his pocket and unlocked one of the drawers in his massive mahogany desk. It was remarkably similar to the one he had in his office at the Calegari house.

He flipped through some files, then pulled out a manila folder and shut the drawer. My heart raced at the implications of the folder.

Dante sat on the couch next to me and held the folder out for me to take, but I refused. He frowned then set the folder on his lap.

"Are you sure you want to hear this?"

Did I?

"No, I don't want to hear any of it, but someone put that envelope in my room. Someone wants me to think that you killed my parents. It's too late to go back now." My voice broke as I finished talking.

Before the last words were out of my mouth, his arm was around me, and my anguished heart felt a moment of relief. He left a soft kiss on the side of my cheek.

"I know you are many things, but I didn't know you were so brave."

I smiled weakly. "I was brave enough to proposition you."

He didn't return the smile. "I'm sorry, Noemi. That will pale in comparison to this." His lips lingered near my cheek. "Are you ready to begin?"

I took a deep breath and nodded. I wasn't really, and Dante's attitude made me think this was more than just getting the name of a killer. Was it someone he knew? Someone... like Michael? Oh, God. What if it was Michael? I didn't know the man very well, but if he hadn't struck me as being a killer when I first met him, then I couldn't be surprised to find out that some of his victims were people that I loved.

Dante moved the folder to my lap, and I flinched. He opened it and pointed to a picture on the inside front cover. "Your parents."

Yes, the picture was of my parents. Dante had known my parents for six years. In true Dante fashion, they weren't close, but Dante spoke to them, waved at them in the street, nodded when they saw each other over the hedge and through the wrought iron fence Dante installed after the Calegaris moved in. Whenever I went to spend the night at the Calegari home, my mother always asked if Dante or Gabriel would be home. Gabriel was much more familiar with them than Dante had been. He was always so formal, calling my mother Mrs. Petrafuso. I don't remember if he spoke to my father very much. I think they just did the head nod thing.

The picture he showed me was my Mom and Dad at a party somewhere. They were smiling and happy. My Dad had his arm around her shoulders while she smiled up at him. They looked the way I always remembered them.

When I didn't comment, Dante picked up a stack of pictures that were inside the folder. He set the first one down.

"This is your father. The man he's having lunch with is Daniel Rubinstein."

"I know him," I interjected. "They worked together at the NSA."

My father had spent years working for the National Security Administration. He rose through the ranks of various administrative positions. I couldn't really tell you exactly what he did. He never talked about it in specific terms and I was just a kid. Jobs were jobs. Did children ever get the details of their parents' work? I began to think maybe I should have.

The next picture he pulled out was my father, Daniel Rubinstein, and a man in a uniform. I took the picture from him to get a better look.

"That's them with General Bailey."

"Joint Chief of Staff General Bailey?" I asked.

"Well done. Yes. He is now. At the time, he wasn't."

He took a deep breath, and I knew the information coming next wasn't going to be more pictures of people enjoying lunch.

The next picture was the same three men at a pool party. But that picture was different. Next to each man, including my father, sat a pretty, young woman. I couldn't tell exact ages from the picture, but my first impression was that they were in their twenties.

My stomach curled. One girl was on Daniel Rubinstein's lap. A pretty blonde sat on General Bailey's lap, and a cute red headed girl sat close to my father on a lounge chair.

Too close.

I blinked as I studied the picture, wondering what it meant. So many questions erupted in my mind.

"Do you want me to continue?" Dante asked.

I gripped the pillow next to me and nodded.

He showed me a fourth picture. I didn't recognize that man, but Dante knew him. His voice hardened when he spoke about him.

"This is Phillip McKenzie. Do you know him?"

"No. I don't think I've ever seen him before."

"Good. He's not the kind of man you want to meet," Dante bit out. "Or, at least he wasn't."

"Why? What happened to him?"

"He's dead."

"Oh," I breathed out. It was on the tip of my tongue to ask, but I had enough to deal with.

"Look through the rest of these pictures and I'll explain."

He handed me eight more pictures. Each one showed either my father, General Bailey, or Daniel Rubinstein, or a mixture of the three of them, at various parties. In each picture, General Bailey and Rubinstein were with different women. Nothing seemed inappropriate if you looked at the pictures quickly, but at closer look, there were hands on knees, hands on backs and shoulders. I had no idea about General Bailey, but I knew Rubinstein was married, and I wanted to throw up at the pictures of my father. The only difference with the pictures of him was that in the other pictures, the other girls were different in each shot. In the pictures my father was in, he was photographed with the same red head. Six. Times.

"What does all this mean? I don't understand."

I dropped the pictures of the other men and focused on the photographs of my father and the mystery red-head, who truthfully, looked no older than I was when my father died.

Dante stood up to move back to his desk. I immediately missed the warmth and comfort his close presence brought me. He opened the desk drawer again and took out another folder.

He sat in his chair and spread open the file on his desk.

"Phillip McKenzie was a billionaire with more money than he knew what to do with. He was a spoiled man who was raised with the proverbial silver spoon in his mouth. So deep, I think he nearly choked on it. He never did a hard day's work in his life, but he surrounded himself with hardworking people. He paid a lot of people a lot of money to keep him out of trouble.

"I'm going to make a long story short, Noemi, because McKenzie's story is sick and perverted, and not something I want to taint you with. I'll just say that McKenzie's boredom led him to a life of depravity. He broke laws. He treated people, women, like they were his property."

I bit down on my lip.

"Don't worry. He paid the price for his actions."

"What happened to him?" I dared to ask, not sure what Dante would tell me and wondering if he'd admit to murder.

He shrugged. "He was found dead in his villa in Italy four years ago. His death was ruled a suicide."

"I don't understand what he has to do with my father. How did they know each other?"

Dante pulled a picture out of the folder and pushed it across the desk to me. I stood up and looked down at it, the most condemning of all. McKenzie, my father and the mystery red-head.

Dread filled my stomach. "Who is she?"

Dante sat back in his chair. "Her name is Lydia Padgett. She was one of McKenzie's victims."

"Victim? She doesn't look like a victim in that picture," I sneered. I didn't feel much sympathy for a woman who had her hand on my father's knee.

"The picture is misleading. At the time it was taken, Lydia had just turned eighteen."

"So, was my father having an affair with her? Why are they together in all these pictures? Dante, stop trying to spare me and tell me what all of these pictures have to do with my parents' deaths."

I didn't want to feel the pain slowly. I wanted all of it at once, like pulling the bandage off quickly, not bit by agonizing bit.

Dante leveled his stare at me. "Phillip McKenzie trafficked young girls. He groomed them and molded them until they became of age, then he whored them out to his friends. In some cases, the girls weren't even aware of it. They were invited to parties. They were made to feel special. And then, usually very shortly after they turned eighteen, like days after, they were seduced by a man who had spent the last few months getting to know them. Each girl was selected and then preyed upon by a wealthy bastard. Sometimes, the seduction led to a brief affair, but most of the time, it was over before it began. McKenzie's client paid hundreds of thousands to be with the girl of his choice. The girl was used, physically, and emotionally. Several of them committed suicide afterward."

"Oh my God. How long did this go on? How many girls did he do this to?"

Dante shook his head. "I don't know, but I'm sure it was dozens. Like most men who get away with their crimes, he started to get lazy and sloppy. His handlers worked harder and harder to keep his activities a secret."

I sifted through the pictures one more time. "How could they do that? How could anyone keep this a secret?"

"The only people who knew about it would never talk," he said quietly. "If they did, they would be admitting their own guilt. They were all complicit, Noemi. And the girls were given a substantial parting gift. There were bribes and payoffs. Most of the girls would have either not realized what had happened behind the scenes or they were too scared to talk. I know there were at least two who disappeared."

"Disappeared," I repeated numbly as I went back to the picture of my father and Lydia.

"My father wouldn't do anything like that," I denied as the pieces clicked like the jagged edges of broken glass, meant to be part of a whole, but not fitting perfectly, making your fingers bleed as you tried to make them fit.

"He didn't," Dante replied, and my breathing became easier. "At first."

All my breath left me. I put the pictures down and hugged the pillow again, listening to his words. I sought out his tone and the deep timbre of his voice, using it as a shield against the oncoming pain.

"Your father had a working relationship with General Bailey and Daniel Rubinstein. Over time, they worked on him. Invited him to some of the parties and eventually, he accepted. From what I know, he behaved himself. He showed no interest in any of the women. Until the night he met Lydia."

I squeezed my eyes shut.

"Even then, he kept her at a distance, but the temptation was great. He started attending more and more parties. He spent more time with Lydia, and only Lydia, not moving from girl to girl like the other men."

"Did he sleep with her?"

Dante didn't want to answer the question. I could see the rare reluctance in his eyes.

"Tell me the truth," I whispered, scared to death of what the truth would be.

Slowly, so slowly I barely saw his head move, he nodded.

Chapter Twenty-Two
-Dante-

Words mattered, but this time they stuck in my throat. I would rather have choked to death on the syllable of a one-word answer than ever see that much pain in Noemi's eyes again.

I wanted to stop there. She didn't need to hear the sordid details. I could skip over all of that now that she knew the relationship between her father and Phillip McKenzie. Her father, unfortunately, was as much a victim of McKenzie's depravity as Lydia was. Lydia was an innocent and didn't deserve to have her name be part of the story any longer.

With what little I'd explained, Noemi was completely focused on her father's infidelity. Perhaps she should have been because it was that infidelity that led to his death, but the person who killed Gerald Petrafuso wasn't the only person who wanted him dead.

"I know this won't be easy to do, but don't get hung up on Lydia."

"Really?" she snorted angrily. "My father was cheating on my mother with an eighteen-year-old and I'm supposed to brush it off?"

The man I was would have taken her comment with pride. She believed in me and believed the story I told her. She had questions, but she was seeking more facts, not questioning my credibility.

The man I had become found no satisfaction in telling her about her father's past and in doing so, ruining the memory of a man who had been a loving father and up until the very end, a good husband.

But I didn't have time to coddle her. I needed to get Noemi past those details and move her on to the truths that would ruin everything she believed.

As if I hadn't done enough to her already.

"I understand how you feel—"

"No, you don't," she exclaimed.

"I do," I insisted. "Noemi, your father was a good man—"

"He was," she agreed angrily. "Until he cheated on my mother."

I moved around the desk to pull her into my arms. "You can't measure the value of an entire lifetime by one mistake. Your father has already paid the price for his indiscretion."

"Indiscretion? That's putting it mildly."

She was stiff with anger, but Noemi let me wrap my arms around her. We were close enough that I felt the strength of her heartbeat.

I wrapped my fist in her hair, not to control her as I'd done in the past, but to soothe myself. Selfish bastard that I still was. It was another way of getting close to her, of becoming a part of her, to have the strands of silk wrapped between my fingers link us together. I wanted her to take from me. She already had courage. I wanted to bolster that toughness with my own resolve.

"Try not to focus on those details."

"Because there's more," she guessed, tilting her head to look up at me.

Once again, I was unable to answer her. Her eyes narrowed.

"Tell me. Was my father murdered because of what he knew about McKenzie and his disgusting parties?"

I had to think about how to answer her.

"The answer to that is yes... and no."

When her shoulders fell, I knew she was reaching her limit.

"Yes, someone wanted your father out of the way. I don't know the details, but I suspect that he felt guilty."

"He should have!"

"I absolutely agree. But that guilt made people nervous. McKenzie could never let this information get out and people in power like Bailey and Rubinstein couldn't afford it either."

"So, McKenzie killed my father to keep him quiet?"

"No," I answered her truthfully.

"Then it was Bailey or Rubinstein?"

I shook my head. "No, Noemi. It wasn't either one of them."

"Then who? Please, just get it over with. Who killed my father? And my mother! Dante, they were killed on the same night. Whoever caused that accident was responsible for taking both their lives."

The tears started again.

"Sit down, baby girl."

I tried to get her to cooperate but in her emotional state, I might as well have been trying to charm a cobra.

"No," she pushed away from me. "I need answers, Dante. Please tell me which one of those men was responsible for my parents' deaths."

"None of them were."

"Then who killed them!" she cried out desperately.

"Your mother, Noemi. It was your mother who caused the accident that killed them that night."

Her mouth fell open, then closed, confusion and disbelief in her eyes. She struggled to understand what I'd said. She shook her head repeatedly.

"That doesn't make sense with anything you've already said. Besides, I already knew that. My mother was drinking, and her drunk driving caused the accident."

"No, Noemi. That wasn't what happened. Your father's guilt caused him to make rash decisions. I'm not sure of the specifics. There was no alcohol in your mother's blood that night. At least, not enough to say that she had been driving drunk."

"What are you implying?"

"What I'm saying is that your mother deliberately caused the accident after your father's guilt led him to confess his affair with Lydia to your mother. I believe, but can't prove, that he told her about McKenzie, afraid that she'd find out some other way."

"No, she wouldn't have done that. She wouldn't have been happy, but she wouldn't have killed him. She wouldn't have left me and Willis alone like that. I don't believe you."

It was the first part of my tale she couldn't come to terms with and I didn't blame her. But I had proof. I picked up the folder from my desk and handed it to her. "There's a copy of the coroner's report and their death certificates. Have you ever seen either one of those documents?"

"No. Willis... Willis handled everything. I never wanted to look at them."

I pushed the file into her hands. "Take your time."

I left her alone on the couch to review the documents that would tell her what the police report and the coroner's report corroborated during the investigation. The motivation was unclear to them, but crystal clear to those of us who knew the facts. Rachel Petrafuso had been driving the night she and her husband Gerald left a party at General Bailey's home. Unbeknownst to Gerald beforehand, in order to keep his guilt in line, Bailey and Rubinstein invited Lydia to attend.

Their actions had the opposite effect. Instead of intimidating him into silence, I suspected that Gerald had a severe fit of nerves and admitted the affair to his wife. The police investigation showed that the accident had been deliberate. Rachel Petrafuso drove her car off the road, into the tree, causing a severe enough impact to end both her life and that of her husband.

I have no idea what happened in the car that night, what words were said, or why Rachel responded the way she did. There was one man who knew more intimate details about Rachel and Gerald's relationship than I did, and it appeared he was good at keeping his secrets. Willis had never told Noemi anything about the truth behind her parents' deaths and had managed to keep the facts hidden from her for nearly a decade.

Until a man in a knit cap decided she needed to know the truth which made no sense either, since he'd left her a note implying that I was responsible.

Like I expected she would, Noemi quickly put the information together.

"I can't believe this." Her hands shook as she put the papers down. "All these years, I thought... He let me believe... Willis had to have known the truth. He was the executor of their estate. He handled these documents. He knew what happened."

"I can only say that I suspect that he knew your mother's actions caused the accident. He wanted to protect you, Noemi. I can't blame him for that. I would have done the same thing. I don't know if he knew anything about McKenzie, Bailey, or the affair with Lydia."

Noemi surprised me when she stood up abruptly and started to leave the room.

"Where are you going?" I followed her to the living room.

She gathered her purse and started digging for something inside. "To ask him. I'm going to New York."

She headed for the door and I jumped ahead of her to block her. "No, you aren't."

"Don't tell me what to do."

"I'm not trying to tell you what to do. But I do need to point out that you can't drive to New York right now. You don't have a car. You can be angry about this all you want, and I don't care, but you've had a shock tonight, Noemi. You're in no condition to be driving, baby girl."

I don't know if it was my nickname for her or the realization that she had no way of getting to New York, but her shoulders slumped in defeat and she dropped her purse.

"You're right. I forgot." With the shock of what she'd learned, her voice became stiff and wooden.

I tugged her back to the living room. "Sit." I nudged her gently onto the sofa then went back to the bar. I didn't know if it was what she'd want, but a shot of scotch wouldn't hurt, and I definitely needed one.

I returned to the sofa with a shot glass in each hand.

She raised her eyebrows as I handed her a glass. "Shoot it or sip it, I don't care, but drink it. It will help."

I tossed mine back, and to my surprise, Noemi did the same, coughing and making a face as the liquid burned down her throat. She fell back against the pillows with her hands covering her eyes.

"I need to talk to Willis," she insisted.

"And you will. I'll take you there."

She brightened up with anticipation.

"Tomorrow."

She slumped down again.

"Listen to me, Noemi. We need to make sure he's even in New York before we go driving out there in the middle of the night. It's possible he's in D.C."

"It's not that much further."

"True, but I think you need to rest, adjust, and think through this before we go chasing your brother down."

"It's so much," she started. "I can't believe it, but I do. I know you wouldn't make all of this up, but also..."

She tilted her head the way she always did right before she disagreed with me.

"I also don't understand," she said slowly, "how you knew all of this. How do you have so many details? *Why* do you know so many details?"

I took a deep breath, prepared to share the last bit of information that no one knew but me. This wasn't something found in the police records or something that Willis would be able to corroborate. And as usual, Noemi was too damn smart.

Chapter Twenty-Three

-Noemi-

He said he'd never killed an innocent person. When I asked him how he knew the people he killed were guilty, he said it was because he thoroughly vetted all his contracts. He investigated each person and knew they were guilty and deserving of the fate.

I blinked up at him as he turned to stone next to me.

"You said you didn't do it. That you didn't kill them."

"I didn't," he said in a lethal tone.

He was close to becoming that man again: the hard, implacable man who was brutally honest and didn't care who got hurt in his wake because he didn't have enough empathy to stop himself.

"Then how do you know all the facts? How do you know so many details that no one else does? The parties, Lydia, McKenzie—my mother!"

My tears started again. It seemed I couldn't keep them at bay for long. My mind played tug-of-war with my heart. I wanted to believe everything Dante said, but unless he made it all up, there was only one way he could have all the details. He knew them too well, told them too convincingly for it to have all been a lie.

I lost my cool, thinking what it all could mean.

"Damn you, don't just sit there," I screamed at his continued silence. "Tell me how you know all of this! If you didn't kill them, if it was all my mother's fault, then why do you know so much about it!"

He stood up, shoving his hands into his pockets. The cold demeanor returned, but I wasn't afraid of this Dante anymore. Not when I had gotten to know the other one. Not when I had fallen in love with both of them.

"I think you already know the answer to that."

He turned his back on me and walked to the bank of windows that ran along the back wall. He pushed the curtain to the side and stared out into the darkness.

With one arm braced on the wall, he let out a breath. "I'll say this for the last time. I know I'm a murdering bastard, but I didn't kill your parents, Noemi."

I started to ask him more, but without turning to look at me, he put up his hand for me to stop talking.

"I'm only telling you this information now because I promised you that I would. I think you've had enough for one night, but since you're determined to have the truth, I'll give it to you."

He turned to face me. "I didn't kill your parents, but it was possible that I was going to kill your father."

He might as well have grabbed the beating heart from my chest. My knees grew weak even though I was already sitting down. I swallowed hard, wanting an explanation but for the first time that night, I was too terrified to ask for one. Dante ran his hand through his hair, but he didn't back down.

"There was a contract out for your father. As soon as I saw it, I was curious. I wasn't interested in fulfilling it, but knowing your father and his family life, my curiosity was piqued. As I told you, I conduct thorough investigations."

"That's why you have all those documents and the pictures. You investigated my father?"

"Yes. But it was unofficial at the time. I never met with anyone or negotiated for the contract. I started my investigation and with the information I found, I decided not to go any further."

That caught me off guard. From what he had told me, this ring of men preyed on vulnerable females.

"I thought these were the kind of men you ... deal with."

I didn't know how else to say it. I didn't know if I'd ever reconcile the Dante I knew with a cold-hearted killer.

"They are. And I used that information later. For other purposes. But in the scheme of what he'd done, your father's actions, while disgusting and immoral, were not deserving of my retribution."

"So, what he did wasn't so bad that you thought he should die for it?"

"Yes, but there was one other factor that influenced me the most."

"What was that?"

I watched it happen that time. I watched the expression in his eyes change as his humanity gained control again.

"That he was your father. Even back then, I couldn't bring myself to contemplate any action that would bring you pain. He would have had to have done much worse than what he did before I could have torn him from your life."

"Like my mother did," I whispered through the tears. "Then why do you have a copy of the police report? You didn't just let it go after you decided not to..." My voice trailed off. There were things I needed to face, but I didn't have to say them.

"I have to apologize for that as well. My nose was out of joint. I was miffed that the contract was still open, but someone had apparently taken the job. I wanted to know who had the audacity to make a move like that. My research led me to the truth. I dropped it after that."

I wasn't sure it mattered but now that the truth had come to light, I wanted it all out there.

"Your ego was bruised because someone killed my father too soon?" He truly lived in a messed-up world. "Who put the contract out on my father in the first place? It had to be McKenzie."

"There's a certain protocol involved in these things. You don't get to pre-empt the contract. That's not how it's done, but once the contract was taken down, there was nothing more I could do. I'm sorry, Noemi, but I don't know who initiated it."

He was genuinely remorseful, and I should have been glad, but it seemed every question, and every subsequent answer, led to more questions.

"My freaking head hurts," I muttered. But I squared my shoulders and forged ahead. "Do you have any clue then, why all this would be brought up now? What does it have to do with me?"

He shook his head. "I don't know yet, but I promise you, I'm already working on it. I also don't know who the man in the knit cap was who planted that envelope on your bed."

"Oh, God, I nearly forgot about that envelope and the fact that someone got into my house when I—How do you know he wore a knit cap?"

It just wouldn't end.

"Surveillance footage," he answered as he returned to sitting next to me on the couch.

"You're recording me?" I asked, or accused, I suppose, depending on how you looked at it.

"No, not specifically. Some of the camera footage from the exterior of our house covers a bit of yours. The street out front, some backyard shots, and a little bit of your front door and driveway. I saw a man pull up after you left with Gabriel. He was wearing a long winter coat and a knit cap. I suspect that he's the one who left the envelope. As you said, he must have had a key or been good at picking locks."

"Is it possible that he could have done that? Picked the lock?"

Dante nodded. "Trust me. It's very possible, which is why I'm installing an alarm system as soon as you return home."

The next few seconds felt like an eternity as the silence grew. When Dante opened his arms, I didn't give a second thought to moving into them. I had questions still lurking in the back of my mind, but I was exhausted, and I knew I wasn't done with the tears yet.

"It's so much," I muttered to Dante's chest as he scooped me into his lap.

"I know."

He rubbed his chin against the top of my head, and I snuggled deeper against him, seeking as much of his warmth and strength as I could steel.

"I know you wanted the truth, baby girl, but I would have spared you this. I would have taken these secrets to my grave with no regrets."

"It's too bad someone else doesn't feel the same way," I muttered with a yawn.

"Whoever that person is, they'll realize their mistake soon."

I wrapped my arms around his waist and held him tighter. His nearness, his conviction—they were the only things making this bearable. I had a long night ahead of me as I struggled to deal with all that I'd learned.

Dante held me through it all. Dropping a soft kiss on my forehead or one on the top of my head every now and then. Letting me soak his shirt until I cried my eyes dry. Covering me with a blanket as he stretched out on the sofa next to me and spooned with me until my tired eyes could take no more and I finally cried myself to sleep.

Chapter Twenty-Four

-Dante-

When remorse is not part of your repertoire of emotions, it leaves an uncomfortable feeling under your skin.

Gingerly, I edged Noemi to the back of the couch and managed to stand up without waking her. She had been sleeping for about an hour. Our nights together had taught me to recognize when her breaths were regulated enough for me to leave her, which was something I had done too damn many times in the last two weeks. I thought about carrying her to the bedroom, but I was afraid she wouldn't fall back to sleep if she awoke, and she needed her rest.

My chest hurt when I looked down at her swollen eyes. She braved my confessions with the heart of a warrior, coming back for more with each wound she received, as each answer to each question revealed more damning information.

When her brain cleared after a night's rest, there'd be more she'd want to know. I didn't really want to do it, but if she was determined to visit Willis and get more answers from him, I would drive her to wherever he was. It would be a tricky conversation to navigate since they both knew some of my secrets, but hopefully, were equally as determined to keep them.

I kicked off my shoes and padded down the hallway to my office. Out of habit, I locked the door when I went inside. I didn't like surprises, especially when I was working. I'd left Michael's office door open on Smuggler's Island because it wasn't my door to lock. I wasn't making that mistake twice.

I wanted to check my emails and see if Marco had made any progress on Delacroix's files. Once he sent them, sifting through them would take time, weeks probably, and after Noemi's visit from the man in the knit cap, I doubted I had that much time to spare. Experience taught me that the situation was growing rapidly, and my sense of urgency needed to move along with it.

I picked up the files and their scattered contents and sat back at my desk.

Noemi's parents' pasts and subsequent deaths, the contract that had been taken out on me, the threats to Noemi's life and her mysterious visitor—three seemingly separate incidents that all converged... somehow. My gut told me these were all pieces of the same puzzle, but I'd be damned if I could make sense of it.

Reluctant to give up for the night, I poured through the papers again. Until I showed them to Noemi, I hadn't looked at those files in four years. Not since Phillip McKenzie's alleged suicide.

The fucking bastard. If I had anyone to blame for all of this, it was him.

Maybe justice hadn't been served. Maybe the head of the snake had been cut off, but the serpent still lived. Noemi's father wasn't alive, but Rubinstein and Bailey were, as well as thirty or more so-called "illustrious" men whose money or lawyers had helped them to escape notice after McKenzie's death.

A fresh new emotion washed over me—guilt.

It wasn't my job to take out the entire club. I had a contract to fulfill at the time, and I did what I was paid to do. McKenzie deserved it. His game was up. Every sordid, salacious, debauched evil he had ever perpetrated was about to be made public, or would have if he had lived. Someone didn't want his escapades brought into the public eye. Someone with money wanted the innocent to be free of reliving their trauma, but that someone also wanted McKenzie to pay for every crime he committed. Before the story of his sex ring could hit the papers, he put a bullet in his temple.

Or so it appeared.

With the information I gathered from Gerald Petrafuso's case, the investigation I conducted before I took the contract on McKenzie was a no-brainer. To avoid any further investigation by law enforcement or any other agency, McKenzie's death had to be ruled a suicide. It wasn't easy, but I made it work. And then I moved on with no regrets.

Until now.

I sifted through the pictures again, looking at the faces of the men who paid the price for their indiscretions and at the men who managed to walk away unscathed. I stopped at a picture of the four men together. I was relieved that Noemi hadn't asked me how I managed to get the pictures. I'm sure she would at some point and my best bet wasn't to lie. She'd see through me. How the hell she'd learned to do that, I didn't know. I would have to be brutally honest with her and tell her that those details fell into the category of things that she was better off not knowing and she'd have to trust me on that.

It would be a struggle, but she'd have to know the information I withheld was for her own good. If we were going to be together, there would be rules and limits. And expectations.

Fuck. I was going to have to throw my "no expectations" mantra out the fucking window, because we *were* going to be together in whatever capacity I could make it work. For her safety, and her sanity, she'd have to learn to accept that our relationship came with limitations. She couldn't know everything; couldn't know the intimate details of my work, the ins and outs of the syndicate, how I did what I did, the where and the why. I'd have to keep her in the dark about how I was able to maneuver through the dark. There were still secrets that needed to be kept, and she'd have to trust me as much as I was learning to trust her.

I tossed the pictures back on my desk and ran a hand through my hair. She was my ultimate distraction, but I couldn't let Noemi go now. Possibly, not ever. I needed to know she was safe. She was mine to protect. I couldn't give that responsibility to anyone else because...

What the fuck?

I picked up the picture of the four men together, studying it with more clarity than I had before.

I missed that detail in the past because I hadn't been looking for it. I probably would have missed it again if he hadn't been fresh on my mind.

There the cocky bastard sat, cocktail in hand, in the background of the picture, lounging poolside with a trio of smiling young ladies. His face was blurred and slightly pixelated. But not enough. I recognized him.

Damn me. How the hell had I missed that face before?

He was already at the top of my list and now, Christian Delacroix earned a big fat star next to his name.

Another piece of the puzzle fell into place, and while I didn't know the connections yet, I knew that the matter was snowballing into something that had the power to devour us all.

I steepled my fingers and thought about the many different scenarios that could play out. I couldn't take part in every single one of them. I was just one man and the variables were too many.

The life of an assassin is a lonely one. Men can't be trusted and there's no such thing as a real friend. Willis. Michael. They were as close as I would ever come to having friendships, but even then, it was all work related. Willis and I never talked about the ballgame, and Michael and I never shot-the-shit over a beer. If I had to put my life on the line to protect Noemi, there was only one man I knew who would have my back, and I wouldn't have to plan for what would happen if he betrayed me. In his world, he held as much power as I did in mine.

I wasn't used to asking for help. It left a bad taste in my mouth, but Noemi was worth it. I'd grovel if I had to. I couldn't leave anything to chance.

I didn't hesitate to call him.

Despite the late hour, Gabriel answered on the second ring.

Chapter Twenty-Five

-Noemi-

My eyes hurt and my back ached, but the smell of freshly brewed coffee was the only thing that could tempt me enough to let Dante see me with my blotchy face, snarled hair, and rumpled clothing. I couldn't have hidden from him if I tried, considering that the living area was open concept and Dante was just a few feet away drinking his morning cup. I had learned over the last few weeks that he was a one-cup-a-day kind of person. I didn't understand that concept, but then again, his portions weren't diluted by rich creamers.

I smiled awkwardly when I stood up and approached the counter. Dante automatically reached for the pot and poured a half cup into the mug that he was sweet enough to have ready for me. I smiled again at his choice of dishes: solid black.

"I'm going to have to introduce you to the color wheel," I teased as I reached for my coffee.

His brow furrowed. "I don't like color."

"I didn't notice," I said, looking pointedly over my shoulder at the black furniture and beige walls.

One corner of his mouth ticked upward, and I wanted to hug him. Dante Calegari and I were sharing early morning banter over a cup of coffee. If my heart hadn't been so sorely bruised from the night before, it would have sung with joy.

"I don't have any creamer," Dante said as he pulled a half gallon of milk out of the refrigerator. "No one ever comes here, and this was all the convenience store on the corner had."

"That will work," I accepted, knowing I wouldn't get the sweetness I craved but all I needed was a shot of caffeine to wake me up.

In the past, the silence between us had been almost eerie, but that morning, it was a welcome peace. There would be plenty more to talk about but in that moment, I just wanted to drink my caffeine and get an eyeful of Dante wearing a fitted black t-shirt and a pair of black lounge pants.

I tipped my head down to take a sip from my mug so I wouldn't get caught ogling him. I loved the way he looked in his suits, and I fell hard for the casual khaki look he sported on the island, but this man, this I-just-got-out-of-bed-so-let's-get-back-in-it look he wore, was enough to make me want to let the past sort out its own details and drag him off to the bedroom.

"Do you want breakfast?" Dante asked, interrupting my dreams of seduction.

"Maybe just some toast or something if it's not much trouble. I'm really not very hungry."

"It's no trouble, Noemi," Dante said softly as his hand reached out to stroke my cheek.

I had no idea what time it was when he left me alone on the couch, but I knew I missed his touch. The warmth of his palm on my cheek soothed me.

"I need you to understand one thing," he said silkily, as he leaned across the counter.

"What's that?" I asked in a hushed voice matching his.

"That you can ask me for anything. Anytime. Remember? Even a fucking piece of toast when you want it."

"Except, that's not true, is it? I can't ask you for what it is I really want. You've already told me. We're through."

God, as if I didn't hurt already, bringing up his rejection was enough to end me.

"Then I need you to understand two things."

His eyes darkened and he got that look, that intense, alpha stare that always weakened me.

"And that second thing is?" I stuttered through the words.

He sunk his hand into my hair and pulled my face toward his. "That I lied. We're not through. I'm not done with you yet."

Maybe some stronger women would have been appalled at his caveman behavior, and if it had been anyone else who said that to me, I might have kicked them in the shins. But this wasn't anyone else. This was Dante, and he had just said the words I needed to hear as much as I needed my next breath.

Even though I had longed to hear them, I wasn't sure how to react, like when you finally get that one thing you've always wanted and you're speechless.

"Good," was the only thing that came out of my inexperienced mouth.

"*Good?*" He smirked at me and shook his head. "Baby girl, we're going to have to get you some lessons in flirtation."

"Oh? We can do that when we sign you up for charm school. I think this is a classic example of the pot calling the kettle black."

"Then we'll make an agreement. If you'll flirt with me, I'll do my best to charm you."

I laughed. "You already have, in your own arrogant, oh-so-special, domineering way. Why are you so hung up on me flirting with you? I thought you didn't like to be teased."

The look in his eyes pulled me into him even deeper. How could this man ensnare me with just the intensity of his eyes?

"I don't like to be teased because it's superficial. It's a promise of something that won't be delivered."

I didn't need to finish my coffee. His touch awoke my entire body when his thumb traced my lower lip.

"But you're different."

I tilted my head to study him even while his thumb stayed where it was. "How so?"

"Because I think I'd like it if you flirted with me. I know you." His voice dropped, pulling on that sexy, husky note he used so well. "If you flirted with me, I'd know you meant it."

I felt the blush start low and spread across my face in seconds. My eyes fell, but he forced me to meet his gaze when he tipped my chin up with his index finger.

His eyes searched mine. "I love the way you blush when I talk to you. If you're not hungry, breakfast can wait."

"I'm not hungry."

My breath hitched when he pulled my hand to his lips and pressed a kiss to the pads of my fingers.

"Come." He stretched his hand out and pulled me towards the hallway.

"Where are we going?"

"To take a shower."

He tugged me into following him. I fought my nerves. This was something new. Something I had wanted to do while we were aboard the yacht, but Dante never indicated that he was interested in sharing a shower. He was usually gone by the time I woke up in the morning.

Taking my hand, he pulled me through his bedroom and into the master bath. Dante's townhome didn't exhibit any of the opulence of the *Mary Theresa* but was still elegant in an understated way. The master *ensuite* was another exhibition in monochromes. Black and white tile. White with gray swirl marble countertops with the same marble floor to ceiling in the walk-in shower.

Dante closed the door behind us. Hooking his fingers under the hem of my cable knit sweater, he pulled me toward him. "You look nervous."

"Unfamiliar territory," I replied.

Nodding, he told me to put my hands up, then he pulled the sweater over my head.

"Another first," he said as he continued to undress me by rolling off my jeans.

Everywhere he touched me my body screamed, but these touches were different than what I was used to from him. He was gentle, removing my bra slowly, and he surprised me when he dropped to his knees. He nuzzled my stomach before slipping his fingers under the edge of my panties and lowering them. I put my hand on his shoulder to step out of them.

When he stood up, he gathered all my clothes and tossed them into a hamper near the shower.

He stood there looking at me with yet another unreadable expression on his face. Never having showered with a man, I didn't know what to expect. Dante's hesitation told me that perhaps he was feeling the same way.

"Would you believe me if I said I'd never done this before either?" he said quietly as he reached into the shower to start the water. He looked at me over his shoulder, then turned away again to stick his hand into the steamy stream to test the water.

I took a step forward, torn between my own awkwardness and a desire to make it easier on him. This awkward man in front of me was another side of Dante that I never thought I'd meet. He was always so confident and sure of himself, cocky even. And while he still exuded strength and masculinity, this timid side of him brought out a confidence I didn't know I had.

"I would," I said, as I reached out to pull on his black t-shirt. When I started to raise it over his head, he had to help me because I couldn't quite get it right, tangling up the shirt when I had to rise up on my toes to get it over his head.

We smiled at each other as the shirt hit the floor. My eyes roved over his chest, glancing over lean muscles and following the trail of hair to his waistline. I reached for the waistline of his pants, confident in knowing the reaction I would get. We've done this dance before. Dante's stomach muscles clenched, and he sucked in a breath when my nails scored his stomach. His pants were tied loosely, so I quickly undid the knot, slid my fingers along the elastic waist, and tugged. Dante took over from there, pulling them completely off and tossing them into the hamper as well.

Without a word, he stepped into the shower then extended his hand for me to join him. It seemed his hesitation was over. He stood in front of me, taking the brunt of the hot water before moving around behind me. The hot stream was a balm on my aching, tired body; bringing to the forefront just how uncomfortable my night had been.

Reaching around me, Dante grabbed some body wash and a washcloth that sat with it on the ledge. Lathering up, he covered my body head to toe and back to front in a soapy massage that had me quivering, but it was almost too much. My body was tired, and my mind was still exhausted from yesterday's journey into the past. If his hands meant to entice, they failed. The pressure of his strong hands molding my body aroused me, but relaxed me at the same time.

When his hands stopped moving, I leaned back against his chest and sighed. His arms encircled me, and his lips hit the sensitive crook of my neck. I felt how hard he was behind me and thought that I should return the favor and wash him, but it felt too good, too relaxing, to stand under the hot water while I practically let him hold me up.

"I could get used to this," he murmured as his lips teased my ear.

"If that's an offer to do this again, I accept." I tilted my head back to look up at him. His arms tightened around my slippery body.

"I should never have walked away from you," he said, surprising me. "That was a mistake. It won't happen again."

The words he chose may have seemed odd, but they suited Dante. He said he didn't know how to do romance, but he knew how to be direct. It was only my self-doubt that made me seek clarification, because if I interpreted his words wrong, the final piece of my heart would shatter.

"What are you saying, Dante?" I turned in his arms to face him, sliding my wet hands over his dripping chest.

"That I want you. Not for a night. Not for a day. Not for a week. Fuck, I don't know what I'm saying. The timing is bad, baby girl. There's a storm brewing. At first, I tried to stay away from you so I could deal with it, but I can't do that anymore."

"You want to be with me so you can protect me?" Why would that disappoint me? That didn't make sense, but in my tired state, that was the emotion that came to the forefront.

"No. I want to protect you because I want you in my life. I want you blushing when I come on to you. I want you wet and hot for me. I want you to wear my blindfold because you're sexy as hell in it, and I want to worry about whether I have the right fucking creamer for your coffee. I want to be with you and if this shit is going to keep us apart, then we'll face it together."

When I looked at him, I saw the first hint of fear I've ever seen in Dante Calegari's eyes.

"Unless that's not what you want," he said hesitantly.

"No, I want that. I mean, I want you too. I want everything you just said."

"Okay then." I thought he would smile at my admission, but he didn't. He reached past me for the shampoo bottle. "Tip your head back," he directed, then proceeded to wash my hair then his own.

It was typical Dante fashion that such a heartfelt conversation would end so abruptly, but knowing that he wanted to be with me was more than enough to make up for the brevity of the conversation.

Chapter Twenty-Six
-Dante-

I wanted her so much my body called me a traitor for not giving it what it needed, but after last night's revelations there was no way in hell I could take advantage of her like that. I washed her hair, running my hands through her dark tresses, and wished that the circumstances were different.

My confession meant changes—for me and her. A change of attitude. A change in my lifestyle. Hell. For the first time in my life, I took a shower with a woman and enjoyed every damn minute of it.

And that scared me.

I turned off the shower and pulled Noemi out. I wrapped a towel around my waist then wrapped the other towel around her like a cape. Tugging on the corners, I pulled her to me. She looked better, but I could tell she was still exhausted. She needed to eat, and if I could convince her to do it, she needed to sleep before we tracked down her brother.

While I still had work that needed to be done, I found myself oddly reluctant to be away from her. I didn't want to miss a moment of being with her now that we crossed that barrier. I wanted to take every minute of her day and make it mine.

Fuck, she scared me. These were feelings that weakened men. This was what had brought down Troy and ended an empire.

I was just one man. I didn't stand a chance.

"What's going through that head of yours?" Noemi asked, tilting her head as she studied me.

I pushed damp tendrils of hair away from her face. I was so raw for her I didn't even hesitate to answer.

"You. I can't stop thinking about you."

Her eyes widened in disbelief, but I couldn't be stopped now that my truth was out.

"You scare me. I've confessed things to you, weakened myself for you. You have more power over me than I have over myself which makes you the only person in the world I'm afraid of," I whispered longingly. "You terrify me. You always have. I'm afraid to be with you, but I'm even more afraid to be without you. I don't know what to do about us, but I know that if I don't do something, I won't be able to breathe. I can't even think right now because of you."

Noemi didn't say anything which was exactly what I needed. I didn't want words...more fucking words. Yes, they mattered, but this was another first in my life. This time, I just wanted her silence because the look in her eyes was enough.

I didn't have to wonder if she'd abuse the faith I had placed in her by revealing my deepest secret yet. As weak as I was for her, I didn't worry that she'd betray my confidence and wield the power I'd just given her against me. Instead, I felt a bolt of energy surge through me when she stood up on her tiptoes and left a soft kiss against my mouth.

She needed to rest, but my body screamed to seal my words with deeds, to love her until *she* was as weak and dependent on me as I was on her. To own her mind, body, and soul the way she had so easily taken ownership of me.

When her lips traveled from my mouth to my jaw, I started to give up, but I held on to my resolve. I wasn't that much of a bastard, not for her. But when her hand slipped under the fold of the towel and I felt her soft touch on my hard dick, I groaned my surrender.

"Are you sure you want this? Now? Last night was hell. Maybe you should rest before we go see Willis."

I tried to give her an out, but she stroked me with more confidence than I could resist. Strangled moans escaped me as I pushed forward, urging her to continue.

"I don't need to rest. The past waited five years to raise its ugly head. It can wait a few more hours. What I need right now is you."

With a growl of need, I stopped arguing with her. Bending slightly, I put one arm around her waist. She squealed as I hauled her up onto my shoulder and walked into the bedroom with her soft breath in my ear. I lowered her to the bed and quickly followed her down. Towels were undone and in the way. I was tangled. She was stuck. She laughed when I couldn't get the intruding fabric away from her body fast enough.

"Fucking hell," I growled as I eventually removed the offenders and tossed them away.

Finally, we were skin to skin. My hardness to her softness. I braced myself over her, searching her eyes for anything that told me this was too soon.

All I found was a need that matched my own.

"I would never lie to you," she whispered as her arms circled my neck. "I want you. I want this. Now."

I don't know the right words to describe such a kiss except to say that I kissed the hell out of her. Every pent up need I had for the last week burst forth. I wanted to devour her. Brand her. Make it clear to myself and the rest of the world that she was mine and no one, *no one*, was going to take her from me.

After the unintended foreplay in the shower, I didn't have the stamina to last. I parted her thighs, groaning with relief to find her soaking wet for me.

"I can't wait, baby girl," I muttered against her lips as I settled between her eagerly parted legs. "I'll make it up to you. Right now, I just fucking need to feel you."

I wasn't sure she understood the last words I groaned as I pushed into her. Feeling her tight pussy taking hold of me was like coming home; like when the man who'd trained for the marathon finally gets his medal. When the lonely miscreant finally realizes he's not alone anymore.

When for one fucking moment, everything in the world was the way it was supposed to be, and all the interlopers and degenerates were consigned to hell.

Only she could bring me that peace.

Only she could make me beg for release: release of pleasure, of pain, release from the past.

"Please, *bambina*," I moaned as I entered and withdrew from her again and again in that search for relief. "Give it to me. Now."

I was still selfish enough to demand what I wanted, to take what she offered freely to me.

Her shattering orgasm was beautiful, but it was my surrender that I sought. It was my admission that this woman was worth everything to me. She was my beginning and my end. I knew as I shuddered with pleasure and came deep inside her that we had sealed a bond that would never be broken. Not as long as there was breath in my gasping body.

"I fucking love you," I moaned, taking her quivering lips in a kiss of pure surrender. "I love you," I repeated. I didn't care whether she said it back, or if I saw that answering echo in her eyes. It was enough that she let me say it to her. She didn't need to love me in return. She just needed to let me love her.

NOEMI FELL ASLEEP IN my arms again, not long after she whispered, "I love you, too," into the side of my neck, making me smile at the return of her shy side. I laid there, her declaration continually whispering in my ear as if she were still awake repeating it. My family showed affection, and I knew how we all felt toward one another. Noemi was the first person to ever use words to tell me she loved me.

My heart thudded loudly in my chest while the blood rushed through my head. She was mine now. Not just physically, but with every bit of my being I claimed her as mine. What awed me more was that I belonged to her as well. Three little words could own a man, and for as long as I lived, I was hers.

I couldn't wrap my head around it. My body wasn't used to the emotion. It created a turmoil within me that wouldn't subside. I needed to do something, to stay busy, to let my mind and heart grapple with this new revelation.

With a restless growl, I gently rolled Noemi to her side and continued my habit of leaving her alone as she slept. I checked my emails when I got to my office and found my first message from Marco. He sent me a section of the files he extracted from Delacroix's computer system. There was more to come, he said, but this was the first chunk he managed to pull out.

I had asked him to find references to me or Noemi, but after seeing Delacroix in the pictures last night, I decided to take a different approach and search for the names Gerald Petrafuso, Daniel Rubinstein, and General Bailey as well. It was another hunch that my gut said would pay off. I could work on the search while Noemi slept. There may have been information that would be valuable during our discussion with Willis. I knew he'd be the soul of discretion. He couldn't afford leaks any more than I could. I needed to go armed with every piece of valuable information I could find, hoping that he would reveal more without knowing that he had done so.

I locked my office door and ran the decryption code on Marco's file. It would take a while, so I decided to fish around and see what the internet had to say about General Bailey and Daniel Rubinstein. Once I was done with a contract, I almost never followed up on anyone involved. Phillip McKenzie was the rare exception to that rule. And since I wasn't bidding on a contract for any of these men, all three were fair game.

I started with Bailey. Back then, he had been the most public figure of the four. McKenzie made the most headlines, but not until his death. I quickly scanned the top three links for General George Edmund Bailey. I didn't pay much attention to politics. It seemed our friend Bailey was a top runner to take over as Director of the CIA. That would be a damn good reason for him to take desperate measures to make sure his past remained in the dark.

"What the fuck would that have to do with Noemi?" I muttered, not seeing a connection.

I should have dug deeper, but my inner voice said not to delay in looking up Rubinstein. Quickly, I found that I could take him off the list. His online obituary nauseated me as it droned on about his accolades and all the prestigious government positions he'd held, including what would have been his highest honor had he lived long enough to accept the position—Director of the CIA.

Fuck. I had to read through the paragraphs lauding his contributions before I found an article that mentioned his cause of death. Accidental drowning. How the hell did a sixty-year-old man accidentally drown to death? I skimmed about ten more articles but couldn't find anything that questioned the coroner's ruling as the cause of death. Rubinstein was found face down in the pool at his Florida estate. Was he drunk? High? Did he have a coronary while swimming? On the surface of what the internet provided, all my questions remained unanswered. Wasn't it fortunate for Bailey that the man who was the original choice to be the new head honcho at the CIA was also a man who could one day testify against him in a sex crimes case and that man met an untimely death?

In my line of work, I learned that coincidences of this magnitude were not just rare, but non-existent. Bailey's greed outweighed his friendship with Rubinstein. Rubinstein wouldn't have talked about the past. If he had, he would have endangered himself. He and Bailey could have taken their secrets to the grave and never have put the other into suspicion. But something made Bailey nervous. Something alarmed him enough to remove his competition.

The picture was getting clearer, but I needed the center, those key pieces that made all the others make sense.

I received the notification that the decryption was done. I wasn't sure I needed those files anymore, but that nagging inner voice told me to run a quick search.

Before I hit the search bar, I read Marco's note again.

This was easy. Too easy if you know what I mean. I'll have more soon. Will probably be done tonight.

I mulled over his words while I typed in General Bailey, Bailey, George Bailey and a few other combinations that came back with zero entries found.

Frowning, I tried again. Rubinstein. Daniel Rubinstein. D. Rubinstein.

Nothing came back for him either.

Delacroix was up to no good, but he hadn't been in contact with, or discussed either one of those men. At least, not electronically.

I went with what my gut told me to do next. I typed his name in slowly, as if typing it too quickly would achieve a different result.

Gerald Petrafuso. Zero hits.

Petrafuso. Thirty-three hits.

Fuck.

I narrowed the search and typed one name. Noemi.

Zero hits.

My eyes narrowed as I was left with one conclusion.

"You fucking son-of-a-bitch," I ground out, pounding out the keys to his name.

W.I.L.L.I.S.

Thirty hits.

I sat back in my chair, willing myself to calm down before I dove into each entry. The number of entries didn't necessarily mean anything yet. Maybe Delacroix did some shady work for the government as well. Maybe we had both become part of Willis' network and didn't know it. And maybe Willis didn't know about the connection between me and Delacroix.

And maybe pigs could fly, and yellow brick roads really did lead to emerald cities.

And maybe I had finally found the puppet master who wanted me out of the way and his sister dead?

"No. No way would he do that."

Taking me out for whatever reason he had come up with was one thing. Maybe he was in hot water and had to clean up his dirty work. Maybe he was just an ass and wanted to betray me. Maybe he was pressured into it by someone else, but I knew one thing for certain—Willis Petrafuso would never hurt his sister.

I sucked in a deep breath, ready to forge ahead with what I anticipated would be the biggest betrayal I'd ever face. If my suspicions were true, he was a dead man. I'd kill him before he could kill me. And I'd make him suffer for even thinking he could kill Noemi and get away with it.

I lingered over the enter button. I shook my head, my instincts screaming. My mind said one thing: to believe what made sense. But my sixth sense told me that I was wrong. I knew him. I knew how much he loved her. There was more to this and the only way I'd find it was to keep looking.

Noemi knocked softly on the door. "Dante? Are you in there?"

I squeezed my eyes shut, torn between what I wanted to do, what I had to do, and the only thing I could do. I hesitated as once again Marco's note came to mind.

"You're right," I said to the air. "It's too easy. Too fucking easy."

Delacroix didn't even make us work for it. He wasn't that stupid. Not as stupid as I'd been for falling for this bullshit. And Willis? Even if I had reservations about Delacroix, I knew Willis knew how to cover his tracks better than this.

"What?" Noemi called from the other side of the door. "I was just wondering if you wanted to go see Willis soon. It's almost noon."

I shut my laptop and walked across the room to open the door for her. She looked like she felt better. Her eyes weren't as puffy and the makeup helped her pale complexion, but anyone who knew her would clearly see that something was wrong.

"Do you feel better?" I asked, dropping a quick kiss on her mouth.

"I do, thank you." She hummed, kissing me back. "I just texted Willis. He said he's at his place in New York. I just told him I was coming up to visit him and he said fine. I didn't tell him why. I can go myself if you're busy," she added hesitantly.

"No, it's nothing that can't wait," I said, closing my office door behind me. "I know you have a lot of questions. I think I'd like to hear what your brother has to say."

Before she stepped away, I grabbed her wrist and pulled her against me. The urge to disrupt the casual feeling was foreign to me but I couldn't take even the illusion of distance between us.

But once I had her against me, I didn't have any idea what to say. Unlike her, my silence didn't stem from bashfulness but ignorance.

"I don't know what to say," I said, staring down at her.

A small smile crept across her mouth. "You didn't have a problem earlier, but that's okay. I love you, too."

Chapter Twenty-Seven
-Willis-

There are those bad feelings you get; the ones you just can't shake.

I lived with those feelings, twenty-four hours a day, seven days a week. I made decisions that affected people's lives: Their ability to make a living, their wages, their medical care, the ins and outs of how a government works and what it is, and isn't, supposed to do for its people. In most circumstances, I made decisions that I thought were good for the general population. On a few rare occasions, I voted for bills I didn't like, but I understood their purpose. I understood what the end goal was.

Mostly, I voted to enhance people's quality of life. I championed projects that I thought would improve the world we lived in.

Sometimes, that meant doing something distasteful, like taking the life of another human being. People who made a living bringing other people down and keeping them there. Drug cartels. Human traffickers. Pedophile rings, just to name a few.

I wasn't a goddamn superhero, and I didn't get my hands dirty. There were a limited amount of people I could rely on and as of that morning, one of them had betrayed me.

I threw back another shot of whiskey and started to reach for the decanter again.

But I stopped.

Alcohol wasn't the solution to my problem.

I rubbed my brow to relieve the pressure. The solution to my problem was already in motion, but everyone else's impatience was fucking it up.

Especially his.

Dante Calegari.

Damn him.

I liked him. I always had. We weren't the best of friends, even though we were neighbors. He was quiet and stayed to himself. I was too busy to get too close to the Calegaris, but Noemi's friendship with them made it inevitable.

I watched it happen for years. Watched from a distance and never said anything as Noemi's feelings for Dante changed from a fondness for her best friend's brother to a schoolgirl crush. I knew she'd grow out of it and was relieved when she called out of the blue one afternoon and announced that she had accepted an archivist position in England. I'd miss her like hell, but I thought it was a good choice for her.

After our parents died, she needed to be the person she wanted to become. She needed her freedom, to be the woman she'd always wanted to become but had been too shy to try.

She needed to get the hell away from Dante Calegari.

I'd always known he wasn't right for her.

The day I faced him across a negotiating table, I was glad she'd moved on from him, even if she had to move to another country.

Who the *hell* would want their baby sister dating a hired killer?

Dante and I spent several years working together after that, but any conversations about our personal lives were off limits. When Noemi called to say she was ready to move home, I was torn between how much I'd missed her and the fear that once she returned, she'd fall for him all over again.

I was right. She hadn't even been back for a month and it was like she'd never left as far as her feelings for Dante were concerned. It was worse than that, what with their trip to Barbados and all.

I pulled strings I shouldn't have. Tried to scare her away from him. I was desperate and not thinking straight, especially with the other shit I have going on. And it backfired.

If I'd taken longer to plan it, I would have seen that, but I made rash decisions and... and she was going to kill me when she found out what I'd done. She was a grown woman and could make her own decisions, but damn, why did she have to choose Dante fucking Calegari, the most lethal, dangerous man I knew? What kind of life could they have together because as her big brother, I wanted her to have a good life, a meaningful, happy life where she had the job of her dreams and a man to love and spoil her. What would happen if she ever found out her lover was a cold-hearted assassin? Would their relationship have ever gotten that far?

Thankfully, no. It was a moot point. Dante had made it clear when he broke into my house that they were through. He had walked away from her. While I knew that would leave her heartbroken, it was for the best. That was probably why she had called and said she was coming for a short visit. I didn't ask her why because I could tell by her voice that something wasn't right. She needed me and I'd be there for her. She'd hurt, and then she'd heal, and then, eventually, she'd find someone who could really make her happy.

And if she and Dante were over as quickly as they'd begun, I could put that issue to bed and deal with the man who was making my life a living hell.

That nagging feeling that something bad, something so bad the hairs on my neck were at constant attention, thatwas about to happen would go away, and I'd get to go back to living with my usual sleeplessness and anxiety.

Despite the premonitions I couldn't shake, my heart felt a little relief when the doorbell rang. She was there, and for a few hours, I could relax, pretend the bastards of the world didn't exist, and feel like a human again.

"Hey, Noe." I grinned as I pulled open the door, blinking into the sunlight as I saw that Noemi hadn't come alone. Dante was with her.

"Hey!" she exclaimed softly, and with a hint of hesitation. *What the hell? She was afraid of me?*

We hugged and I looked over her shoulder to glare at Dante, who crossed his arms and glared back.

That feeling of dread returned like a wrecking ball. My eyes narrowed as I stepped out of Noemi's hug.

"Come in," I said, moving out of their way and not taking my eyes off one of the world's best assassins as he walked into my home with the person I loved most.

They took a few steps into the foyer, then we all stood there. Dante glaring at me, me staring back, and Noemi staring at the floor.

Fuck it. That feeling told me that the game was over. Noemi looked like she had cried for days. No amount of makeup could hide that from me. And the fact that Dante was with her, looking pissed as hell, after he had said they were through. The man was many things, but he wasn't a liar.

And neither was I.

"Are you okay?" I asked Noemi. The love I felt for my sister took precedence over underworld shenanigans.

"Better, but... There are some things I wanted to talk to you about."

I nodded, wondering which one of the things on my list she had discovered.

"Okay." I tried to play along like I knew why she was there. "I guess I'm not surprised."

Whatever it was, I'd be as honest as I could be, but it wasn't like they were my secrets alone to keep. Some of them could get me in hot water with the U.S. government. Others would get me in hot water with some not nice people, like Dante Calegari. Others could get me killed. It was a delicate balance. I'd have to take my cues from her and Dante and rely on my instincts for the rest.

"Come into the living room. Can I get you something to drink?" I used social niceties to give me time to think, to try to read Dante to see if I could pick up on a clue as to why the hell he was there with her.

"Do you have some iced tea?" she asked. "I need some caffeine but no coffee."

"Sure." I got three glasses and the pitcher of sweet tea my little sis knew would be in my refrigerator. It was my go-to drink when my nerves weren't driving me to the amber contents of a shot glass.

I poured our drinks then pushed one glass towards each of them before taking a sip of mine and waiting. The silence killed me. And acting like a coward didn't sit well with me. It was time to poke.

But before I could speak, Dante apparently had come to the same conclusion.

"She knows." He ignored his glass of tea and fixed me with his steady gaze. I tried to read him. *What? What the fuck did she know? About him? About me? About what I'd done in Barbados?* I needed more information than he gave and the smug expression on his face as I deliberated my next move made me think he knew that and was enjoying my discomfort.

So, I played his game. "I'll tell you anything you want to know if I can. Just ask."

There the ball was in his court. *If I can* meant if it won't get one of us killed. *Just ask* meant I would only answer specific questions. No fishing expeditions. Noemi wouldn't analyze each word, but Dante sure as hell would.

Noemi hesitated until Dante put his hand on the small of her back. She looked up at him, her expression changing before she faced me again.

"I wanted to ask you about Mom and Dad. About... the night they died."

I closed my eyes and took a deep breath. For years, I prayed this day wouldn't come, and now it had. Something must have tipped her off if she were suddenly having doubts about what I'd told her. They were just a few white lies to protect her. And them. But if she'd learned that I had lied to her and everything she thought she knew about that night was fabricated, then that would explain why she looked like she had spent the entire night crying.

But I wasn't sure, so I had to remain vague. "What do you want to know?"

My sister had a backbone. She didn't use it unless she had to, but she wasn't pleased with my evasiveness. "You could start with the truth then move on to why you've lied to me about it."

"I told you," Dante said. "She knows."

I thought it odd but as he continued, I began to understand.

"She knows about the coroner's report, about the cause of the accident."

He didn't say anymore, and Noemi nodded.

"Okay, Noe," I said softly. "If you've found out the details, then what more do you want to know?"

Dante snorted and Noemi glared at him before turning her ire toward me.

"Why didn't you tell me the truth? It's there on the official records. I don't understand why you lied."

That was the easiest answer I had to give. "I lied because you were in enough pain and it wasn't a lie at first. The initial thought was that it was a drunk driving accident. They didn't test right away because... there wasn't a need to, or so they thought. It was several days later that the results came back, and I had already told you that the accident was caused by alcohol."

"You were so distraught, Noemi." My voice broke as I recalled that night in the Calegari kitchen. "I couldn't bring myself to put you through that a second time. To know that Mom—"

"So, it's true, then? Mom deliberately... she killed them?"

"That's what the investigation revealed."

"And you believed it? How could they possibly know something like that from just tire marks and broken glass?"

So, she didn't know everything. "Because there were witnesses."

"Witnesses to the accident?"

"No. To the argument they had before they left the party. Mom was angry. Dad tried to calm her down. The investigating officer said the argument was left out of the report, but due to her mental state at the time... It wasn't conclusive, according to the investigator."

"So, they filed a false report?"

"Not false. They just omitted a few details."

"Did the investigator tell you what they argued about? People have arguments. It doesn't make them drive cars into trees."

"I'm not sure," I said.

"Don't lie to me. Was it her? Lydia? She was at the party. Is that who they fought over?" Noemi's voice rose as she brought up a name I had hoped she'd never hear.

I glared at Dante who shrugged. "I told you. She knows."

I gave up then. If she knew about Lydia, she knew enough. "Yes. He wouldn't tell me specifics, but... the witness said Mom accused Dad of having an affair with... a child. She wasn't," I insisted. "She was legal."

"Barely," Noemi sneered though her eyes teared up. "Part of me thinks it doesn't matter how old she was. He still cheated on Mom, but the very idea that he... I just can't believe it."

"I made sure, Noe. Even though it wouldn't have mattered to some, she was a legal adult at the time." I felt like I was going to be sick. "They interviewed her. She said they had just started seeing each other right after her eighteenth birthday. There was nothing between them before that."

Noemi looked at Dante who frowned and shook his head. Something was going on between them and I realized that we weren't just talking about the night of our parents' car accident.

I said their names just to see what Noemi's reaction would be. "Bailey and Rubinstein."

Noemi's tears started to fall faster. Dante put his arm across her shoulders and kissed the top of her head.

"I told you. She knows."

"How much does she know?" I ground out. I was tired of running around in circles.

His eyes didn't leave mine. "She knows about your father's affair and Bailey and Rubinstein's involvement."

"I just didn't know how or why anyone would think that Mom..." Her voice trailed off, shaking with her tears.

"They said the conversation was pretty damning, but not conclusive. Out of respect for who Dad was... they left those details out of the official report. I'm sorry, Noe. I should have told you sooner, but it didn't seem like there was any reason to."

"I guess no one thought it would come up again ten years later," she said resentfully.

Which brought a whole new set of questions. "How did you find out?"

"Someone got into the house and left an envelope on my bed with pictures and copies of the police and coroner's reports."

That didn't make sense. She had mentioned things that weren't in the reports. "Bailey and Rubinstein aren't in the police report," I said.

Noemi tilted her head. "I know they aren't. So now will you tell me how you knew about those two? Please, just tell me the truth, Willis."

I looked at Dante who gave me that cocky "what now" look.

I could have played stupid and asked her how she'd found out, but it didn't matter anymore. It was clear that Dante had more connections to the past than I thought he did. His affection for Noemi forced him to tell her the truth after the reports were planted in her room.

"Noemi deserves the truth, Willis. She's been through hell the last few weeks. In fact, someone tried to kill us when we were in Barbados. I stopped him just as he was about to enter her bedroom," Dante said.

Part of the game was still afoot. He mentioned the incident in Barbados as if he'd never told me about what had happened to them that night. As if any of it were a surprise to me.

And then he decided to play hardball. Sneaky bastard. I had to give it to him. He was good. Leaps and bounds above me when it came to subterfuge.

"If someone is trying to kill your sister, she has the right to know anything about the matter that you can share."

"No one's trying to kill you, Noemi," I said before downing the last of my tea and wishing it were something stronger.

"Dante's not lying, Willis. I woke up and saw the man myself. I—"

I shook my head and leaned against the bar. "It was a sham. A fake attempt."

Dante's eyes narrowed with suspicion, but Noemi wasn't buying it.

"That's not true. I saw him. Dante—well, he dealt with the guy, but there was two more of them, Willis. They were going to kill us."

Dante put his hand on Noemi's shoulder. "It's time to end the charade, Willis. Whatever you're involved in has put your sister at risk. I can't allow that."

Who the hell did he think he was to imply that I didn't care about my sister's life?

"You can't allow that?" I raged. "What the fuck do you think I've been doing here? Every move I've made has been to save her life!"

"But you just said the attempt was a sham!" Noemi cried out. "Make up your mind, because right now, Willis, I don't believe a word coming out of your mouth."

"For fuck's sake," I muttered. "You were never in any danger, Noemi. Those men were planted there on the island. Well, they didn't know they were a plant. They thought they were there—"

"To kill me," Dante interrupted.

"Yes."

"The first man I killed specifically told me that it wasn't about me," Dante said, pushing me for the truth.

"It wasn't. It still isn't. It wasn't about you or Noemi. It was and still is about me. Unfortunately, your *relationship* and your impromptu trip to Barbados gave him the leverage he needed."

"Who?" Dante demanded to know. "Rubinstein is dead, so it must be Bailey."

"Yes. He's running scared. Worried that the truth about his past will come to light somehow."

"I don't understand," Noemi said. "What does Bailey have to do with you? With Dad, McKenzie, and Rubinstein dead, why would Bailey think that you knew anything at all about what they were involved in?"

I crossed my arms over my chest. "He knows I know because he's the one that told me."

"Holy shit," Dante muttered under his breath.

"Yeah, exactly." I stalked across my kitchen and grabbed a beer from the fridge. I popped the top and gurgled half of it to gain the fortitude to tell them what I'd been dealing with for the last month.

When I turned around, I decided to tell the truth. Noemi and Dante knew bits and pieces of it anyway. Especially Dante. Now, he'd get the full picture.

"Bailey has been tapped to be the next Director of the CIA," I explained.

"Rubinstein was the choice before him," Noemi added.

I shook my head. "Not really. It looks that way from the way it was revealed to the press, but there were three men who were top runners for that position. General Bailey, Daniel Rubinstein and me."

Noemi blinked. I watched Dante turn on his heels, walk through the dining room to the bar and help himself to a shot of whiskey. He downed one shot, refilled it and another glass, and brought them over to me.

I tossed back the shot he handed me and forged ahead. "Rubinstein died conveniently, but a week before he died, Bailey approached me with this story about Dad. I didn't believe him at first, but then he convinced me. I'm not telling you how." I didn't know what specifics Dante had shared or even why the hell he knew so much to begin with, but Noemi didn't need the disgusting details. Dad may not have been involved in anything more explicit than his affair with Lydia, but he'd be guilty by association and our family name would be stained forever. My career sure as hell would be over. And Bailey knew that. He wanted to control me, at any cost.

"Why did he tell you?" Noemi asked. "That doesn't make sense. He'd be the one in trouble if the truth ever came out."

"To get Willis to drop out of consideration for the position. He wanted it all for himself," Dante explained.

"Exactly. Basically, he blackmailed me. He'd reveal Dad's past if I didn't turn down the position."

"Turn it down? You mean it was going to be offered to you?"

"That's what he thought, at least. No one ever specifically told me that, but Bailey was scared. Even if he got the job legitimately, he would still have his involvement with McKenzie hanging over his head."

Noemi kept shaking her head. "So, he told you the truth then threatened to use it against you, but he didn't have any leverage."

"But he did. He does," Dante answered for me. "He has you."

"Bailey made some unsavory insinuations about what would happen to you if any of this information ever became public."

"So, then he's the one who hired those hitmen?" Noemi asked.

"No. I chose them."

Noemi palmed her face. "Who *are* you?"

I had been asking myself the same question for weeks. I made some poor decisions, out of desperation and fear. What I'd made was a tangled mess that I couldn't unravel.

"Let me explain, Noe. I know it doesn't make sense. Bailey told me he'd kill you. He knew you were going to Barbados with Dante."

I had no idea if she knew who Dante really was, but while I hated the idea of the two of them together, she was safer with him than anyone.

"How could he have known that? *I* didn't even know where we were until we were leaving."

That didn't make any sense either, but I wasn't surprised by Dante's mysterious behavior. I hired him to do jobs and he did them. I never asked for details.

"Delacroix," Dante told her. "Christian Delacroix knew that someone was interested in my whereabouts because he saw the contract that had been taken out on me. He's the one who told Bailey where to find us and he must have told him early because those men showed up within the first twenty-four hours of our arrival."

Noemi turned from me to Dante. "So, then it was Delacroix who took out the contract on you?"

Noemi didn't even blink while listening to Dante talk about contracts, hitmen, and killings. It appeared I didn't have to worry about Dante's secrets any longer.

"No, it wasn't, baby girl. But Delacroix knew who did."

"Then who was it?" Noemi asked, her eyes going back and forth between me and Dante.

"It was me. I drew up the contract for Dante's murder."

Chapter Twenty-Eight
- Dante -

I didn't think he'd have the guts to admit it, but when he told us about Bailey's blackmail, everything started to fall into place. Willis had been walking an oiled tightrope with a pit of alligators below him. His scheme was well-played. I could appreciate the intricacies of it even though I wanted to punch him in the face for his betrayal.

"You're making my head hurt," Noemi groaned.

I massaged her shoulder, willing her to keep going. None of this was pleasant to hear, but I finally understood what Willis' end game was. I knew he was good at what he did, but I didn't know he was a master manipulator as well.

"Let me see if I understand this. When Bailey started blackmailing you, insinuating that he would hurt Noemi, you decided to fight fire with fire. I'm guessing you already had Delacroix in your pocket for some other reason. Doesn't matter what," I added, wondering if Delacroix was Willis' puppet or the other way around.

"You knew Noemi and I had left together because as soon as I asked Delacroix to borrow his plane and told him I was bringing a guest, he immediately informed you when he found out who the guest was. Then, you posted the contract, knowing that Noemi was vulnerable. Not because you wanted to hurt me, but because…"

"Because I couldn't exactly call you and tell you what was happening. I needed you aware and alert. And ready to kill anyone you had to," Willis interrupted.

"To protect me," Noemi added softly as she started to connect the dots. "But you said those men weren't there to kill us?"

"They weren't. Not really. I had to make the contract look legitimate. I posted it for a low amount, knowing that would eliminate anyone who might have a chance of executing it. It would be a hard sell at any price. You know that," Willis said, looking me in the eye.

"Who were those men you sent to their death?" I asked him, curious why he allowed three innocent men to face me when he knew they wouldn't succeed.

"I can thank Delacroix for that. I'd say he's not what he seems, but he's a slippery S.O.B. Those men deserved what they got. They were on our list. I won't go into details, but through his connections, Delacroix managed to convince them to take the assignment. We knew they wouldn't come out alive. Justice was carried out."

Guilt washed over me. Maybe those men had done something heinous and their lives were forfeited because of it, but there was an innocent man who got caught up in this.

"And the man in New Orleans?" I asked softly. "He said Delacroix paid him to visit me that night?"

Noemi looked at me in confusion and started to ask a question. I put my finger over her lips. She didn't need to hear about that encounter. "Later, *bambina*. It's a long story."

Willis pulled up a stool and sat next to Noemi. "It wasn't Delacroix who hired him. But when you confronted Delacroix and told him the man was dead, Delacroix couldn't tell you the truth. The person who hired him used Delacroix's name, but we suspect he was one of Bailey's henchmen."

That explained why Delacroix was upset that the young man had died.

"Why? That doesn't fit either. Why would Bailey suddenly want to hurt Dante? How did he know where he was? Are you sure it wasn't Delacroix?" Noemi was unconvinced of Christian's innocence and I didn't have a way to prove it to her. "I don't trust that man."

Willis shrugged. "I can't say more than that, Noe. I trust Delacroix. If it hadn't been for him... and," he pointed to me, "Donald didn't die in that room that night. He's pissed and recovering from you shooting him in the leg, but the gunfire into the room missed him. He was cut up by the glass, but he'll survive."

Noemi turned alarmed eyes my way, but I quieted her again. "Later," I promised.

"I should ask how you know about Donald, but now I see that you and Delacroix are closer than I thought. Perhaps in the future, you won't play games with my life," I warned him.

"They weren't games. If I had any idea that you already knew about Bailey and Rubinstein, I probably would have enlisted your help instead."

"Instead of manipulating me?" I growled.

"Yeah. And it's not over," Willis reminded me.

There were still many unanswered questions, but I no longer gave a damn about any of it. There was only one man who needed to be held accountable for his actions. Everything else was just noise.

"Yes, it is over." I felt my mask start to slip into place. "The truth is out. *All* the fucking truths are out. Me, Delacroix, your parents, Rubinstein, McKenzie, and fucking Bailey. And yes, it's going to end. I'll be damned if I let that bastard continue to try and run our lives. I understand why you did what you did, Willis. But as far as I'm concerned, you're done now. He's pissed me off, and he's going to pay for it."

Willis shook his head without conviction. "You can't assassinate a four-star general who's going to be the next Director of the Central Intelligence Agency. If it were that simple..."

Willis let the words hang in the air. I almost laughed. If it were that simple, he would have hired me months ago.

The dynamics had changed. I looked into Noemi's frightened eyes.

"The fuck I can't. I've taken down worse than him. I don't want or need your assistance and I don't give a damn if this isn't sanctioned by the U.S government. In fact, the less you know about it, the better. Pack your bags, Senator. You're taking a trip, a junket, whatever the fuck you call it."

"I have responsibilities, Dante," Willis said. "I can't just leave."

"And don't try to send me away. I'm not going anywhere without you," Noemi argued.

The other man returned. Torn between the cold-hearted killer I had to be to protect them all and the man who loved her to distraction, the killer won that time.

"I'm sorry, Noemi. But that's not possible. I have work to do, baby girl, and I can't have you around."

I only prayed that she'd forgive me for what I was about to do.

Chapter Twenty-Nine
-Noemi-

"I don't want you to go." I didn't whine when I said it that time. My voice was firm, but he still ignored me.

He kept his eyes on the road. Cold, unmoving Dante was back, and there wasn't anything I could say to reach the man who had told me just that morning that he loved me.

With a loud "harrumph," I crossed my arms over my chest and sat back in the seat of Dante's Lincoln.

"You'll be in good hands," he said drolly. "Nothing will happen to you while I'm away."

"I'm not worried about myself. I'm worried about you. I don't think you should do this alone."

He let out an irritated sigh. "I work alone, *bambina*. I always have. This topic is not open for discussion."

"But you're not alone anymore," I whispered.

Dante was going off to confront Bailey, and my heart couldn't take it. We'd come so far in such a short time, and now I faced losing him.

"When it comes to my work, I'm always alone," he said, not taking his eyes off the road.

I wanted to scream, yell, grab the wheel—do anything to make him listen to me. A cold chill spread through my body. He was so confident in his abilities that he couldn't see that I was terrified.

I didn't say anything else until we arrived at Dante's townhome.

"We'll stay tonight. Then tomorrow, I'll take you home." He opened the front door and ushered me into the black and beige living area that echoed his personality.

"Home?" I gnawed on my lower lip, anxious at the thought. Someone let themselves into my house. How was I going to be safe there?

"Not your home," he explained. "Unless you need some more clothes or something. I'm taking you to the only place I know you'll be safe."

My heart warmed a little. "Your home?"

Dante nodded. "I know it's secure. There's surveillance and an alarm system. And you'll have Lilly and Ma for company." He reached out and tucked a strand of hair behind my ear. "I'll still worry, but I know Gabriel will take care of you."

His honesty softened me. I was angry with him, mostly out of fear for his safety. This was a premonition of what our life would be like. Every time he went away, which was often, I would worry about whether he would come home to me.

"Would you? Worry about me?" I asked, selfishly needing to hear the words again.

Two arms snaked around my middle, and I softened just a little more.

"Of course I'm going to worry about you. Why would you think that I wouldn't? I'm only doing this because of you."

His breath tickled my ear as he leaned down. "I love you, remember?

I sighed and leaned against his chest. With my ear plastered to his shirt, I listened to the steady beat of his heart. Mine was racing with fear, but his set a calm rhythm I willed myself to match.

"I love you, too. And that's why I'm so scared."

Dante threaded his hands through my hair, letting the strands filter through his fingers repeatedly. "I understand."

I wanted to tell him that he didn't. He couldn't possibly understand how I felt. I had no control over any of this. He at least had a
response for Bailey's greedy behavior while I was supposed to sit back
and wait for him to fix things.

Before we left New York, Dante and Willis locked themselves in
Willis' office. I didn't hear what was discussed and when I had asked,
Dante replied in typical fashion that it was none of my business. I
argued against that point and lost. Not because my argument wasn't
sound. I mean, Bailey was using my life to blackmail Willis so it certainly was my business, but I lost because once Dante Calegari made
up his mind about something, nothing I could say would change it.

"I know you're scared, baby girl," he said to the top of my head
where his cheek rested. "To be honest, so am I."

Shocked, I tilted my head to look up at him. He hadn't lied, I
could read him. I saw the fear, and the love, in those dark eyes which
were suddenly a whirlpool of emotion.

"I didn't think you were afraid of anything," I teased.

"Then you're wrong."

He didn't offer more but his arms tightened around me.

"Aren't you afraid of Bailey? He's dangerous, Dante. That's why I
don't want you to go alone. I—"

"Fuck Bailey," he growled. "I will never tell you the details of my
work, Noemi. I can't. But I've taken down men with more power and
blacker hearts than George Bailey."

Dante nuzzled his head against the top of mine. "I need you
right now, Noemi. I need you to trust me and to believe in me. It's
not Bailey I'm afraid of."

"Then who?"

He tipped my chin up and pulled me up into a hard kiss that
didn't last long enough but left me breathless when he raised his
head.

"I told you this morning. *You* terrify me. This is the first time I've gone on a job and thought twice about it. You've made me think about who I am and what I want from this world. No, you won't change my mind, baby girl, but that doesn't mean I don't wish things were different. Come here for a minute."

He tugged my hand and pulled me to the overstuffed black suede sofa. He sat first then pulled me onto his lap. He played with the ends of my hair while I waited patiently for him to speak.

"You know I can't give you details. What I'm about to do is rare, even for me. There's no contract to uphold. There's no exchange of money. I'm not being solicited by a third party."

He ran his hand up my neck and cupped the back of my head. "This isn't an assassination—it's murder."

I gasped at his bluntness; the hair on my skin stood on end. He was always direct, but this time, it came with a sense of foreboding that set my body on edge.

"I don't want to scare you more, but you need to know that the aftermath of this could get ugly. Bailey's a public figure and a high-profile government official. His death won't go away as quietly as Rubinstein's and McKenzie's did."

He was quiet and couldn't look me in the eye.

"What are you trying to tell me?" I felt sick. This wasn't the conversation I thought we'd be having, and it didn't feel good.

He squeezed his eyes shut, then squared his shoulders as he opened them and stared into mine. "When this is over, Noemi, I need to lay low for a while. Until things blow over."

I scrambled off his lap despite his attempts to keep me there. "What does that mean? Are you leaving?"

He didn't stand up to follow me but steepled his fingers between his knees and stared at the oak floor. "Yes."

I couldn't believe what I heard. "You said you loved me."

His head shot up quickly. "I do love you. Which is why I'm doing this."

I shook my head. "No. If you loved me, you'd come back when you were done. Or you'd take me with you. But you wouldn't leave me. People don't leave the people they love."

But they did. I knew that. People left the ones they loved all the time.

My parents had.

Dante stood up and tried to reach for me, but I moved away from him. "You could take me with you. Or leave me here and come back. We could go away together."

"We can't, Noemi. I told you. This isn't the same as my other jobs. It's... trickier. There's more work here than just... Fuck it. I can't tell you. You're going to have to trust me."

"Trust you? I trusted you and now you're walking away from me. Again! For how long? How long will it be before I can see you again?"

He shook his head. "I don't know. Six months to a year? I doubt it would be any sooner."

"A year? You want me to wait a year?"

His eyes narrowed as he glared at me. "This isn't going to happen overnight, *bambina*. The planning alone could take months."

"Months? So, I'm supposed to move into your house and live with your family for months, maybe even a year? Are you crazy?"

I didn't care that my words made him angry. I was pissed at him, hurt by him, and I didn't care how I made him feel.

"You seduced me," I hissed at him. "You knew how I felt about you. You let me fall in love with you and you told me you loved me. Now, you want to leave? You've got what you wanted and now conveniently, Bailey gives you an excuse to bail."

I was angry, but nothing that came out of my mouth was the truth. But that didn't change anything. He hurt me and I tried to hurt him back, using the only weapon I thought I had.

"If I didn't love you, I wouldn't be doing this," he said between clenched teeth.

"If you loved me, you *wouldn't* do this. There has to be another way," I insisted as the damn tears started to fall. Damn, I was tired of crying. I hadn't cried this much in the entire five years I lived in England. Now, I couldn't be around Dante for more than a few hours without my emotions getting the better of me.

"We can't be together right now, Noemi," he said, shoving his hands into his pockets and walking to the window. "Don't you understand? It's not just Bailey. There are others involved. The people who hired Donald, whoever the hell they are. Delacroix. I don't trust him, despite Willis' endorsement. And there's whoever the hell planted that envelope in your bedroom. I still don't know who the fuck did that and why. I can't leave a trail of bodies all around you. Willis didn't have all of the answers either, but we both agreed that there's more to this than what we're seeing."

"Are you kidding me? Isn't this enough? Just deal with Bailey and walk away."

"I can't do that, baby girl."

"Yes, you can," I lashed out at him. "You can do whatever you think has to be done." I still couldn't bring myself to say it. "And then we can leave. Just us. We can go anywhere."

Turning his back on me, he shook his and sighed. "It's not that simple. You don't understand."

"Because you can't explain it. You just tell me little bits and pieces and then expect me to trust you."

His back stiffened and my breath caught in my chest. Slowly, he turned to face me again. His eyes returned to the black voids where his emotions should have been.

"I do expect you to trust me, and if you don't, then we're done. I told you, the only person I'm afraid of is you. I'm afraid of exactly this: that you won't trust me. That your love for me was just a manifestation of a crush that should have died ten years ago. I'm doing the right thing. I know that as much as I know that I do love you. I've never let anyone get as close to me as you have. And now, I'm fucking terrified that you won't wait for me, that you don't need me as much as I need you. Maybe, this entire affair was just you getting what you wanted, hmmm?"

Oh, God. Being on the cutting end of Dante's blade hurt so bad I wanted to crawl away and start licking my wounds. He didn't pull punches, but then, neither had I.

"After all, you made the initial offer, didn't you? I was just the poor damn fool who accepted. But you know what, *bambina*?"

His voice softened and I fell for his trap.

"What?" I whispered cautiously.

"It wouldn't have mattered. You could have never made the offer at all. I believe that I was always meant to love you. That's why I stayed away from you. I didn't want this," he waved his hand in the air. "I didn't want to one day face the fact that you couldn't love me, so I kept my distance. It seems I was right to do so. I've always known, you see. Why would a girl like you ever love a monster like me?"

"But I do!" I blurted out. "I love you."

He took a step forward and trailed a finger over my lips. His expression was once again unreadable. Or rather, he didn't have one. He was blank again. No anger, no fear, no sadness.

And no love.

"I believe you," he said in his classic monotone voice. "Now, go get your things. I'll take you home."

Chapter Thirty
-Dante-

"Are you ready?" Gabriel asked.

I nodded. I was ready weeks ago. A sense of urgency to end this madness drove me to work tirelessly toward my goal. Willis did his part from afar, but Bailey was slow to take the bait. I anticipated that, but Gabriel grew more irritated by the day.

He blew out a breath. "I can't hear you nodding over the phone, Dante. Can I assume your silence is a 'yes'?"

Fuck, he irritated me. I pinched the bridge of my nose. This was why I worked alone. I loved my brother and I trusted him, and right now, I needed his help. Willis was right, I couldn't just assassinate a four-star general, no matter how much he deserved it. Gabriel's assistance gave me more options than I had working alone.

"Fuck you," I growled.

Gabriel laughed. "That's better. How many men do you want?"

"Three. And choose them personally, Gabriel. I only want men you would vouch for."

"I choose all of my men personally."

"Really?" I couldn't pass up the opportunity to throw it in his face in good, brotherly fashion. "Is that why Jacko still drives Lilly around?"

"Shut up or he'll be the one and only man I send."

One corner of my mouth ticked upward. "Do that. Maybe he'll finally learn something."

I missed hearing his laughter. Each week when we spoke, I heard less and less of it. He tried to hide it but helping me take out Bailey wasn't the only pressure he was under.

"I'd like to return the favor when this is over, Gabriel, but—"

"Don't worry about it, Dante," he said quietly but with strength. "I've got it under control. You just worry about taking care of whoever the hell pissed you off. I will expect the details someday, by the way. That's the price I'm charging you."

That's how good of a man my brother was. He gave me weapons, men, and his support without even asking me why I needed them.

He took care of Noemi for me as if she were one of the family and never once asked me why I had left her.

I nodded again. I would never tell him, and he would never really expect me to, but he'd enjoy holding it over my head, probably for the rest of my life.

"Someday," I said.

"Someday," he answered. The only detail I had given him was that once this job was done, I'd be leaving for a while. Walking away from him, Lilly, Ma and our home like a coward. But it wasn't cowardly to put distance between us, to keep them safe while I tried to figure out who else was involved in this mess. I had my suspicions, but I couldn't go home every few months and keep breaking Noemi's heart every time I walked through the door.

"I'm sorry." I must have been getting soft in my old age. The words were out before I could stop them. I knew I was leaving him with a huge burden.

"You have nothing to be sorry for. You'll pay me back. I know that."

"How is she?" If he told me about anyone but Noemi, I'd go mad.

"She's doing better. She got that job she wanted. The part-time one at the library. And yes, I have people with her. They drive her to work, wait until she gets off and then bring her back home. She doesn't like it, but... she's adjusting."

I smiled. "Adjusting, huh? She's giving you an earful, isn't she?" I knew her. There was no way she just sat back and let Gabriel call the shots, not without telling him what she really thought.

"Every. Fucking. Day," he exaggerated.

I laughed into the phone as I stretched my feet out in front of me.

"Holy shit. Did you just laugh? Brother, I haven't heard you laugh in years. Since we were kids," he added softly. "You miss her, don't you?"

I ignored his question. Those were places I wasn't willing to go yet.

"Have your guys meet me in New York on Saturday. I'll text you the address."

"Got it."

"I'll try to call one more time, to talk to Lilly and Ma, but I can't guarantee it. Gabriel, if anything happens—"

"Nothing's going to happen. You've spent weeks planning this. I've got your back. I'll take care of it."

"Sure, but just... Noemi..."

"Don't worry. I'll take care of her, too."

We hung up. It was the first time in my life that I had doubts about what I was doing. Not whether Bailey deserved it. Not whether I could accomplish it, but whether I had made the right decision to leave her. Maybe she was right. We could run off together. I could buy us a fucking island like Michael had we could build on, live our own lives. I had enough money to turn it into our own tropical paradise. Fuck. We didn't have to ever surface again... if it weren't for the other people in our lives.

Ma. She was starting to have health problems. She still had years left in her, but she wouldn't live forever. I couldn't disappear for years. It'd break her heart. And mine.

And Lilly. She was immature and spoiled, but she was fun, and light-hearted. When I came home from doing things good men don't do, Lilly's smile was one of the things I looked forward to the most.

And Gabriel - the best friend a man could have when he was otherwise friendless. I owed him after this, and I couldn't repay him by permanently dropping off the face of the earth.

Then there was Willis. I'd be fine if I never saw him again, but I couldn't ask Noemi to give up her best friends either. If she couldn't see Lilly or Willis, she'd lose another piece of herself. I'd always be there to pick up the shattered pieces, but she wouldn't be the same. I couldn't do that to her. I'd already done enough.

Gabriel was right. I missed her. I put this plan together in half the time it usually took me because it was the only thing that kept me from thinking about her. I couldn't sleep. I only ate because I had to. A year without her would kill me. Fuck.

I was wrong. The whole damn situation was wrong.

I picked up my phone and hit redial.

When he answered, I didn't wait for him to speak. "Listen to me and don't argue. I have a change of plans."

THE FAT FRAUD WALKED into the garage like he owned the fucking place.

"Nice," he sneered, looking around at the machinery, tires and cars like a working man's life was beneath him. Bailey glared at Willis. "This was the best you could come up with?"

Willis played it cool like he always did.

"Does the atmosphere really matter?" he said as he shrugged.

Bailey stopped a few feet away from us. "No. But a man's word does. Who the fuck is that?" He jerked his head in my direction.

"Nobody," Willis said, pushing away from the large toolbox he had been leaning on. "Who the fuck are the four guys you have surrounding the place? You agreed to come alone."

Bailey shook his head. "I've been doing this longer than you have, kid. Never, ever, go anyplace alone."

"Good advice," Willis winked at me as he crossed his arms over his chest.

I nodded but kept my eyes on Bailey. He wasn't armed, but the men outside were. Heavily armed from what Gabriel's men whispered in my earpiece.

Bailey threw up his hands. "Fine. You have your guy; I have mine."

"You have four," Willis pointed out.

"It's just a number. Besides, we're just here to talk, remember? So, what does it matter who I brought with me?"

"It matters," I said quietly, "because it means you're not a man of your word."

"Then neither is he." Bailey gestured to Willis. "He brought you."

"No, he didn't." I pushed away from the workbench I leaned on and stood beside Willis. "I didn't give him a choice. He's actually here to stop me."

"From doing what?" Bailey asked, his fat jowls dangling. The man had led a good life if his portliness was anything to go by.

I shoved my hands in my pockets. "From killing you."

The son-of-a-bitch had the nerve to laugh. "Really? You have a reason to want me dead, do you?"

I nodded. "I do."

"Care to enlighten me, whoever-you-are?" He turned to Willis, still thinking he held the upper hand. "Who the fuck is he?"

"I'm sure he'll tell you soon."

"He's not telling me anything, because I'm not here to talk to him. As a matter of fact, I'm done talking to you. I don't know what kind of game you're playing—Where are you going, Petrafuso?" he barked when Willis nonchalantly picked up his jacket and started to walk out of the garage.

"You said you were done talking to me, so I'm leaving. You can talk to him," he said over his shoulder.

Bailey watched Willis leave, then turned back to me.

"Why the fuck should I talk to you? Where is he going?"

I shrugged as I unbuttoned my black blazer. "I don't know, and I don't care. He did tell me that a United States Senator couldn't be an accessory to murder, so I imagine he's trying to avoid what comes next."

"You're insane." He pulled a cell phone out of his pocket and hit a button. "Yeah, come in and get me. I don't know what the fuck is going on."

"Gerald Petrafuso. Lydia Padgett," I said as I took my jacket off.

He stopped talking and looked at me.

"Daniel Rubinstein," I added as I unbuttoned my sleeves. "Phillip McKenzie, although, granted. You didn't kill him. I did."

"You killed him? What the f—? Who are you?"

"Jennifer Dales committed suicide. So did Anne Morehead, and Theresa Baxter."

"Hold on. I'll call you back." Bailey hung up and stared at me. "You have something to say to me? Say it."

"I am saying it. Now, shut up and listen." I started to roll up my other sleeve. "At least their families knew what happened to them. Karen Johnstone and Maria Perazinski's families weren't that fortunate. They're still waiting for their children to come home. But they're not coming home, are they, you fat fuck?"

Now, he started to put it together. Beads of sweat formed on his forehead. He jumped when the door to the garage, the one we'd entered through, slammed shut.

"What the fuck is going on here? Who the fuck are you?" He mashed on the button of his phone as he walked to the door. "Hello? Hello?" he yelled into the phone.

"I don't think they're going to answer, George," I said.

He started frantically pulling on the door.

"I don't think that's going to open, either." I circled around him, crossed my arms, and leaned on the door of a mint green Dodge that I'd bet my life on was stolen.

"I'm going to ask you one last time. Who the fuck are you?"

"You don't know me, I don't think. But you may know my girl-friend."

"Who's that?" He started looking around the area for something to use as a weapon.

"Tire iron, right there," I gestured to a workbench cluttered with tools. I don't know how Willis arranged it, but it was turning out that the garage was a perfect location. At least here, Bailey would feel like he had a fighting chance.

Bailey didn't hesitate to reach out and grab iron.

"Noemi," I answered his question. "Noemi Petrafuso. You know her. She's Willis' sister. The woman whose life you threatened."

"I don't know her," he denied.

"No, of course you don't. But you have no problem threatening the life of a woman you've never met just to get Senator Petrafuso to step out of the running for that job you wanted. What's the position? Director of the C.I.A.?"

He pulled his phone out again, and I lost my temper. "They're not coming to help you," I bit out as I kicked the phone out of his hand.

He waved the tire iron at me. "You don't know who you're fucking with."

"That's where you're wrong," I unbuttoned the top two buttons of my shirt. "I know all about you and your past. I know the dirty secrets you want to keep hidden. And I know that you've been blackmailing Senator Petrafuso. The thing is, you would have gotten away with it all if you hadn't brought Noemi into the picture."

"You're not going to get away with this. You're not even going to get out of here alive. I'm a four-star general, you son-of-a-bitch. I have people—"

"Sure, you do. But so do I," I said. Reaching into the waistband at my back, I pulled out the small gun I had hidden there. "And right now, they're dealing with the assholes you have outside. I'm guessing we don't have to worry about taking them out. I mean, it's not like you're running around with a government entourage. Those men aren't the kind you should get caught up with. I know. I checked."

He paled, holding the tire iron up defensively. "I'm going to ask you one last time. Who the fuck are you? Besides a dead man."

I nodded as I leveled the gun at him. "So are you. And my name is Dante Calegari. Now put the tire iron down."

"No. You want to fight this out, put the gun down and fight me like a man."

"Fair enough." I set the gun on top of the car. "I'll even let you keep the tire iron."

I didn't wait for an answer. Did I fight fair? Fuck, no. He didn't deserve fair. There was no honor among thieves here. I kicked his hand, knocking the tire iron to the ground. He grabbed his hand and howled.

"You're making this too easy, George," I said as I circled him again. "Why is that? After all, you're a military man. But you've gotten fat and lazy in your prestige. I expected more of a fight than this."

I narrowed my eyes then smiled. "You think the cavalry's coming, don't you? No one's coming, George. You see... Delacroix? The man you think is waiting out there to help you? He's not on your side at all. How do you think we put it all together to begin with? He turned on you. He's been ratting on you, telling the good senator everything he knows. You're in this alone, my friend."

"I'm gonna kill you," he yelled, finally showing his balls and lunging at me. He hit the side of the Charger, knocking the gun onto the floor. Laughing, he started to grab it, but I kicked it away.

"I'm getting tired of our game, George. I only kept playing as long as I did because I wanted you to know why you were here. I wanted you to know why you were going to die."

George doubled over, grabbing for the gun. I let him grab at it, not surprised when he stood up with it, laughing with his cocky confidence.

"I don't know who you are, Dante Calegari, but you're not very good at this."

"I guess not. Go ahead. Take your shot," I said, taking a step back. I didn't want the blood splattering my shirt.

"Now who's making this too easy?" He raised the gun with a nasty grin on his face.

It was the last thing he did. The bullet went into his chest from behind, staining his blue shirt. He clutched his chest and turned around.

Gabriel walked down the steps of the small loft above the shop. Shakily, George waved the gun at him. He fired, but he missed as he fell to the floor. I walked up to him and kicked the gun from his hand.

"Get out of here," Gabriel said to me. "My guys are cleaning up the mess outside. There's a car waiting for you."

He stood over Bailey with the gun pointed at his head.

"Willis?" I asked as I unrolled my sleeves.

"Long gone. Left before even one man went down. This chop shop doesn't have any cameras. No one will ever know he was here."

"Delacroix?"

"We still can't find that bastard. But don't worry. I'll take care of it."

I sighed. I never left my business unfinished, but Bailey had paid the price for what he'd done. For the girls he ruined; the lives he'd taken.

I stepped over Bailey and shook Gabriel's hand.

"I owe you," I said. "I'm leaving you with a fucking mess. This should have been my kill, I should be the one cleaning it up."

"It was the only way. You know that. And yes, you do owe me. I'll call in the favor someday. Trust me."

I wanted to hug him, but he had his gun on Bailey as the general gurgled his last breath, so I just stood there, feeling awkward and lost. I'd never had a job go down like this. It was... uncomfortable.

"I know," Gabriel said. "Now get the fuck out of here, will ya?"

I nodded, grabbed my blazer, and walked to the door where one of Gabriel's men waited.

But I couldn't walk through it.

Shaking my head, I turned to look at him. "It was too easy," I said. "It shouldn't have been this easy."

"I know. I've got your back on this, Dante. Delacroix will get his, too, and Willis will never find out that Delacroix was the one who betrayed him. Now stop stalling and let me deal with this piece of shit."

I turned to leave, but I paused when I got to the door. I didn't know how long it'd be before I saw my brother again. Walking away didn't feel right. I hesitated.

When I turned around, Gabriel was on one knee next to Bailey's body.

"I told you to stay away from my family. You should have listened," he said in Bailey's ear.

"He won't let you... get away with this," Bailey gurgled.

I didn't hear what Gabriel said back to him. I turned around. He thought I was gone. I was never meant to hear those words. It was probably for the best that I didn't.

I drove to my hotel room, unable to get Gabriel's words out of my mind. He never mentioned that he knew Bailey. Not once. I hadn't told him everything, but when I had called him back the night I changed my mind about how I wanted to handle Bailey, I gave him a brief description of why Bailey had to go. If he was going to take the risk of helping me, he deserved to know why Bailey had to die, beyond my own selfish reasons. It was his idea that he be the one who pulled the trigger.

And now I knew why. It wasn't because he was trying to protect me like he said it was. He carried out his own vengeance. No, I couldn't have single handedly dealt with the four men Bailey brought with him as well as Bailey himself, but I had no qualms about killing Bailey. I let Gabriel talk me into giving him that option because he said it'd be better for Noemi if I kept my hands clean. My fucking hands had never been clean, but Gabriel didn't know that, did he? He thought I was a fucking stockbroker. If he suspected more, he never said it. He never once questioned anything I asked of him while we made our plans to deal with Bailey and Delacroix.

I never told him that murdering people was what I did for a living.

I pulled into the hotel parking lot, shut the car off and laid back on the headrest.

Noemi. I missed her. It'd been three months since I'd left her at the house with Gabriel, Lilly, and Ma. The alarm system was installed at her house even though she wouldn't be allowed to stay there. Gabriel made a point when he told me she couldn't live with them forever. But it wouldn't be forever. He promised me that. "I'll take care of it," he kept saying like a broken record.

I spent weeks going through the files Marco sent. It may have been easy for him to retrieve them, but what they revealed was invaluable. Delacroix was a lying, double-crossing bastard, and now, he couldn't be found anywhere. He played Bailey and Willis against one another, thinking he'd come out on top. What he'd gain by that, I didn't know yet. I thought he was the man in the knit cap at Noemi's house, but I couldn't prove that either. There were too many things left unexplained.

I told myself they didn't matter.

I told myself Bailey was gone. He was no longer a threat to Noemi or Willis.

But in my soul, I knew it wasn't over. All the secrets mattered: Mine. Delacroix's. Willis'. And now, Gabriel's.

It all mattered if it meant that it'd be another year or even longer before I could get Noemi back. I didn't think I'd live that long. I'd become a melodramatic bastard without her. Loving her was the motivation I needed. Having her back in my arms was the only thing that would keep me sane.

In a few months, the furor over Bailey's death would die down, and I could start working again. Gabriel had a plan, but he didn't share it with me. Another thing he convinced me would be for the best. He just told me he'd take care of Bailey's body. And I trusted him.

So, what the fuck had he meant when he'd said those last words to Bailey?

I sucked in a breath, blew it out slowly, and got out of the car. My brother always said he knew me, but he really didn't. I knew that my brother was the head of an organized crime family, but we never discussed his business in detail. Maybe I didn't know him very well, either.

Chapter Thirty-One
-Noemi-

One week led to six weeks, which led to three months. Spring was on its way, and I was still stuck at the Calegaris. I knew I had free will, but I trusted Dante. When he left, he told me he'd come back for me as soon as everything was resolved. He didn't say anything else. He didn't tell me he loved me. He didn't even kiss me goodbye.

It was of my own free will that I stayed at the Calegari home, waiting and worrying. Dante was dealing with the demons from our past and I was in his home being "guarded" by his stifling, over-protective younger brother.

"Dante will kill me if anything happens to you," he said one night during dinner. "Whether it makes you mad or not, you stay here," he shrugged as if I had no say in my own life.

"But the alarm system was installed weeks ago," I protested.

"An alarm system is just one security measure, Noemi."

"But if you add that to the goons you have driving me around and following me everywhere, I'll be fine. I need some space, Gabriel. I need to breathe."

"We have plenty of air here," he said, his tone changing.

I tossed my fork down. "I'm an independent person, Gabriel. You can't keep me locked up here if I want to leave."

"Can't I?" he mocked me.

The table got quiet. Lilly started to say something, but Gabriel waved his hand at her and she snapped her jaw shut.

"So, what?" I challenged him. "Am I a prisoner here now?"

"Do you need to be?" he said quietly.

There it was. The family resemblance. Dante used that tone daily. He lived with that deadly intense look on his face. Both were a part of him that I missed so much I nearly burst into tears. Gabriel didn't use either very often. This was a side of him I had never seen before, but it seemed the Calegari traits ran true.

But I didn't cower to Gabriel the way I submitted to Dante. Gabriel wasn't Dante. There was no pull, no magic. No urge to please.

"No," I answered with conviction. "But you can't blame me for wanting to leave, Gabriel."

He sat back in his chair. "I didn't realize you were so unhappy here."

"Of course I'm unhappy here," I lashed out. "I wake up every day, and everything I see around me reminds me of him. From the black coffee mugs in the cupboard to the columns of the back porch. I miss him so much, but I can't get any peace because he's everywhere around me. And do you know what's worse? He's out there, wherever the hell he is, and he has nothing of me. There's nothing to keep him awake at night. Nothing choking the memories from him until he can hardly breathe."

"Oh, Noemi," Lilly gasped next to me.

I shook my head. "Don't any of you get it? I love him, and being here, with all of you... I can't do it, Gabriel. I can't stay here much longer."

Lilly rose from her chair and hugged me. She'd been such a comfort. I felt bad for the things I said, but they were all true.

"I understand," Gabriel said, once again sounding just like Dante. "I just ask that you stay strong, Noemi. I know my brother. He'll be back as soon as he can, and he'll come for you. Just have faith in him. Don't let him down now."

"Dante loves you, too," Lilly whispered to me. "He never shows it, but I know he does. I don't know where he is or what he's doing, but if he said he would come back, Noemi, then you have to believe him. Dante never lets anyone down."

"I told you, *carina,*" Dante's mother added. "My son is worth waiting for."

I could only nod and let Lilly hug me some more. Dante's family's love was exhausting and comforting at the same time as it was stifling and controlling. Just like the man himself.

"I need to make some calls. If you ladies will excuse me. Noemi, please remember what I said."

With barely a glance in my direction, Gabriel left the table. I watched the doors swing behind him.

"I need some air. Excuse me," I muttered, tossing my napkin down. I nearly ran out the side door, around the side of the house to the porch at the back.

I leaned against the column, sucking in air and thinking about that night, about our first kiss and about how Dante had pressed my body against the cold stone but all I could feel was the heat between us.

I closed my eyes, imagining he was there with me, but I couldn't get the dream to take hold. It was too quiet. The moon was behind the clouds and the air wasn't cold enough. I worried that the memory would start to fade. I worried that the distance between us would grow. We didn't have enough time together. Just a few weeks. Maybe that wasn't long enough to bond us together when we had been separated for months? What if they were all wrong? What if he didn't come back for me?

IT WAS LATE, BUT EVERYONE else was gone. Lilly had left hours ago. I suspected that she was working on her boutique idea, but she never gave me an answer when I'd asked her about where she'd been spending all her time. I would have pushed her, but if she meant it to be a surprise for her family, I didn't want to ruin it for her.

Gabriel had taken Mrs. Calegari to Martha's Vineyard for the weekend. She had a cousin who owned a house there and was supposed to stay for the week. Gabriel said he'd be back in a few days. He'd taken several trips the last few months but was usually only gone for a day or two. Earlier this month he'd stayed away longer, for about a week. He acted more and more like Dante every day, from his domineering attitude to his travels. Either that, or I was just seeing what I wanted to see.

The house was quiet without all of them in it. I ate a sandwich for dinner, watched a movie, made sure the alarm was set, and called the men in the black car who drove me around and watched the house like hawks.

"Who's this?" I said when one of them answered the phone.

"Manny," he answered.

Manny was okay. He was one of the few who talked to me like I wasn't someone's property.

"I'm going to bed, Manny. Have a goodnight."

"Yes, ma'am. You, too."

I hung up, feeling like an idiot. Calling people to tell them I was going to bed. I thought it was crazy, but when Gabriel left, he insisted on it. When this was all done with, I had a lot of things I was going to hang over his head for a very long time.

Provided we were still on speaking terms by then.

I put on my pajamas, brushed my teeth, and crawled into bed. I never fell asleep easily. Usually, I had to keep myself busy until I was too exhausted to keep my eyes open. That night, however, my eyes got heavy after just a few pages of the book I was reading. It must have been the solitude that brought me peace of mind for a change; a chance to be alone with my own thoughts, thoughts that were never very far away from him.

I AWOKE TO COMPLETE darkness and rough hands all over me. My feet were being held down while someone else held my arms behind my back. I struggled. I fought by twisting my body around. I barely got out a yell and someone shoved something round and chewy into my mouth right before they covered my eyes with a blindfold. I shook my head from side to side to get them to stop, but after a few seconds I gave in. All I achieved was to give myself an ache in my neck and they were too strong for me anyway. One of them held my head still. A blindfold wasn't enough. They covered my head with some kind of sack.

My heart raced uncontrollably. I was being kidnapped. What happened? How had they gotten into the house? Where were they taking me? I tried desperately to fight them off, but there seemed to be so many of them. My feet were quickly tied together so I tried to buck with my entire body. Then my hands were tied together and some long sack was slipped over my entire body like I was in a cocoon. With the amount of hands holding me down, I wasn't almost completely immobile.

I was picked up and carried off, slung over someone's shoulder like a sack of potatoes. What happened to everyone? Where were the men who guarded the house? Where was Manny? What happened to the alarms? They were silent alarms possibly. Maybe someone was coming. The police would be notified. One of Gabriel's employees would come, surely?

They carried me away from the house and to, I assumed, a car outside. I heard their feet, felt the air change. I wiggled harder, but whoever was carrying me tightened their grip. I couldn't move too much. My air was cut off from the pressure on my stomach. Struggling too much started to hurt as well.

Was this it? Was this how my life was going to end? I heard feet shuffling and tried to figure out how many people there were, but my fear and the blood pounding in my head made it hard to focus.

I was lowered into what had to be the trunk, but before I could get my body to move the way I wanted it to, the trunk lid slammed shut.

Where the hell was everyone? With all the security measures Gabriel had in place, how had someone gotten into the house?

I was going to die. Suffocated in the trunk of a car. Taken to some field, shot in the back of the head and left to die there. Or even worse, buried in a shallow grave, not to be found again until the farmer tilled his soil for the next planting season.

Screams raged from my throat, but the ball gag suppressed them. I wanted to pound on things, kick the trunk lid, but with the full-length body jacket, I was immobile. My heart hammered in my chest so fast I thought it would burst. I knew my screams wouldn't be heard, but I made them anyway, until I got tired. It was the one thing I had control over—scream or don't scream. I wiggled until I maneuvered my body into the most comfortable position I could find.

I needed to rest. I didn't know if I had hours, days, or just minutes left to live. Or... there was a chance that... I wouldn't be killed at all? Maybe, I would be held for ransom? Locked away until Willis paid for my release?

Willis! Willis would come for me! He was wealthy. He had resources. Willis would do everything he could to find me.

And the Calegaris. Lilly would come home soon. She'd wonder where I was. She'd look for me. She'd call Gabriel and the police.

There'd be video footage! Dante had told me about the surveillance cameras. My kidnapping would all be on video. As soon as they came home, as soon as someone saw the video footage, they would come for me.

If I wasn't dead already. If they had any clue where in the world to look.

Oh, God. I was going to die. I knew it.

Dante sent me to his home to be safe, but they'd found me. Whoever "they" were—Bailey's cohorts? Delacroix? I didn't trust that man and I questioned my brother's judgment where he was concerned. My quiet, happy world had been invaded by murders and predators.

Never mind the good I could find in Dante. He left me to keep me safe, but it didn't matter because he wasn't the only one who could hurt me. There were others in the dark, other people who didn't want me, who didn't love me. People who wouldn't give a damn whether I lived or died, and those people now had me shoved into the smelly trunk of a car.

Dear God, how many other people had met their end via the trunk of this stupid car!

I took a deep breath to calm myself. I was on borrowed time, but I had to stay alert, aware. If an opportunity came, I had to be prepared to make the most of it. I thought about Dante. About his confident swagger. How nothing seemed to get to him. I know that was part of who he was. He could detach himself and look at a situation without any emotion getting in the way.

My body squirmed with desperation. Tears poured down my cheeks. The fear of dying didn't bring the waterworks; it was the idea that Dante loved me, that we could have had some kind of life together, and now that life would never be realized because I would be dead. I couldn't even think through the pain. I eased into the most comfortable position I could find and let the tears take over. Eventually, the noise of the road fed my exhaustion and I fell asleep to the memory of piercing, dark eyes and the warmth that always surrounded me when he was near.

I woke to the smell—not the stench I had been lying in, but a familiar scent that flooded my mind and body with memories. That salty brininess, so heavy I felt it against my tongue even through the gag. Memories of another time, of ocean waves, and sanderlings along the shore. Of a tropical paradise where the shadows of palm trees played across bamboo huts.

The ocean. We were near the ocean. And the car was stopped.

Was this it? Was this the end? Were they going to throw me into the ocean in my cocoon and let me sink to the bottom of the sea?

I heard doors slamming and for the first time, voices. All my other senses were unreliable and useless. My hearing was all I had. I remembered something Dante had said one night. "When your other senses betray you, channel everything into the one you have left."

I kept as still as possible so I wouldn't inadvertently make a noise. I needed to hear anything and everything I could. Find the opportunity, if one existed. Take it and make that bitch my one chance to get away. What else had Dante told me? So many things. Even though I didn't know where he was, he was helping me get through this and he would never know it.

The voices approached the back of the car, but I didn't recognize them. The trunk lid popped open. All I heard was, "You carry her."

They said little, revealing nothing, and didn't speak at all when one of them reached in to pull me from the trunk. I wanted to struggle, but I let my body go limp, so they'd think I was unconscious. I expected to be thrown over his shoulder, but instead, he cradled me in his arms and started walking.

Someone finally spoke.

"Is she okay?"

"How the fuck do I know? She's breathing, I can feel it."

"He doesn't want her messed up."

He? Who was *he*?

"She didn't get hurt while we were taking her, so unless she hurt herself somehow, she's fine."

The other one grunted. "There's the boat."

It was a boat. So that was it? Drowning in the middle of the ocean? My heart continued thundering in my chest. It was so loud they had to be able to hear it.

I thought about flopping around. Maybe I could get him to drop me, but I had no idea where I was. Would I land on rocks and knock myself out, or hasten my own demise by inadvertently throwing myself into the water? It was close. The smell... the salt... it was as if we were right over the water.

He continued walking and the sound of his footsteps changed, becoming heavier, like soft thuds. He started walking up an incline. Gravity pulled me back against him. A pier. No—a gangway! We were going up a gangway onto a boat!

I fought the panic welling up inside me. The only release I had for it were the tears that continued to fall.

I heard the slide of what I assumed was a glass door.

"I'm going to set you down," one of the unknown voices said.

I stumbled when he set me on my feet, then I had to lean uncomfortably against him while I got my footing. He kept one hand on my shoulder, barely touching me, making it even more difficult for me to get my feet steady. Jerk! *First you kidnap me, then you leave me to wobble around like some inflatable clown?*

I didn't care if I was going to be killed or not, once this gag came out, someone was getting a piece of my mind before I swallowed my weight in seawater.

I searched for something to keep me calm. Something to help me get through this. I found Dante's voice in my head.

"Easy, baby girl," he'd whisper to me. "You got this."

I took a deep breath and righted myself. I heard the swish of doors again. The atmosphere changed. It felt... cooler. We were indoors, on a boat. I strained to hear... anything... but it was quiet. The slap of water against the side of the boat. The screech of a gull. A slight hum from the mechanicals of the boat. Nothing to tell me where I was or why I was there!

I felt a movement as someone approached me. The ties of my cocoon were undone. I would soon come face to face with the person who would murder me.

Hands moved to undo the clasp that kept my arms immobile. A clasp around the hood was undone, then the suit fell away from my body. The first thing I noticed was the cool air against my skin. I shifted uncomfortably on my heels. A hand reached up to pull the gag from my mouth. As soon as it moved, I started to speak, to yell, but then it was shoved back into my mouth, so I stopped. I'd be quiet as a church mouse if they would just remove the gag. I stood as still as I possibly could to let them know I was ready for the gag to be removed. Whoever it was stepped even closer to me. I could feel the heat from his body.

He was still for a minute, then once again the gag was removed, I sucked a deep breath into my lungs and noticed the scent. Not the ocean. Not the filth of the trunk of a car. But a crisp, clean, manly scent. A woodsy, citrusy scent.

He stepped around behind me. His hands fumbled on the ties that bound my hands behind my back.

The scent overwhelmed me, reaching around me, pulling me into not caring that I was still trussed up like a turkey ready for the oven.

"Oh, God," I cried softly as the smell of him wrapped around me. The ties were tangled, and he struggled to undo them.

"Hurry."

Tears started to well up again. It couldn't be. This wasn't real. How could he be here?

He tugged unsuccessfully on the ties again.

"Fuck it," he growled, spinning me around. I lost my balance and fell against him.

Dante's mouth crashed into mine. His mouth, strong and hard. I opened my mouth at his urging, and he devoured me. I couldn't reach him, couldn't touch him with anything but the length of my body, so I pushed against him, rubbing over his body. He groaned, tightening his grip and pushing his hips against mine, grinding his rock-hard cock against me.

"Blindfold," I gasped between desperate kisses. "I want to see you."

He never broke contact with me but reached up and pulled the blind fold over my head in one quick movement. "Dante," I moaned into his mouth.

"Right here, *bambina*. I'm right here."

The blindfold fell away, and dark eyes stared down at me, moving over my face repeatedly before his eyes came back to mine.

Dante was breathing as heavily as I was. "Did they hurt you?"

"No, I'm not hurt, but... did you kidnap me?"

"No. Here. Let me cut these ropes. Sons-of-bitches. They didn't have to make it this convincing."

Dante pulled a knife out of his pocket and easily sliced through the bindings on my legs.

"I don't understand. What happened? You did kidnap me!" I accused. "You could have just come to the house and not scared the hell out of me. As soon as you untie my hands, I'm going to—"

I didn't get any further.

"Shut the fuck up, Noemi," Dante growled as his mouth claimed mine again. I didn't care if he'd kidnapped me, as long as he kept kissing me. The pressure of his mouth was divine, awakening a body that had slowly started to die without his presence. Desire breathed life back into me.

"My arms," I whispered frantically as his mouth traveled across my face. "I want to hold you. Untie my arms."

"Are you going to hit me?" he growled.

"I will if you don't untie my arms," I growled back.

The warmth of his laughter was a sound I'd remember for the rest of my life.

"I fucking missed you, baby girl," he said, cocking his head to the side, "but... I don't know. Maybe I'll leave the ties on for a while."

"Please? My arms already hurt, and I want to hold you."

He didn't say anything but studied me for a second before walking behind me and cutting through the ties. His hands replaced the rope. Slowly, he massaged my wrists as my hands fell to my sides. His fingers worked my muscles, moving up my arms to knead my shoulders. One arm snaked around my chest and pulled me back against him as the other splayed across my stomach.

"I'm sorry. This was Gabriel's idea. I didn't even know about it until this morning. He sent a text. Told me what time to expect you. Are you sure you're not hurt?"

"I'm fine. Your brother and I... I know Gabriel was taking care of me for you, but we're going to have words someday."

"Don't be too hard on him. If he hadn't helped with Bailey—I still have secrets to keep, Noemi. I used my brother, at his insistence, so I could be a selfish bastard and keep them."

"Then Bailey is gone?"

I felt Dante nod behind me.

"How?"

"I won't tell you."

His lips settled into the crook of my neck.

I settled into his arms and sighed. This was where I belonged. I couldn't bear to be ripped from him again.

"You're wearing pajamas?" Dante said as his hands traveled past my stomach to my thighs.

"They took me from my bed, Dante. In the middle of the night. What were you expecting?"

He spun me around in his arms, his dark eyes never leaving mine. "I'm sorry."

"It's okay. Gabriel works in mysterious ways, but I'll survive."

"No, not for that," he said. Dante took my hand and pressed a kiss to my fingertips. My breath caught at his gentleness. "For leaving you. I did what I had to do, Noemi. I can't promise that I'll never leave you again, but it won't be like this. It will never be like this again."

He rested his forehead against the top of my head. "I love you, but... I'll never change, Noemi. My laughter may be heard more often, baby girl, because you're good for me. But I'll always be both men. Can you live with that?"

"I love you and that love isn't conditional, Dante. I fell in love with both men. I understand one of them more than I do the other, but I don't love him any less. I told you," I cupped his jaw, "I want you. All of you."

"This isn't a temporary thing, Noemi. I need you to be sure. If you have doubts, this is the only chance you'll get to walk away from me. After tonight, you're mine." He pulled me roughly to him and that deep thrill started low in my stomach. My breath quickened and the hunger in my heart grew. "I want you with me, beside me. Always a part of me. Words matter, *bambina*. Say it," he whispered in my ear. "Please."

"I'm yours, Dante. With you. Beside you. Always a part of you. Always."

I SIGHED AND STRETCHED out beside him, his heavy warmth keeping the chill at bay.

"This boat is colder than the *Mary Theresa*," I muttered as I snuggled against his hard stomach. "Is this yours, too?"

"No," he yawned. "I borrowed it... from a friend."

I stiffened in his arms.

"Relax. It's Michael's. And it's temporary."

He turned me beneath him and braced himself over me. "If it makes you feel better, my crew is here, too. People I can trust."

"I don't care who's here." I slid my arms over his neck. "You're the only person who makes me feel safe."

He kissed me hard on the mouth then stood up. "I have something for you."

"Then you're going in the wrong direction," I laughed, watching him walk naked to a chest of drawers across the room.

He pulled something out of the top drawer then sat on the bed next to me. "Are you teasing me?"

"Yes?"

"Is that a question or an answer?"

"Both?"

Dante chuckle-growled as he pushed me back onto the bed. "Stop teasing me so I can give you your gifts and make love to you again."

"I don't need gifts." I kissed the side of his throat. "Make love to me again."

"I will," he groaned, "but first, you have to put this on."

He opened his fist in front of me.

I smiled at the silk scarf I knew so well.

I bit my lip. "I missed this."

"I did, too. I carried it with me these last three months, in my breast pocket, close to my heart. Other than the memories that wouldn't fade, this was the only piece of you I had. Well, there was one other. Open it," he said, pressing the silk into my hand.

The silk had a weight to it. Not heavy, but something was wrapped inside. I held the scarf over my other hand and gasped at what came rolling out.

"Where? When? How long have you had this?"

Dante didn't smile as he put the simple coral and shell bracelet from Barbados on my wrist.

"Since that afternoon in Barbados. I went back for it before I returned to the yacht."

"There was so much going on then. I forgot about it." I gently touched the inexpensive stones, touched that Dante had remembered.

"I didn't. I wanted you to have this, Noemi. I wanted to give you your 'one thing.'"

"I love it," I said, shaking my head and kissing him gently on the mouth. "And I'll treasure it always."

I looked up into the dark eyes where in the past I'd seen fury, anger, lust, and sensuality. That morning, I saw something different.

"But you already gave me my 'one thing.' I have your heart." I smiled at him. "And that's all I've ever wanted."

From the Author:

Thank you for reading Caprice Langden's debut duet. It's not a secret that Caprice Langden is a new pen name for author Debra J. Falasco. Why two names? Caprice Langden Romance is a darker, edgier style than what I usually write so I wanted to separate the two brands, but no, I'm not keeping it a secret. If you love a good romance, I think you will enjoy all my books. For the latest updates on both Caprice Langden and Debra J. Falasco, follow me on:

Facebook: www.facebook.com/debrajfalasco[1] and www.facebook.com/Chapelhallproductions[2]

Goodreads https://www.goodreads.com/author/show/18270175.Debra_J_Falasco and https://www.goodreads.com/book/show/50520366-the-virgin-clause

Amazon https://www.amazon.com/Debra-J-Falasco/e/B07FZFK5H5 and https://www.amazon.com/Caprice-Langden/e/B085HN6C7W

MY BOOKS ARE AVAILABLE on Amazon and are currently in Kindle Unlimited. You can also subscribe to my newsletter by entering here: https://www.facebook.com/debrajfalasco/app/100265896690345

As Caprice Langden

The Virgin Clause, the Calegaris, Book One[3]

---

1. http://www.facebook.com/debrajfalasco

2. http://www.facebook.com/Chapelhallproductions

The Virgin Temptation, the Calegaris, Book Two[4]
Princess of Pride, the Calegaris, Book Three[5]

As Debra J. Falasco
Contemporary Romance
Man with Money[6]
Man with the Mafia[7]
Historical Romance
Inevitable, the Tales of Chapel Hall, Book One[8]
Inhibition, the Tales of Chapel Hall, Book Two[9]
Lord Ravenspur's Christmas Wish[10]

3.   https://www.amazon.com/Virgin-Clause-Calegaris-Book-ebook/dp/B085DCLWR8

4.   https://www.amazon.com/Virgin-Temptation-Calegaris-Book-ebook/dp/B085RY2777

5.   https://www.amazon.com/Princess-Pride-Calegaris-Book-3-ebook/dp/B091NNY-DX5

6. https://www.amazon.com/Man-Money-Debra-J-Falasco-ebook/dp/B07R4NK5S1

7. https://www.amazon.com/Man-Mafia-Debra-J-Falasco-ebook/dp/B07PS6R3YL

8. https://www.amazon.com/gp/product/B07FYTW44S

9. https://www.amazon.com/gp/product/B07VJJNXSP

10. https://www.amazon.com/Lord-Ravenspurs-Christmas-Wish-Novella-ebook/dp/B081DNWT23

Don't miss out!

Visit the website below and you can sign up to receive emails whenever Caprice Langden publishes a new book. There's no charge and no obligation.

https://books2read.com/r/B-A-QTJN-EZHNB

BOOKS 2 READ

Connecting independent readers to independent writers.

Did you love *The Virgin Temptation*? Then you should read *The Virgin Clause* by Caprice Langden!

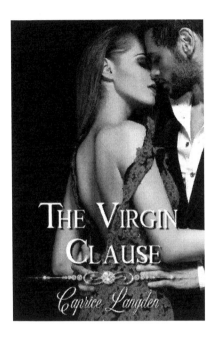

He's my best friend's older brother; the man I always wanted but couldn't have. He wasn't my type - tall, dark... dangerous. My stomach flip-flopped whenever he was around, and I got so tongue-tied I could never get words out of my mouth. But it didn't matter. He never talked to me. Barely knew I existed. So why did I just spend the last decade dreaming about him? I'm shy, quiet... still a virgin. A man like Dante Calegari would never be interested in a girl like me. But I made up my mind. I wanted him, so I made him an offer he couldn't refuse.She thinks I don't know how she feels, thinks she's hidden it all from me. She couldn't be more wrong. I've known Noemi since she was twelve years old. I watched her grow up. She was sweet back then; a little shy, too quiet. Never talked to me. Just smiled, nodded, and walked away. Then the sweet girl I knew went away to college, traveled the world and came home to torment me. But it could never happen between us.I'm a ruthless killer and she's the girl next door.Then she made me an offer that changed things. She handed me what I needed: a pass to my own personal paradise, or a one-way ticket to Hell, depending on how you looked at it. She gave me permission to ruin her. She asked me to agree to the Virgin Clause and I wasn't strong enough to say 'no.'Now, she's all mine.If I can keep her alive.

Read more at https://www.amazon.com/Caprice-Langden/e/B085HN6C7W.

Also by Caprice Langden

The Calegaris
The Virgin Temptation

Watch for more at https://www.amazon.com/Caprice-Langden/e/
B085HN6C7W.

About the Author

Caprice Langden is a pen name for romance author Debra J. Falasco. Edgier, darker and steamier, Caprice Langden romances feature alpha males and the good girls who bring them to their knees. She lives in a historic home in Colorado with her husband, son and two kitties.

Read more at https://www.amazon.com/Caprice-Langden/e/B085HN6C7W.

About the Publisher

At Thorned Heart Press, we are a new publishing company specializing in helping exceptional romance, LGBTQA+, and interracial authors share their words with the public and publish our titles in paperback, ebook and audiobook format.

Visit us on our website:
https://thornedheartpress.com
Like us on Facebook:
https://www.facebook.com/thornedheartpress

Printed in Great Britain
by Amazon

62283286R00156